Praise for *Last Call*

"*Last Call* is *Cheers* with bodies, set in North Florida, with Carla tending bar. Smart, funny. You'll want to run a tab."

—Hallie Ephron, New York Times bestselling
author of *You'll Never Know, Dear*

"[Maggie] will break your heart and have you laughing out loud!"

—Annette Dashofy, *USA Today* bestselling
author of the Zoe Chambers Mysteries

"Raise your glass to Paula Matter for creating Maggie, a positively intoxicating bartender in North DeSoto, Florida."

—Nancy Martin, author of the Blackbird Sisters Mysteries

"You will love Paula Matter's delightful debut mystery. Her misfit heroine will win your heart and keep you guessing."

—Victoria Thompson, bestselling author of *Murder on Union Square*

"A heroine who's not only feisty, but sometimes downright funny as well."

—*Kirkus Reviews*

"Fans of Terry Shames, Bill Crider, and Steven F. Havill will want to get to know Maggie."

—*Booklist*

LAST CALL

PAULA MATTER

LAST CALL

CLOSING TIME IS ABOUT TO GET DEADLY...

MIDNIGHT INK
WOODBURY, MINNESOTA

FIRST EDITION
First Printing, 2018

Book format by Cassie Willett
Cover design by Shira Atakpu
Cover images: istockphoto.com/182177971/nico_blue
istockphoto.com/175432672/FrankvandenBergh
shutterstock.com/238811824/Everett Historical
Editing by Nicole Nugent

Midnight Ink, an imprint of Llewellyn Worldwide Ltd.

Library of Congress Cataloging-in-Publication Data
Names: Matter, Paula, author.
 Title: Last call : a Maggie Lewis mystery / Paula Matter.
 Description: Woodbury, Minnesota : Midnight Ink, [2018] | Series: A Maggie
  Lewis mystery
 Identifiers: LCCN 2017058664 (print) | LCCN 2017059857 (ebook) | ISBN
  9780738757926 | ISBN 9780738757827 (alk. paper)
 Subjects: LCSH: Murder—Investigation—Fiction. | GSAFD: Mystery fiction.
 Classification: LCC PS3613.A8438 (ebook) | LCC PS3613.A8438 L37 2018 (print)
  | DDC 813/.6—dc23
 LC record available at https://lccn.loc.gov/2017058664

Midnight Ink
Llewellyn Worldwide Ltd.
2143 Wooddale Drive
Woodbury, MN 55125-2989
www.midnightinkbooks.com

Printed in the United States of America

For Mom, who didn't consider my early scribbles a waste of paper.
If you knew Ann "Tiny" Peres, you know why that's meaningful.

One

Refusing a ride back to the VFW was maybe the stupidest thing I'd done that morning. But if Bobby Lee thought I was riding in the backseat of his police cruiser twice in one day, he had another thing coming. And now my stubborn streak was proving costly. Not moneywise, thank God, but there I stood in the town square outside the North DeSoto Police Department, stranded because I wouldn't accept the chief's offer of a ride.

I sure couldn't afford a cab, no buses ran on Sundays, and returning to the police station with my tail between my legs was not going to happen. I had a choice: walk three miles to the club and my car, or one mile in the other direction to get to my house. I'd figure out later how to get to work.

Work. All of this—the murder, my arrest—may have started at work two nights ago.

———

I lost count of how many times I threatened to pull the damn plug.

The jukebox plug, that is. From the time I opened at five o'clock, Sinatra and Crosby had crooned until seven. Now, thanks to the younger working crowd converging with the older retired guys, the Rolling Stones blasted from the speakers. For the past three hours, I'd listened to my customers complain about each other.

Maggie, turn up the lights. Maggie, it's too bright in here. Maggie, lower the volume. Maggie, I can't even hear my song.

Another typical Friday night at the North DeSoto VFW. I'm Maggie. Welcome to my world.

All I could do was fiddle with the dimmer switch and the volume control, pour beer, sell gambling tickets, remind them to sign the daily book, smile, laugh, tell jokes, and generally try to keep everybody happy. Not easy because they simply could not play nice together. Totally up to me to show my customers a good time. So to speak.

Their bickering wasn't helping me with my recent goal to be nicer. Nothing worse than a grumpy bartender when people are out for a good time. I needed to take action, turn the mood around. I ducked into the little kitchen behind the bar, pulled out a strip of clear plastic wrap, cut it to the right size, then hurried back to the bar. Just in time. My next victim got up from his bar stool and walked to the restroom. Scott Nelson had left a half-full glass of beer on the bar and I quickly confiscated it. Unfortunately, Scott had also left a burning cigarette butt in his ashtray. I stamped it out and emptied the ashtray in the metal bucket I keep behind the bar.

I stretched the clear wrap over the top of the glass, smoothed down the edges, and set it back on the coaster. Chuckles, whispers, and elbow nudging from the folks sitting close by. Except for my two least favorite customers: Jack Hoffman and Pam Nelson.

Pam, Scott's mother, is the Ladies Auxiliary president. She reminded me of a ferret. If ferrets were tall, dyed their hair, and got their nails done every week.

Jack Hoffman sat next to her. Jack, a Korean War vet who still wore the Marine buzz cut, had been mouthing off all night worse than usual, and scribbling in his little notebook. His big ears and beady little eyes resembled an opossum.

I ignored the dirty looks they both gave me. While I washed the glasses, I watched Scott sit back on his bar stool. He raised his glass to his lips and bam! Beer sloshed against the cellophane. Everyone—excluding Pam and Jack, who scribbled in his notebook—laughed.

"Got me again, Maggie," Scott said. He peeled the wrap off his glass, crumbled it up, and threw it at me. "Good one. At least that was better than the ginger ale trick."

I'd become very good at making watered-down ginger ale look like beer. In my five years at the VFW, I'd played these tricks on most of the members. Fortunately, they were pretty good sports and liked watching others fall for the gags. Plus, my own grumpiness eased up by making others laugh. Win-win.

But it was ten o'clock and I'd been on my feet for five and a half hours. I needed a break. On tiptoes, I reached for the cord of the bell hanging on the wall.

Before I got the chance to pull it, Pete Snyder, our resident flirt and general womanizer, came in with another one of his young ladies. Seems each week he's with a different one. Some of the girls he's brought in made me wonder if he's running some kind of shelter for wayward souls of north Florida. I've always assumed he picks them up along his delivery route. Lots of women for a trucker to meet between Pensacola and Jacksonville. As far as I knew, he'd gone through all the available ladies here in tiny North DeSoto. Had to give him credit, though: he'd never hit on me. I guessed he stayed away from short middle-aged widows. Well, middle-aged if I make it to ninety-two. While he signed the daily book, I turned away from the bell and poured his usual glass of Coors Light.

That's the nice thing about working in a club—every night it's the same people drinking the same drinks. It can also be the worst thing—serving the same drinks to the same people. Night after night, ad nauseam.

"Hey, Pete, how's it going?" I set the glass of beer in front of him.

"Hi, Maggie, thanks." Turning to his friend, he said, "This is Abby Kwon. Abby, this is Maggie, my favorite bartender—the one I told you about."

I smiled at Abby and said, "I'm the only bartender, hon. That's why I'm his favorite. Now, what can I get you?"

Tall and lithe, with shoulder-length silky black hair, she clung to Pete's arm and softly asked for a virgin frozen strawberry daiquiri. I looked up at Pete, hoping he'd set her straight on how things worked here. No frozen drinks because my bosses were too cheap to buy a blender. Hell, I couldn't even get them to buy fresh limes for the occasional gin and tonics.

I wondered why Abby wore sunglasses. At the moment, the lights in the club were pretty dim. The next words out of her mouth made me question her own dimness.

"Oh, okay. How about a Virgin Mary—no pepper, Worcestershire, or hot sauce."

Alrighty then. She was asking for a friggin' glass of tomato juice. I smiled at the bimbo and added a straw to her drink. "Here you go, hon."

"Thank you, ma'am. Petey, where's the ladies' room?"

Ma'am? I bit my tongue while Pete pointed her in the right direction. We both watched her walk away. She reminded me of a panther with her shiny black hair and gracefulness.

"Sheesh, *Petey*, where'd you find this one?"

"Aw, c'mon, Maggie." He ran his fingers through his short highlighted blond hair and grinned. "She's not used to places like this."

Uh-oh. That was sure to get things going.

Sure enough, Jack Hoffman sat up and took notice. He narrowed his already beady little eyes and said, "What? We're not good enough for her?"

Pete rolled his eyes. He pulled a dollar out of his wallet and handed it to me. "All I meant was because of her age, Abby's probably used to younger crowds. Maggie, get Jack a beer on me, willya?" He leaned over and whispered, "Bet that'll be going in his little book, huh? Probably say that you're serving minors." He winked, took his drinks, and sat down at a nearby table.

"Here you go, Jack, this one's on Pete. Now, leave him alone, okay?" I tossed a plastic beer chip in front of him. Maybe a free beer would shut him up. I was wrong.

"This ain't no bar or nightclub, y'know," Jack snorted. "Damn women anyway. Never should've let 'em join. It was better when only men belonged. Back when I was Commander, things were done right. Everybody knew what was going on, we trusted each other, did right by each other. Too many funny things going on around here now." He mumbled a bit more, but I stopped listening. Jack Hoffman. Leave off the last syllable and the name fits. I remembered too well the last time Jack had stirred up trouble. Him and those stupid notebooks of his.

"Mr. Hoffman, there's lots of women in the military nowadays," Scott piped up. "Times have changed."

Jack waved his hand as if to shoo Scott away. Hunched over his spiral notebook, he wrote something down that I'm sure would eventually get back to me. Jack brought his notebook to the monthly board of director meetings and, like a little tattletale, told the officers about all the so-called infractions committed in the club. Silly things like someone letting the F-word slip, or accidentally breaking a glass, or if I gave away a free beer. He even kept track of how much big winners won at gambling and who won the daily book.

Time for my break. I pulled on the bell cord and clanged it a couple times.

"Okay, ladies and gentlemen, don't everybody jump at once, but who wants to play bartender for ten minutes? Give a girl a much needed break?"

"Since I'm the only one not drinking alcohol, it would be up to me now, wouldn't it?" Pam said. She set her can of diet soda down and came around, stashing her purse on the shelf next to mine. Hands on her scrawny hips, Pam looked miffed. I had no idea why since she'd covered for me lots of times, but she sure seemed tenser than usual. Whatever.

"Okay, kids, Pam's in charge. Y'all play nice." I double-checked that everyone had fresh drinks in front of them, then hightailed it into the restroom where I counted to ten twenty-seven times.

I do this nightly, and it gets me through the rest of my shift unscathed. Inside the restroom, I could escape the *thwack* of darts, the *click clack* of balls on the pool table, the sudden roars of victory or groans of defeat, Mick Jagger going on about not getting any satisfaction.

Still, none of that compared to when someone played "Unchained Melody" by the Righteous Brothers earlier. Our song.

Terrific. Here came the tears. I wished I could get through one entire day without bawling. It'd been two *years*. I pulled the scrunchie from my hair and laid it on the sink. I turned on the faucet and splashed water on my face. I rubbed my sore jaw, trying to loosen the fake-smile muscles. Working behind the bar was like being on stage, one big performance. I stuck out my tongue at my reflection.

"You okay?"

Oh, crap. Little Miss Bimbo stood behind me. She must've been in one of the stalls the whole time. I dried my face, balled up the paper towel, and slam dunked it. I restrained myself from kicking the metal trash basket.

"Yeah, I'm just dandy, hon. Shouldn't you be out there with Pete?" I turned to face her. That was when I noticed the shiner. Her entire right eye was puffed up and bruised. "Sheesh, hon, what happened to you?"

"Nothing. I'm fine." She put on her sunglasses and headed toward the door.

"Hey, hold on." I reached out to grab her arm. "Are you okay?"

"I said I was fine." The door swung shut, leaving me alone in the room.

Okie dokie. Poor kid. I'd ask Pete later what her story was, if I could do anything.

My ten quiet minutes were up, so I plastered a smile on my face and headed back to work. The smell of the popcorn I'd made and passed around earlier still hung in the air. The guys who'd been playing darts had settled at a table with their pitcher of beer. The jukebox, thank God, was silent. While his beer was still on the bar, his stool was empty, so it looked like I'd get a break from Jack's whining.

"Thanks, Pam, for watching the bar for me," I said. I glanced at the sink. She hadn't lifted a finger to wash the few remaining glasses. Typical.

She looked me up and down and said, "Can't you do something with your hair? Really, Maggie. Aren't you a little old to wear your hair so long?" She took her purse and returned to her stool. I made a face at the wall, grabbed another scrunchie from my purse, and tied my hair back.

Time for the daily book drawing. I reached under the shelf and hoisted the large, heavy snack tin up onto the bar. I removed the lid, dug my hand in the can, and swished the plastic chips around. "Okay, y'all ready?" A resounding "Hell yeah!" told me they were, indeed. I lugged the can to Pam since she was the only officer present at the bar.

Pam pulled out a chip, looked at it, and handed it to me. I hollered, "Number 910!" A bunch of groans followed. Looked like we didn't have a winner in the house. I replaced the chip and the can back under the shelf and looked through the member roster for the matching number. Not a familiar name, so he probably hadn't signed in the day before. I checked anyway, of course, and confirmed my hunch. I wrote the name, his number, and a big fat "NO" on the whiteboard along with the amount he'd lost out on. $2,108.

It was a pretty simple lottery meant to encourage members to visit the club. Each night a chip bearing a member's number was drawn. If the winner had signed in the previous day, they got the pot. If the winner hadn't signed in, the cash carried over. We hadn't had anyone win in a few weeks, so the amount was slowly creeping up. I checked the daily book to make sure I'd remembered to sign my name for tomorrow night's drawing. A couple thousand bucks would sure come in handy. Hell, a couple hundred would be helpful. Although I'm not a veteran, Rob was. When we moved here five years ago from Miami, he joined and I signed up as a member of the Ladies Auxiliary. Shortly after that, an opening for bartender came up. I'd been working here ever since.

Two hours later midnight finally rolled around, and I clanged the bell and announced last call. Shortly after everyone drank up and left, I restocked the cooler and cleaned up the bar. After closing out my drawer and cashing in my measly $36.82 in tips (who the hell left me two pennies?), I was finally out of there. Unfortunately, the only place to go was my house. I grabbed my purse and keys, tapped in my security code, jiggled the locked back doorknob, and hurried to my car. A streetlight in the parking lot provided some light, but I hated facing this time of night alone.

Of course, I wasn't truly alone considering Gussie, the creepy neighbor whose house bordered the VFW's property. I'd never seen her in person, but as with my numerous bill collectors, we were on a first-name basis. Like clockwork, she called to complain about the noise on Band Night, the fourth Saturday of every month. I always stammered an apology, thanked her, and went about my business. I glanced over at Gussie's house. I'm pretty sure I saw a curtain in her window move.

Damn. Diane Reid had struck again. I yanked the flyer from my windshield wiper. This time it was a fundraising event for the local SPCA later this month. Bless her little heart of gold—there wasn't a cause Diane couldn't be talked into adopting. I slipped the flyer into my purse and backed out of the parking lot. Instead of getting on the faster main street, I took the long way, which was still only a ten-minute drive this time of night. The streets were quiet and empty, and I used this time to unwind. I turned onto River Walk Road, the street that took me behind the downtown square. The back of the courthouse, police station, and post office were to my right, and the magnificent St. Johns River to my left. Up ahead I could hear the soft gurgling natural spring in the little riverfront park. A couple of centuries ago, North DeSoto was popular among wealthy tourists looking for therapeutic relief from the natural spring. I'd have to try it one of these days. I could sure use some relief, and it'd be cheaper than therapy.

Actually, my job was my therapy. I had a reason to get out of bed every day. The money sucked, but at least it was money coming in. I knew how fortunate I was to have a job, especially in this small town. I liked most of the people, even though I had too many bosses (the entire VFW board of directors), and the hours were good.

My house, a huge dumpy Victorian duplex, stood on the corner. I parked my trusty paid-for Honda in the driveway, wishing for the millionth time that street parking was permitted. Nothing to do but walk all the way around to the front door. Blustery March winds had loosened the blue tarp covering the porch roof—I'd have to climb up there again tomorrow and put some more bricks down.

My tenant Michael's side of the house was dark, and the only light on my side came from the blinking red light of my answering machine. Good news: The electric company hadn't turned off my power yet. Bad news: I had a hunch the four new messages were from bill collectors. This was one of those times when I wished there really was treasure buried somewhere in my house. Too bad it was only a rumor. I tossed my keys into the bowl on my secretary desk and turned off the machine. I flipped the light switch and headed upstairs.

My cherished Paris Leaf chandelier lit up the staircase and upstairs hallway. A birthday gift from Rob, it was a treasure I'd never sell, no matter how desperate my finances. If I ever finished renovations to the point where I could sell this place, the chandelier was going with me. I walked past the stacks of boxes in the hallway. They looked about ready to topple over.

Exhausted as I was, I headed to the back of the house to brush my teeth. My bathroom, my sanctuary. With the exception of the cheap toilet, it was the only room that had been totally renovated on the upstairs side. I'd insisted on it when Ron bought this old dump. We'd planned on doing our bedroom next.

Yeah. Make plans and God laughs.

Too damn early Saturday morning, the phone woke me. *This had better be important.*

"Hey, Maggie, good news. We've hired another bartender and she'll work your shift tonight. Take the night off," the voice of Sam Keller, my favorite boss, said in my ear.

I plopped my head back on my pillow. "Finally." I looked over at the clock. Almost ten. "Hey, wait, Sam. Who's going to train her? Has she tended bar before? In a club? Is she going to call in sick every time she has a hangover or a hangnail? When—"

"Whoa! Yes, she's experienced. She's new to town and can start work immediately. Pete brought her over this morning. She's filling out the job application now. I'll train her like I trained you. If she does okay tonight, you can plan on taking tomorrow off too. I'll call you later."

I hung up the phone and rolled over, all ready to be lazy for the rest of the morning. Maybe even the whole day. This would be my first Saturday night off in five years, and if she worked tomorrow, that'd make two nights off in a row. A whole *weekend* off.

Then it hit me. Pete. Brought *who* over this morning? The last woman I'd seen him with was Little Miss Bimbo. Remembering her black eye, I immediately felt ashamed for calling her that. In the bathroom, she had seemed much less bimboish. Bimbo-y? Bimboie?

I also felt bad because I never got Pete alone to ask him about her. They'd had one drink and left. Abby was pretty young for Pete—late twenties/early thirties, compared to his forty-something. Maybe I'd find out more when I went to the club later to pick up my paycheck.

Another thought crept in. What if Abby turned out great and took my hours from me? The members would probably love having a pretty young thing behind the bar for a change. No way could I afford to lose this job. I'd been lucky last year when the bosses had shortened the club's hours to save money. In their infinite wisdom, they cut the daytime

11

hours—and the daytime bartender—leaving me to continue working the 4:30-to-midnight shift. Cleaning Pam and Diane's houses helped, but I still couldn't seem to make ends meet. Maybe I should relent and talk to Diane about selling Avon. I had to get out from under all this debt.

Damn it, Rob. I punched the empty pillow next to me.

I told myself to quit whining and get up. I stripped the bedsheets, tossed them into the laundry basket piled high with dirty clothes, and dragged it down the hallway to the kitchen. Hoping there was a saint in charge of old appliances, I whispered a prayer and turned the dial on the harvest gold washer. Water gurgled into the tub, and I sent up a thanks.

Not my favorite room, I spent as little time as possible in the kitchen. My microwave and Mr. Coffee sat on the chipped Formica countertop. The avocado refrigerator hummed quietly, thank God, in the corner. Next to it sat built-in bookshelves crammed with medical textbooks and cookbooks left from when the hospital owned the house. Another item to add to my growing to-do list: Get rid of all those books and replace them with my own favorites, which were still packed in boxes. An old desk with my even older computer was on the other side of the room.

Between loads of laundry, I tackled the rest of the housecleaning chores. Considering I don't use the other rooms, that left making the bed and cleaning the bathroom. After scrubbing the bathtub until it sparkled, I was tempted to take a nice, long, hot bath, but I was anxious to get to the club. I had to deposit my paycheck fast. This week I was playing Beat the Bank with the electric company. I cleaned myself up enough to be presentable, brushed my hair, tied it back with a scrunchie, and I was ready. Time to find out if it was Little Miss Bimbo working behind my bar.

I locked my front door, grabbed the garbage bag to bring out to the bin, and ran into Michael and Chris as they were going in their side door. Close to the driveway, my tenants were fortunate to have the side porch. They didn't have to go all the way around to their front door to get in. Michael Bradley reminded me of a German shepherd. His always-alert eyes were the darkest brown I had ever seen with thick no-man-should-have eyelashes. A touch of silver at his temples reminded me how men age much more gracefully than women.

"On your way to work?" he asked.

Before I could answer him, Chris pinched my arm. Only ten years old, Michael's daughter was my height—and she's an average-sized kid. I imagined it wouldn't take long for her to shoot up past five foot two.

"Hey, what'd you do that for?"

"You're not wearing green, so I get to pinch you," she explained. "It's St. Patrick's Day, Maggie!"

"Okay, here's the deal. On your birthday I get to give you an extra smack. Fair enough?"

Chris giggled and nodded, her ponytail, the color of butterscotch, swinging. "Sure. As long as you give me a good present."

"Now, to answer your question"—I turned to Michael—"no. They finally hired another bartender. I'm going in now to get my check."

"And to check out the new bartender?" He grinned.

I wasn't sure how I felt about him knowing me so well after only a few months, so I shrugged and said, "Leave it to a PI to figure out my motives."

"What can I say? You're easy."

"Hey, I'm not as easy as I used to be." I regretted it as soon as the words were out of my mouth. I looked at Chris. Was ten too young to catch the innuendo? I knew very little about kids. "Sorry," I said to Michael, and pointed at my mouth. "Sometimes stuff just comes out." I was relieved when he smiled, but still kicked myself as I walked to my car.

The club was pretty full by the time I got there after five. Not surprised to see Abby with Sam behind the bar, I said hello to everyone, signed the daily book, and grabbed the only empty stool. Which was next to Jack Hoffman.

"Can't stay away from this place, Maggie?" Sam asked. "Glad you came in. This is Abby."

"Hi, hon. We met last night, Sam." She'd replaced her sunglasses with thick smears of foundation and powder.

"Hi, Maggie, nice to see you." Abby tucked strands of shiny black hair behind an ear.

"Sam, can I get my check, please?" He went to his office to get it while Abby and I checked each other out. Judging by her bright-green blouse and the dangling leprechaun earrings, she had known it was St. Patrick's Day. Score a point for her.

"Sure would be a nice place to open a bar," a voice hollered.

I looked down at the other end of the bar and saw a few empty beer mugs lined up. Abby didn't budge, so I said, "Uh, hon, you've got some thirsty customers down there."

"Oh, sure," she said and moved on down to serve them.

"She won't last long, I tell you that right now. Too damn slow." This from Jack, who never had anything good to say about anybody. I agreed, but I sure wasn't going to let him know that. I shrugged.

"And next time," he continued, "she'd better not give me any of that damn green beer. Tastes awful. Makes it bitter. I only drank this one 'cause I wanted to be a good sport."

Good sport, my ass. He probably drank half his beer before looking at it. I shrugged again. I knew there was no taste to green food coloring, but I wasn't going to waste my time arguing with him. Fortunately, Sam returned and handed me my paycheck. I took it, thanked him, slid off the barstool, and got the hell out of there. I looked forward to a Saturday night off losing myself in Dennis Lehane's latest novel while munching on potato chips and M&Ms.

———

The next morning the phone woke me up again. Only eight thirty this time. I growled a hello.

"Maggie, it's me."

Oh, yeah, like that was real helpful. "Who?" I mumbled.

"Sam. Listen. We got a problem. Bobby Lee's here and may want to talk to you. Come straight over, okay? Don't take time to stop at the cemetery."

That woke me up. Boss number one mentioning the police and me in the same sentence couldn't be good.

"Explain, please."

He did and I nearly dropped the phone.

Two

I pulled my heap of a Honda into the VFW parking lot and saw that the police sure were there. Along with Sam and my three other illustrious VFW bosses, Pete, and Jack Hoffman's truck. Poor Jack. I didn't like him, but I never wished him dead.

I stayed in my car waiting for my legs to stop shaking. I remembered too well the last time I'd seen Bobby Lee, North DeSoto's police chief. Two years had done nothing to diminish the memory. I hadn't been happy then either, but at least there'd been a reason for me to be involved. Unlike today. But since Sam's the only boss I actually try to obey, here I was. I put on my big girl panties and got out of the car. I waved at Sam and Pete. Both turned their heads away, not waving back. Weird. Whatever.

The chief broke away from the huddle of men and waddled over to me. He'd always reminded me of the Michelin Man.

"Morning, Maggie." Bobby Lee tipped his Jacksonville Jaguars ball cap at me. "How you been?"

"Chief." No way would I exchange pleasantries with this man. "Why am I here?"

"Well, I know Sam called you to come down, but I don't see as how you can be much help. You didn't work last night, ain't that right?"

I nodded. "The new girl, Abby, worked." Time for him to answer my questions for a change. "How did Jack die?"

"Sam didn't tell you?"

I gritted my teeth. "No, that's why I'm asking. He told me to get on down here, that you might want to talk to me. I was half asleep when he called, and I'm barely awake now. Can we go inside so I can get some coffee?"

"Okay. Inside ain't the crime scene."

"Crime scene? All Sam told me was Jack was found this morning in his truck, that he had died. It wasn't a heart attack or something?" I looked over at Jack's truck as one of North DeSoto's finest wrapped yellow crime scene tape around it. I turned my attention back to Bobby Lee.

"I don't reckon, not with all that blood, but we'll have to wait and see what Doc has to say when he's done looking at the body. We'll know more after a bit."

The body. All that blood. Goose bumps broke out on my arms despite the mugginess of the morning. I brushed them away and followed the men into the club.

We filled up one end of the L-shaped bar. Nobody sat next to me, and I felt like a leper. I hadn't taken time to shower, but still.

Wondering why the hell I was there, I knew better than to ask so I kept my mouth shut and waited. Being the gentleman he is, Sam filled my coffee cup first and I watched as he served the others. Kevin

Beamer, president of the corporation and youngest officer of the group, winked at me. Kevin was my best-looking boss—his hair was still full and naturally dark, and he had gorgeous cobalt blue eyes. No matter the time of day or night, Kevin seemed to have a five o'clock shadow. He pushed his motorcycle helmet aside to give room for Sam to fill his cup. I smiled back. At least he was being friendly.

Tapping his fingers impatiently on the bar, quartermaster JC Nelson bounced on the last barstool. With those initials, he thinks he's God. The others go along with him because he's in charge of the money. I merely tolerated him because he signs my paycheck. Short but twice the width of his wife, Pam, JC reminded me of the Tasmanian Devil. Loud and always on the move like a tiny tornado. I call him Taz behind his back. Sam gets a kick out of it.

Dick Reid, commander of the post and JC's sidekick, looked like he'd rather be drinking a Bud. I was pretty sure he'd already had a few even at this time of the morning. A bit more quiet and older than JC, Dick looked like KFC's Colonel Sanders without the southern gentleman charm. I didn't need to come up with a nickname for Dick. His real name fit perfectly.

I hated having all these bosses, but there it was. Someone had to run this VFW and these guys were the ones to get re-elected each year. Year after year after year. They liked the power, and none of the other members wanted the jobs.

JC stood, pushed his stool away from the bar, and in his three-pack-a-day voice, spoke up. "Let's get this show on the road. I have to open the store in forty-five minutes." He pulled his stool back to the bar and sat down. He reminded me of a jack-in-the-box.

Jack. Oh, man. Poor Jack.

Taking a sip of coffee, Chief Bobby Lee held up one finger to quiet JC. Not the finger I would've used, but it worked because JC didn't say anything more. "Sam?" Bobby Lee hollered.

"Be out in a sec. Making another pot," Sam answered. A minute later he came out of the kitchen. I moved my purse from the stool next to me to make room, but he sat down next to Kevin instead. What the hell? I lowered my head and discreetly sniffed my armpit. Seemed okay.

"Okay, now." Bobby Lee reached into his shirt pocket and pulled out a little notebook and a ballpoint pen. "Who found Jack and what time was it?"

JC jumped up again as if he had a spring up his ass. I guess it was better than the bug that's usually there.

"Sam did. Dick and I both showed up about seven o'clock this morning and saw Jack's truck. We didn't think anything of it, and came on in as usual. When Sam got here a half hour later, he looked in the truck and saw Jack."

I looked over at Sam and noticed his red eyes. Had he been crying? Over Jack's death? Weird. Maybe finding a dead body is what upset or bothered him.

Dick nodded. "That's right, Bobby Lee, just like JC says. We figured Jack had left his truck here last night and walked home. He did that a lot, y'know. That's why we didn't look."

Bobby Lee snorted, then said, "I'm the one who told him to do that. Too dangerous for him drinking all night then driving home when he lives less than a mile away. Safer for him and the community to walk."

"Looks like he wasn't so safe this time," Kevin said. "How was he killed, Bobby Lee? You saw him before the ambulance took him away."

The police chief scratched his balding head. "I ain't at liberty to say just yet. We'll know more after Doc's done with him. Jack could be a real mean cuss at times, but shoot, he survived all these years before getting himself murdered. Do any of y'all know who might've had it in for him?"

All eyes turned toward me. What the hell? Guess the time had come for me to stop keeping my mouth shut. "Why are y'all looking at me? You think I killed Jack? That's—"

Bobby Lee's radio crackled, interrupting me. He got up from the bar and moved several feet away. He spoke into his radio. "Go ahead." He didn't move far enough away because we all heard the loud voice answering back. Bobby Lee cringed and didn't have time to adjust the volume.

"Chief? Yeah. Heard from Doc Shenberger and he says after cleaning up the body, he found two stab wounds. One in the belly, the other in his left thigh. Victim had been dead maybe four to eight hours when he was found. Doc's not positive on the time yet, but says that should be about right. He'll know more later and send you the autopsy report."

"Copy." Bobby Lee clicked off the radio. He sat back down, wrote a few lines in his notebook, then looked up at all of us. "Well, I reckon y'all heard that. Someone stabbed Jack Hoffman sometime early this morning."

Before any of them could look at me the way they had earlier, I spoke up. "It wasn't me. I was home in bed early this morning. Alone as usual." God, what an incredibly stupid thing for me to say.

"Uh, Maggie, I'm pretty sure the chief here doesn't suspect any of us. We got called in to help, not to provide alibis."

"That's not necessarily so, Kevin," Bobby Lee replied. "I have to suspect everyone until I can prove differently. I'm not saying any of you did it, or that any of you had reason to do it. But y'all knew Jack and saw him more than most of us in town."

A lot of heads nodded. Sam said, "Yeah, you got that right, Bobby Lee. This was a second home to Jack. He was in every day as soon as we opened and always stayed until closing."

JC snorted. "Yeah, writing in that notebook of his. He was—"

"A pain in the ass, always causing trouble," Dick finished.

"Jack wasn't so bad, not really," Sam said. "He liked things to be done like in the old days. Jack was set in his ways, that's all."

"Were y'all in here last night?" Bobby Lee raised his hand at me. "I know you didn't work last night, but were you here yesterday?"

"For a few minutes to get my paycheck, and that was around five thirty or so." I glanced at the others waiting for confirmation. No one made a sound. "I imagine the rest of these guys were here, since they usually are every night." I leaned back, crossed my arms against my chest. If they weren't going to back me up, I sure wasn't going to help them.

"Okay. Gentlemen?"

Dick spoke up first. "JC and I left at the same time, about eleven thirty, wasn't it, JC?"

"Yeah, it was right after the news ended, and Jack was still here when we left," JC answered. "And we saw Kevin come out about the same time." Kevin nodded.

"What time did Jack leave last night, or better yet, this morning, Sam? You closed up, right?" Bobby Lee asked.

"I was training the new girl." He took a sip of coffee. "Not real sure when Jack left. I didn't pay too much attention."

I bit my tongue to keep from making another outburst, then thought better of it. Clearly I was on my own. "Yeah, where is Abby anyway? She should be here instead of me."

Pete, who had said nothing at this point, leaned forward. "Abby's going back home. Said she didn't like the small town, and that she missed Ft. Walton Beach." He shrugged his broad shoulders. "I stopped by this morning to let Sam here know."

So much for having two nights in a row off, I thought.

"I'll bet this is the first time a woman left you for a change. What? You weren't man enough for her to stay?" Kevin said, laughing.

"Shit," Pete answered, grinning. "More like she was too flaky for me." He puffed out his chest and sat up straighter.

Bobby Lee said, "Y'know, Pete, I'm gonna want to talk with her sometime." He jotted something down in his little notebook.

My coffee had become cold and I stood up to get another cup. I headed into the little kitchen behind the bar, grabbed the second pot that Sam had made, and brought it around to refill cups. Dick glanced longingly over at the beer tap as I freshened his cup. JC placed his hand over his cup and I was sorely tempted to not notice and pour coffee anyway. I emptied the pot and went back into the kitchen. I took some time to rinse out the pot, empty the filter basket, and wipe up the coffee grounds Sam had somehow managed to spill all over the counter.

By the time I returned to the bar, the men were shuffling away, heading to the back of the room near the offices. They generally used the tables in the back to hold private meetings, and it was obvious I wasn't included. I thought about leaving, but curiosity got the better of me. I slid up onto my barstool and did the only thing I could do.

Wait.

And watch. A huge mirror took up the back bar wall, and I positioned myself so I saw them all getting settled at one of the long tables. I could easily see over the rows of liquor bottles lined up on the shelves. I doubted any of the men would pay much attention to me, and if by chance one of them did, I could easily look away. I'd pretend to take a deep interest in the row of bottles. I practiced shifting my eyes from the bottles to them just in case. I couldn't hear them, but I could watch them.

JC hadn't sat down, and he pulled something out of his pocket and showed it to Bobby Lee. The police chief examined the object, then he looked up and our eyes met in the mirror. Nice bottle of Jack Daniels. When I looked up again, Bobby Lee was holding the object in one hand and scratching his head with his other.

Curious as hell, I forced myself to stay rooted to my stool. My gut clenched, always a good signal for me to keep alert. Four times out of ten, I listen to my instinct, and it was screaming for me to stay put.

A flurry of movement caught my eye. The men were moving back up to the bar. Pete and Kevin made a quick turn and went out through the front door of the building. The others continued toward me. I swiveled around to face them.

Bobby Lee stopped in front of me and held out his palm. "Maggie, is this yours?" A wadded up piece of purple fabric with long strands of red hair lay in his hand. A scrunchie?

My hand automatically went to the back of my head, touching my ponytail. "It might be, Bobby Lee. I don't know. Why?"

Instead of answering me, he glared at the men. "Y'know, y'all shouldn't have touched this seeing as how it could be evidence. Somebody get me a baggie or a paper bag so I can put this away for safekeeping."

Sam made a beeline for the kitchen.

Bobby Lee reached to unclip his handcuffs from his waist.

"Oh, c'mon, Bobby Lee, is that really necessary?" Dick asked. "I think she'll go along without creating a fuss."

"Go along?" I asked. "Where am I going?"

Bobby Lee took his beefy hand off the handcuffs and rubbed it across his mouth. "Maggie, I need to take you down to the station for questioning in the murder of Jack Hoffman. This"—he held out the scrunchie—"was found on the floor of Jack's truck."

Three

This had to be some kind of joke. I'm on my way to the slammer and Bobby Lee decided to get an Egg McMuffin. I figured he'd leave me in the backseat while he went inside, so I planned my escape. No door handles, but I was pissed off enough that maybe I could kick the door out. Yeah, right. I couldn't even stop my legs from shaking.

He pulled the cruiser into the drive-thru lane. Turning his head to look at me, he asked, "Want anything, Maggie?"

Yeah, I want you to let me go. I want to cry. I want to throw up. I want to kill the bastards who've done this to me.

Not one of those things could I say aloud, so I just shook my head no.

"You sure? I'm buying."

And then I wanted to laugh. Hysterically. Loud enough that I'd wake up from this horrible dream. Instead, I closed my eyes, rested my head on the back of the seat. Suddenly feeling as though someone was staring, I opened my eyes.

Peggy Dougal, fast-food server extraordinaire, gaped at me through her little window as she passed a bag of food to Bobby Lee. Terrific. The news of my riding around in the back of the police chief's cruiser would be all over town within the hour.

I leaned forward and, loud enough for Peggy to hear, I said, "Hey, Bobby Lee, thanks again for letting me ride with you this morning. Sitting back here gives me a good sense of what it must feel like to be a prisoner. Great research for my book."

Bobby Lee turned to me, his mouth open.

"Drive," I muttered. "Get me the hell out of here."

Minutes later, I walked through the front door of the North DeSoto Police Department. Bobby Lee led me gently by the arm behind the counter, through the small station, and stopped at a closed door. He pulled a ring of keys out of his pocket and just as gently said, "Here you go, Maggie. I need you to wait in here." He unlocked and opened the door. "This is our holding cell, make yourself comfortable."

A stainless steel toilet, sink, and waste can on one side of the six-by-six room, a wooden bench bolted to the floor on the other. No computer. No desk. No phone.

Phone. I'd watched enough *Law & Order* to know my rights. "Hey, don't I get to make a phone call?" I'd need somebody to take me back to the club to get my car.

"In a bit. Go on and have a seat." He nudged me forward a little. "You can use the phone after I've written up my report. I won't be long."

Whoa. Report. A quick memory flashed back to two years ago when I'd been part of one of his reports. As if a fog had lifted, I came to my senses. I slapped my palms against the doorjamb, locked my knees, and took a deep breath.

"Now, Maggie—"

"Chief. I am not going in there. If you have any questions for me, we'll talk in your office. We both know how you handled your last murder investigation, don't we?"

Bobby Lee cleared his throat, reached around me, and closed the steel door.

Last year the county built a new police station after the last bad hurricane wiped out the old one. The police chief had his own office now, and that's where Bobby Lee led me. He stopped at a coffee station inside his door, pushed the power button, then pointed to the two chairs in front of his desk. I sat on the edge of one of them, my back straight, hands in my lap. The window behind his desk offered a view of River Walk Road, and the St. Johns just beyond.

His chair squeaked as he sat down. Steepling his pudgy fingers, he looked at me across the desk. His nameplate read Robert E. Lee. Bob E. Lee. Oh, now I got it.

"Well. Maggie. What we have here is a very serious situation," he began. "That piece of evidence was enough to bring you in, but I'm sure there's more information you can give me. Like, who helped you? A little thing like you wouldn't be able to tackle someone Jack's size."

I took a deep breath. "A scrunchie? You consider that evidence?"

"I'm not at liberty to say—"

Unbelievable. I blinked a couple times.

"Aw, Maggie, you ain't gonna start crying on me, are you? No need for that. Just tell me what happened."

Crying, hell. More like screaming and spitting and pitching a fit. Another deep breath. My hands felt clammy and I wiped them on my jeans. Never let them see you sweat.

"Bobby Lee, when can I make my phone call?"

"We'll get to that." He waved his hand and said, "Right now we're talking, that's all. Trying to get to the bottom of this. Now, Maggie, what can you tell me?" He leaned back in his chair, hands clasped behind his fat neck.

"I'd like to make that phone call now, Bobby Lee. Please."

He leaned forward, causing the chair to groan. "All right, all right." He turned his desk phone around and pushed it toward me. "Go ahead."

My hand froze in midair over the phone. Who could I call? My friend Brenda would come in a heartbeat, but I had no clue where she was. Mom and my brother Tony were in Miami. Sam? His behavior toward me earlier made me wonder how helpful he'd be. My hand jumped when the phone suddenly rang.

Bobby Lee pulled the phone back and answered. For a split second I considered leaving. That meant I'd have to walk all the way back to the club, so I stayed put and listened to his side of the conversation. Which apparently was all about me. Terrific.

"You were able to get verification? Okay. Three thirty a.m. Definitely Maggie's. Got it." He talked, listened, stared at me, and scribbled on his notepad paper. His multitasking almost impressed me.

Bobby Lee hung up and stared at me for a full minute, a frown creased on his sweaty forehead. He scooted his chair back and walked around behind me. I tensed, waiting to see what he was up to. Who had he been talking to? I relaxed when I heard him at the coffeepot.

"Milk, sugar?"

Sugar? I sprang from my chair. "How dare you call me—" Oh. He held a sugar bowl in one hand, a spoon in his other. *Get a grip*, I told myself. "I'll do it," I answered. He took his mug and waddled over to his chair. I fixed my coffee—lots of sugar and milk—and sat back down. I took a gulp from the cup.

"Maggie, care to explain why you were at the VFW at three thirty this morning?"

Coffee spewed. Everywhere. Across his desk, on his little name sign, all over my lap. I jumped up, brushed the legs of my jeans, looked at him, and said, "What? What the hell are you talking about?" I let loose with a slew of words that'd make any sailor proud.

"Sit down." He wiped his handkerchief across papers, his notebook on his desk.

I glared at him. "Answer me." I pressed my hands flat atop his desk. I hoped he couldn't see my legs shaking. I wished my body would get its act together. The madder I get, the more my hands and legs shake and it makes me look like I'm scared. And that only pisses me off, so I shake more. Vicious cycle.

"Maggie, sit down." Bobby Lee's hand rested on his gun. He shifted in his chair and placed his other hand on his handcuffs. "Now."

Okie dokie. My mother didn't raise me to do the *yes sir, yes ma'am* shit, so I simply sat. But I wasn't going to be quiet.

"C'mon, Bobby Lee, you know I had nothing to do with Jack's murder. I mean, I never liked him, but if I went around killing all the people I don't like, I'd be one busy person." That certainly didn't come out right. I'd try again. "Y'know, I'm not the only person who didn't like Jack. He was always busy writing stuff down in that little notebook of his. He kept track of the stupidest things to bring up at the monthly board meetings. Most of the members didn't like him, and didn't want to wind up in his notebook."

Good one, Maggie. Now it sounded like I had an accomplice—exactly what Bobby Lee suspected in the first place. Maybe it was time I shut the hell up.

Before I could stop myself, I said, "Besides, if I had wanted to kill Jack, I would've poisoned his beer." Ouch. I closed my eyes, lowered my head, and waited.

"You done?"

Keeping my head down, I nodded.

"That was Dick on the phone calling to tell me the security company verified you—"

My head shot up. Bobby Lee raised his hands, the scowl on his face warning me.

"They said your code had been used early this morning. Now, that doesn't prove that it was you, just that someone used your number."

Whoa. Could he be starting to believe me? But who the hell was out to get me? Well, apparently Dick topped the list.

"And this"—he held up the baggie with my scrunchie—"is another piece of evidence because of where it was found. It's all I have to go on. Now, tell me. Were you or were you not at the VFW at three thirty this morning?"

"Oh, please. Lots of people have a security code. And keys." I ticked their names off my fingers. "JC, Dick, Sam, Kevin, Pam, Diane. Why aren't you asking them questions?"

"I'll get to all of them. Right now I'm talking to you, little lady."

Little lady? I almost lost it again. I counted to ten, took a deep breath, and stood. "Are we done here? Because I've told you all I know. Just like the last time."

He recoiled as if my words had hit him. Good.

"Chief, I promise you I will not let you screw up this murder investigation. Not like you did two years ago." I turned and started to walk out.

"Aw, shoot, Maggie, I'll give you a ride home. Or back to the club to get your car."

"I'm fine on my own," I said and walked out onto the town square.

On my own. That's exactly where I was. But I sure wasn't fine.

Four

Aw, hell, might as well start walking. Behind the police station, and the courthouse and post office on either side of it, was where I headed. A riverfront walk from the town square more or less meandered its way to my neighborhood. I couldn't remember the last time I'd walked a mile. I swear, I could sometimes kick myself for being so stubborn. And mouthy. And grouchy.

But I was working on it. About four months ago, Thanksgiving to be exact, I had decided to embark on a get-your-shit-together-and-find-something-to-be-thankful-for journey. The club was closed for the holiday, but Sam had written me up the day before. Members were complaining about my crappy attitude. He felt awful about it, but JC and Dick demanded something be done.

I shivered as a cool breeze off the choppy, gray St. Johns River blew past me. I pulled my jacket collar closer, leaned against the railing, and looked southeast toward St. Augustine. I'd have to go back there someday.

"Good morning," a voice near me said.

Turning my head, I watched an elderly couple approach. I smiled and answered his greeting. She wore a light cardigan across her shoulders, and curly gray hair poked out from underneath his Detroit Lions visor. Tourists. The shorts, brown sandals, and white socks were a dead giveaway.

"Have a nice day, dear," she said, and they continued on down the path.

Sweet couple. Nice they were able to grow old together.

I pushed away from the railing and went on my way. I strolled past the gazebo, the community swimming pool, and the gurgling spring. I could just make out the tall sign of the North DeSoto shopping center in the distance. Another ten, fifteen minutes until I got there, then five minutes more to the house.

Daily walks. I'd add them to my get-my-shit-together plan. Today's walk could be the beginning. About sixteen blocks. Not too bad for my first time. Maybe I could lose the extra twenty-five pounds if I kept this up every day. I could even buy one of those rolling carts like my neighbor has and do my grocery shopping every week.

Right. Who was I kidding? I shopped twice a month and that was mainly for coffee, frozen pizza, and microwave dinners. My stomach grumbled, reminding me I hadn't eaten anything today. I'd stop at Winn-Dixie and get myself a reward for walking all this way. Something healthy, nutritious. Fresh fruit, maybe a carton of orange juice. Eager to get started on my new plan, I entered the store and was wandering up and down aisles when it hit me. I had no cash in my wallet, and my debit card would be laughed at if I tried to run it through the scanner. I dug into my pockets and came up with some lint and three quarters. Terrific.

I ended up buying a king-sized Snickers bar on sale. Usually I eat them frozen, but I tore into it. I picked up my pace, crossed the main road, which led me into a mostly residential section. Between the nearly fifty hours or so a week I worked at the VFW, cleaning Pam's house once a week, and Diane's once a month, I had little time left to really explore my neighborhood. We'd moved up from Miami when Rob got transferred to run the local Radio Shack six years ago. We'd been so busy with the renovations, we'd only met one neighbor—a little old lady named Dottie who'd brought us flowers—and we hadn't ever ventured too far from the house. The places we needed to go to—Winn-Dixie, the credit union, Lowe's—we found our first week here. We never had to drive far to get anywhere. Living in this small town had been an adjustment for us, still is for me. I remembered how we laughed the first time we saw the sign welcoming us to NORTH DESOTO POP. 2,214.

One good part of living in North DeSoto was the weather. I'd learned to love the changing of the seasons. At least from summer to fall anyway. Temperatures dropped all the way down to the thirties or lower, and leaves actually changed colors on some trees. I sure didn't miss the stifling heat and humidity of south Florida. Not that it didn't get hot here, but it just felt different somehow.

The big old houses I passed were similar to my own. I wondered if any of them were in as bad a shape as mine. From the looks of the manicured lush green lawns, the trimmed hedges, and freshly mulched flower beds, I guessed not. Professionally landscaped. Rich people lived in these homes, and each house seemed more elaborate than the last. Maybe it was a matter of impressing the neighbors, keeping up with the Joneses.

That thought made me think of Diane Reid and how she always tried to keep up with JC and Pam Nelson. Crap. I'd have to call both of them and find out if they still wanted me to clean for them. I imagined Pam would have a problem having a suspected murderess as her cleaning lady. And if Pam dropped me, there'd be no reason for Diane to keep me.

I reached the corner of my block and I stopped and stood directly in front of the hospital that used to own our house. A five-story white building with a red Spanish-tiled roof, the hospital took up a half block. It housed an emergency room, a twenty-five-bed nursing home unit, the county morgue, an in-patient psychiatric ward, and sixty patient beds. I had learned all that while mindlessly flipping through the numerous pamphlets as I sat in the ER waiting room two years ago. The details were apparently burned in my brain.

I moved on. All I wanted was to sink into my nice clean tub and take a bubble bath. I'd figure out later what to do about getting a ride to the club for work that afternoon.

The red blinking display on the answering machine told me I had two waiting messages. The first was a hang-up at ten thirty. Let's see. I would've been at Mickey D's about that time. The second call was Sam telling me how sorry he was and that he'd work my shift that night. Well, good. Now I wouldn't have to face any of those people. It also meant I was out some good old cash for one night. Sunday nights were usually slow, but a few bucks was better than no bucks. Numbness had totally taken over, and I let it. My legs felt like lead as I climbed the stairs.

Afraid I'd drown, I skipped the bubble bath. Instead I curled up on my bed with the library book I'd started the night before. After fifteen minutes, I was still on the same paragraph. Pretty bad when even one of Dennis Lehane's PI novels couldn't help me escape. Maybe watching some mindless television would help. I flipped through the limited channels my cheap little digital TV antenna provided probably a dozen times without seeing what was on.

Enough of this spaciness. I had to move, feel something. Feel anything. I turned off the TV, picked up my novel again. PI. That's what I needed. And I happened to have one right next door.

———

I rushed downstairs. The double front doors were original to the house, and the doorbell rang only on Michael's side. Rob and I had considered replacing the heavy oak doors, but we didn't have the money. Instead we scraped away layers of paint and restored them back to their original beauty. After pushing the bell, Michael answered and moved aside to let me in.

I froze. I couldn't go in there. Michael stared, waiting for me to move.

"I need advice from a PI. Can we talk out on the side porch?" I pointed to the torn blue tarp flapping over our heads. "It'll be more comfortable."

"Sure," he answered. "I'll tell Chris where I am. Be right out."

Rob and I had never gotten around to joining the front and side porches. We'd longed for a nice wraparound porch. Without it, I had to walk all the way around the house to the side porch. I sat down on one of the rockers, something I hadn't done in ages. Michael came out and sat in the rocker next to me.

"Okay, what's up?" he said. "Go ahead."

So I did. It came pouring out of me. I even blurted out that I'd consider lowering his rent if he helped me.

He smiled at that and asked, "How much were you going to lower it?"

It was my turn to smile. "So. What do you think? Will you take my case?"

"Of course, he will! Right, Daddy?"

Startled, we both turned to the window behind us. Ten-year-old Chris, her face pressed up against the screen, grinned. Michael looked back at me. "No, seriously, how much were you going to lower my rent?"

"That's so not funny, Dad," Chris said with a groan. "You're supposed to be a private investigator, so investigate already."

Michael shook his head. "Grown-up talk, Chris. Beat it."

"Yeah, yeah," she mumbled and her head quickly disappeared.

"So, Michael, what do we do first?"

He stared at me for a full minute before answering. "Maggie, I'll be willing to offer tips, advice, answer questions, but I haven't even obtained my Florida PI license yet. Right now I'm still getting adjusted to being a single dad and that's my top priority."

I knew all about needing to get adjusted. I'd make it a point to only come to Michael when I really needed his guidance. "Sounds fair to me," I said. "So, what do I do first?"

Michael cleared his throat. "First of all, you should let the police handle the situation. That'd be my most important advice."

"Yeah, okay. I have no faith in our so-called police chief, so what's your next idea?"

"I had a hunch you'd say that." He smiled, then became serious and said, "Okay, don't ever forget that there's a real killer out there. This isn't a game."

The only danger I felt was allowing myself to be set up for Jack's murder. Sitting around not doing anything to prevent that from happening was out of the question. "I promise to be careful and will always remember that. But you know about my husband's murder, how and where it happened. I wouldn't have rented to anyone without revealing that much. I definitely am taking this seriously, but I don't trust the police to do their job, and I don't ever want to wind up anywhere near Bobby Lee's holding cell again."

Michael gave me another good long look, then stood. He said, "Okay. I'll be back out in a minute."

I breathed out a huge sigh, feeling a lot less tense. Some of the numbness had worn off and I felt like I was on track. I was rubbing my neck when Michael came out. Instead of sitting, he frowned as he looked over my head. I turned to see what he was staring at.

Crap. Bobby Lee, in his police cruiser, sat at the stop sign on the other side of the street. I wondered how long he'd been there. With the small amount of traffic in this neighborhood, he could've been idling several minutes without another car coming up behind him. Even then, he'd probably just make them move around him. I turned my head and saw Michael had sat down. He held a legal pad and a pen in his lap.

"Is he still there?" I asked.

Michael shook his head. "No, he turned down the road." He handed me the pen and paper and said, "Here's the first thing to do: Make a list of all the people who could have been the last to see Jack Hoffman. Then you'll go talk to each of them, get their story, find out what each of them knows."

I wrote down all the names of the people who are usually at the club at closing time and showed him the list when I'd finished.

"Okay. Most of these are your bosses, right? And what about the new bartender—which one is she?"

"That's Abby, but I don't know where she is. She left town this morning."

Michael arched an eyebrow. "She left town? Why?"

I shrugged. "I don't know. Pete said she was leaving, or had left this morning to go back to Ft. Walton Beach. Is it important?" As soon as the words were out of my mouth, I wanted to slap myself upside the head. What a stupid question. Of course her leaving was important.

"It's important that you talk with everyone. Don't interrogate, just casual talk. And listen. Give people enough time, they'll keep talking. Who knows what you'll learn. Everything has to be taken into consideration. Then we sift through all the bullshit."

"And I bet there'll be lots of that."

"Oh, you can count on it. There always is. It's amazing what people will lie about. How well do you know these guys?" He tapped the pad with his finger.

I opened my mouth to answer, then stopped. How well did I really know them? I'd known them all for five years. Of my bosses, Sam and Kevin were the only ones I liked, and both of them had bailed on me this morning. "Until this happened, I would've thought I knew all of them pretty well. Now ... who knows?"

"You want to find out as much as you can." He looked at the list again and said, "The first name you have is Sam. Start with him."

I made a face. "Sam wouldn't hurt a fly. I can't see him killing Jack."

"Suspect everyone at this point. Talk to everyone so you can rule them out. For all we know it could've been a random killing. Was Jack robbed?"

I bit my lower lip. "No, I don't think so. At least Bobby Lee didn't say so."

"You'll want to find out immediately. Chances are he wasn't, because the way the chief brought you in tells me he didn't have much to go on. He was grasping at straws when they gave him that scrunchie. Someone had a reason to kill Jack, to eliminate him. Why?"

Damn. Another good question. I had been wondering who and why me, but not why Jack had actually been murdered.

"Maggie, what kind of guy was Jack?"

"A real ornery, opinionated man who didn't give a shit what people thought about him. He spoke his mind, not caring whether or not we wanted to hear it. Jack was constantly writing stuff down in his little notebook."

"What kind of stuff?"

"Oh, who won the daily book and how much it was worth. If I gave a free drink to someone, how much gambling was going on and who was winning, if I or someone else broke a glass or spilled a beer, or just about anything."

"Why did he do that—take notes?"

I shrugged. "Beats me. I always thought it was because he was a mean, hateful person. He blabbed to the officers during their monthly meetings. A little tattletale."

"Sounds pretty harmless to me," Michael said. "Is that enough for someone to kill him? Has anyone actually read the stuff he writes down?"

"I wouldn't think so. Jack always keeps his notebook close to him. He's been like that for as long as I've known him." I chuckled. "I remember one time, shortly after I started working there, his notes actually panned out into something. Turned out Jack had been right about his suspicions that the drawing was rigged. Of course, nothing official was really ever done to the people involved since they're board members, but we did have to change the way we do the daily book. Jack was a little less ornery for a while after that."

"I don't understand. How does the daily book work?"

I explained the procedure.

"How much money are we talking about?"

"It ranges from thirty bucks all the way to thousands. All depends on how long it takes for it to build up between winners. When it's real high, the woodies come out."

Michael frowned. "The woodies?"

"Members who never come in unless the book's high. They come in out of the woodwork."

"Okay, I got it. And what did Jack notice—how was it possible to rig the book?"

"The same guy, a social member, always volunteered to pull the number. He'd look at it, call out the number, and toss the chip back in the bucket without showing it to anyone. Dick or Diane Reid conveniently won a couple times just before going on a trip with Pam and JC Nelson. Their son Scott is married to one of the Reid girls and they spend a lot of time together. Pretty sneaky, huh?"

Michael laughed. "I'll say. But why didn't the guy just call his own number?

"I always wondered that too. Too obvious? Maybe they paid for his beer or slipped him some cash."

"And it was because of Jack Hoffman's notes that they were caught?"

"Yeah. He'd been keeping track of the winners and brought the evidence to the board meeting one night. Nothing happened to the Reids—hell, Dick's been an officer for years. So has JC. It takes something really big for one of them to get in trouble. In the end, they decided it was simply a coincidence. Diane always acted guilty about it though.

"But now the bartender has to make sure there's an officer present to pull the number, shows it to everyone, and there have to be at least six people at the bar." I rolled my eyes at Michael. "I don't know why six—just some number they pulled out of the air."

"So, if the Reids didn't get in trouble back then, and Jack's notes seem pretty harmless, why would someone kill him now?"

Excellent question and I wished I had the answer. I shrugged. "Damned if I know. I wasn't there that night. Hey! Could that be it? They waited for me to be out of the way, making sure I'd have no alibi?"

"But why you?"

Another excellent question. I couldn't wait until I was the one asking questions from other people. I shrugged again. "I don't know. Some of the officers don't like me because I'm mouthy." I told Michael about being written up last Thanksgiving. One more write-up and I'd be out of a job. "I guess I get along with everyone else. But my scrunchie being in Jack's truck makes it seem like someone's out to get me, to set me up."

"You might want to keep that as a possibility for now." He glanced at his watch and said, "I need to help Chris with her homework. Need anything else?"

"Um, my car is still at the club ..."

"No problem at all. I'll give you a ride."

"Michael, thank you. I can't tell you how much I appreciate your help." I felt hot tears starting, so I shut up. I had to hold onto the little amount of control I'd regained. "Anyway, thanks. Want to leave about six? I'll treat you and Chris to dinner." *As long as it's someplace cheap.*

"Sure, that'd be great. We'll meet you out by my car."

I handed Michael his pen and started to tear off the pages I'd written on.

"No," he said, "keep the pad and use it to make notes, keep track of anything you learn."

I thanked him again and walked around to my front door. Crap. My stomach flip-flopped, my pulse sped up, a flash of fear stopped me. Bobby Lee's cruiser was parked across from my house again.

Five

Being scared ticked me off. I needed to get rid of some of this negative energy, do something productive. Even as that thought crossed my mind, a gust of wind pulled up a corner of the tarp. I hadn't gotten around to fixing it yesterday. Until the magical day came when I could afford a new roof, or even some patching, I'd become used to climbing up and moving the tarp and bricks around.

If only there were a way to get used to owning this big dump. After Rob's murder, I couldn't stand living downstairs, so I'd moved into the upstairs. I chose one of the bedrooms and made do with the shabby appliances and furniture that had come with the house. We had never gotten around to tearing down the dividing wall around the stairway, so it was still a two-family house when I listed it with a realtor.

But selling the house with only the bottom floor and the upstairs bathroom being completely renovated was next to impossible. The realtor had done his best, but with no nibbles at all, I didn't bother renewing the contract with him. No one in their right mind would buy the place.

The hospital administrator in charge of the sale must have seen Rob coming. It had been used as a dorm for nursing students before the local college eliminated the nursing program. The house was vacant for two years, and with upkeep and taxes, the costs had become too much. The hospital administration wanted out. Rob had told me how happy the guy had been when he handed over the keys. I bet he was happy he'd finally gotten rid of the dump. Let it become someone else's headache.

And turning it back into a single-family home was a huge headache. In three short years we used all of our savings to renovate the downstairs and master bath. We'd looked forward to celebrating our twentieth wedding anniversary in our finished home. Missed that by eight months.

Whatever. I had to get past this. Somehow I had to get focused. First things first. Having Michael to go to for advice was a start, a good start. Tonight we'd get my car, then I'd go from there.

I climbed down off the tarp-protected roof and headed upstairs to the bathroom to clean up. I skipped the shower to avoid taking time to dry my long hair. I brushed it and started to tie it back with another scrunchie. Bobby Lee's voice creeped into my head.

On the floor of Jack Hoffman's truck.

Hell, I had scrunchies lying around behind the bar. Anybody could've taken one and used it to frame me. But who?

Plenty of people came behind the bar. Sam did the ordering, JC got money out of the safe, Diane cleaned the club every Monday morning. JC and Dick were always in there early when no one else was around. Pam covered the bar for me just about every night so I could take breaks. Pete sometimes helped stock the beer cooler or lugged heavy garbage bags out to the back porch for me. I didn't remember Kevin ever being back there, but he had keys just like the others, so he could get in any time he wanted. With the exception of Pete, they all had keys and security codes.

Any or all of them could be in on it.

That's ridiculous. Now I was getting paranoid, like there was some VFW conspiracy.

I stared blankly at my reflection in the mirror. Paranoid? Well, duh. And with good reason.

I resolved to treat all of them with suspicion until Michael and I had it figured out. I finished tying my hair back, grabbed my purse, and headed out to the driveway, where Michael stood by his car. He whistled and Chris came skipping up the sidewalk.

"Look, Daddy, that nice lady gave me these." She showed us a small box of multicolored geraniums. "Aren't they pretty? Can we plant them? The lady said they need to be in the ground so they won't die."

"What lady, Chris?" Michael asked, frowning.

"She said her name was Dottie and welcomed me to the neighborhood."

"It's okay, Michael, I know Dottie. She's an elderly lady who lives somewhere down the street. She's harmless."

"Can we plant them now, Dad?"

Michael shook his head. "Tomorrow. If it's okay with Maggie."

"Sure, Chris. We'll find a good place for them. How about putting them on the concrete steps for now? They'll be fine."

"Why are those steps there by the house where there's no door?" Chris asked when she came back to the car. "They look really dumb."

"Okay, kiddo, backseat," Michael said. He waited for both of us to get buckled up, checked his mirrors, then asked, "Where to?"

Alrighty then. I guess we were going to ignore Chris's question about the steps. They did look stupid sitting several feet from the house, leading nowhere. At the time it was cheaper to leave them there. No way I could spare the additional hundred bucks they wanted to haul them away. I remembered the puzzled facial expressions on the contractors I'd hired to demolish the perfectly refinished mudroom after Rob's murder. That soon after his death, everything seemed easier to put off for another day. Top priority that day had been getting rid of the room where he'd died, even if it meant closing off the whole back of the house. Bobby Lee had been pissed when he found out. He suspected me of getting rid of evidence.

"Maggie, where to?" Michael repeated, bringing me back to the present.

Definitely not Mickey D's, I thought. Or maybe I should show my face there. Peggy Dougal would see for herself I had my freedom. At the very least, she'd probably think I'd made bail.

"Maggie?"

"I'm sorry, Michael, daydreaming again. Can't seem to stop doing that." Turning my head toward Chris, I asked her where she wanted to go.

"Pizza!"

"Fine by me," I said.

We spent the next couple hours stuffing our faces with pan pizza and soda. A beer or two would've gone down good, but I figured sober was better. Chris entertained us with stories of elementary-school happenings. A fifth grader now, she and her classmates were the big shots in school. Next fall she'd be right back at the bottom of the pecking order at the junior high school.

"And she's my BFF, for real!"

Michael frowned. "BFF?"

"Best friends forever," Chris and I spoke at the same time. I grinned and said, "It's a girl thing, Michael."

Chris just rolled her eyes.

The waitress dropped off the check, and Michael grabbed it.

"Hey! I'm supposed to buy dinner tonight," I reminded him.

"With the way Chris ate? All that pizza, all those bread sticks?" He winked at her, and I swear to God, I think she winked back. I let it go.

Michael handed Chris the check and a few bills and asked her to go pay. "Ready, Maggie?"

"As ready as I'm going to be. I'm really dreading this. Just the idea of going back in the club makes me—I don't know. I'm glad I have tonight off, but I do need my car." Truthfully, I would've preferred a root canal and a pap smear topped off with a mammogram to setting foot in the club. Not something I could say to Michael.

He asked, "Since you're just getting your car, why do you need to go inside?"

"I want to sign the book. With my luck, if I skip one day, that'll be when my number's pulled."

"So, might as well get it done?"

I nodded.

I always liked the way everything was so close in this town. I could do all of my errands without driving all over the place. One of the few things I liked about North DeSoto.

Until tonight.

It took us no time at all to get to the club. As Michael pulled into the parking lot, I looked to see what cars were there. I wanted to be prepared for who would be inside. Surprisingly, I didn't see JC's car or Dick's truck. I studiously avoided looking at the corner where Jack's truck had been as Michael parked next to my car. I felt sad for a second, as if no one had wanted to be near my little blue Honda. *Oh, sheesh. Get a grip, Maggie.*

"This is a funny-looking place," Chris said. "It looks like a spider with three legs. A red body and her legs are white. Weird."

I'd never thought about it before, but looking at it, I saw Chris was right. The main red-bricked building where the bar and dining area were had three white rectangular annexes jutting out. Over the years, depending on how much money the post had, these additions were built. One held the offices, another the big kitchen used for the monthly dinners, and the third was the hall that was rented out for special functions. The hall was also used for the many funeral receptions we had. I imagined there'd be one scheduled soon for Jack.

"Thanks again for the ride and for dinner," I said, reaching for the door handle. "Have a good night."

"Nope, we're going in with you. I want to check out the place."

Cool. My first shot at watching Michael be a detective. "Okay, but Chris is going to have to sit at a table, she's not allowed at the bar."

"Sure," Michael said.

"What does VFW stand for?" Chris asked as we crossed the gravel lot.

"Veterans of Foreign Wars," Michael and I answered at the same time.

I reached into my wallet and pulled out my key card. Since we were a members-only club, all nonmembers had to ring the buzzer to gain access. I slid my key card into the slot. It still worked. Exhaling a deep breath, I realized I'd half expected them to change the locks.

"Here we go." I opened the door and let Michael and Chris walk in ahead of me. The bar, off to the left, was full. All eyes turned toward us. That's the way it usually worked. Any time someone entered the building, everyone at the bar had to see who'd come in. Not too nosey, huh?

I led Michael and Chris to a table and walked up to the bar. Sam stood waiting for me.

"Hey, Maggie. Hurry up and get to work, we need a real bartender back there," someone hollered. Laughter followed, then silence as it became clear I wasn't going behind the bar to start working.

My hand shook as I signed the daily book. I dreamed of the day I'd actually win. Five years and nothing yet. It was worth a quarter a day to keep trying.

You could've cut the friggin' air with a knife. I'd never heard the place so quiet. Of course, it didn't last long.

"Sam? Maggie?"

"What the hell?"

"Hey, Maggie, did you hear about Jack Hoffman?"

"What's going on?"

"Why isn't she working?"

I shrugged, kept my eyes on Sam the whole time. He looked down, then away.

"Seriously, what's going on? Why aren't you working?"

"Maggie, did you quit?"

A low rumbling started from the others. I heard my name whispered up and down the bar. A few words drifted back to me. *Quit. Arrested. Fired. Murder.* The bolder members spoke louder.

"Nah, she wouldn't quit, she loves us too much to leave us."

Oh, yeah, feel the love.

"I want to buy Maggie and her friends there a drink."

Kevin Beamer. God love him. I looked over at him and smiled. My face didn't crack as I thought it might if I'd dared show any emotion. He walked over to me. Kevin slid his arm around my shoulder and squeezed. His wispy beard tickled my cheek as he said, "This really sucks, Maggie, and I'm so sorry. I know you had nothing to do with Jack's murder." He pushed away, pulled out his wallet, and tossed some money on the bar. "Sam, whatever they're drinking." He returned to his barstool.

I turned to Michael, and he joined me at the bar. Time, finally, for a beer for myself. Michael ordered two sodas, took one to the table, then came back to me. "Chris said she'll be fine. Introduce me to your friends, Maggie."

My friends? Was he nuts? Oh, I get it. Sam still stood in front of us, so I guess he'd be first. He and Michael shook hands, neither one saying a word. A very large man, Sam towered over Michael.

"And how about the gentleman who bought us drinks? I'd like to thank him," Michael said.

We made our way down the bar to Kevin, stopping as members reached out to hug me or pat me on the back. I smiled and nodded to each one, never really saying much.

"Kevin, this is Michael Bradley. Michael, Kevin Beamer and Pete Snyder." Handshakes all around.

"What's this, Pete? No girl with you tonight?" I teased. I explained to Michael how Pete is our Casanova, always bringing in a different gorgeous girl practically every week.

"Aw, knock it off, Maggie," Pete said. "You're embarrassing me."

"Oh, so this is Abby's boyfriend?" Michael asked. Very innocently.

Pete did look embarrassed this time. He rubbed his hand across his clean-shaven chiseled jaw. "Um, actually, no. Abby decided to move back home. This town wasn't big enough for her."

"What wasn't big enough for her, Pete?" someone hollered out, with loud guffaws following. "Are you sure it was the town that was too small?" More laughter.

Michael asked Pete, "So, where's Abby from?"

"Korea, I think," he answered.

"No, I mean where's home for Abby?" Michael asked. Again very innocently.

"Ft. Walton Beach, over in the panhandle."

"What does Abby do?" Michael asked. He sipped his soda. "Did she have a job to go back to, I hope?"

Pete frowned. I knew he was wondering just who the hell this guy was asking all these questions.

I jumped into the conversation. "My guess is she's not a bartender." I batted my eyes instead of rolling them. "Just kidding, Pete. I thought she was a nice girl."

"Yeah, she is. She'd just broken up with a boyfriend and wanted to get the hell out of that town. I offered her a ride and that's it."

"Pete's a trucker," I explained. "A knight of the road."

Michael tipped his glass toward Pete and said, "I admire you. I'm sure that's a tough job."

Pete shrugged his broad shoulders. "Hell, it's just a job. The guys you should admire are some of the ones in here." He pointed at Kevin and continued. "Kevin here is the hero. And Sam there was in the Navy during the Cuban Missile Crisis in the early sixties."

"Oh, c'mon, Pete, you know I don't like to talk about it. Besides, I'm sure Michael isn't interested in hearing any war stories," said Kevin. He swallowed his beer and pushed the empty glass to the edge of the bar. Sam shuffled away to refill it. Kevin's remark surprised me because he usually liked swapping war stories. Maybe he somehow knew Michael had never served in the military. I've learned vets are funny that way. Some of them will only share stories with other veterans. Some won't talk about their war experiences at all.

"Let me buy that one for you, Kevin. A way of thanking you." Michael pulled his wallet out of his back pocket, reached inside, and pulled money out.

I grabbed the five-dollar bill out of his hand. "No can-do, Michael. We have rules. Only members can buy drinks here." I placed the bill on the bar and slid it toward Sam, who'd come back with a full glass. I told Sam, "I'd like to buy Kevin's beer."

"You got it, Maggie," Sam said and took the money.

"Thanks, Michael, cheers." Kevin clinked his glass with Michael's and winked at me.

"There's always ways to get around proper procedure," I explained to Michael. I laughed when I saw the expression on his face when Sam returned with his change.

"Wow," Michael said. "Sixty-five cents for a glass of beer?" He left the coins and a dollar on the bar, then flipped three bills around until they faced each other and slipped them into his wallet.

The others laughed along with me. God, it felt good to laugh. I had forgotten for awhile how terribly screwed up my life had become. Michael, though, apparently hadn't because he turned his attention to Sam, who leaned against the bar.

"Sam, will you be around tomorrow morning? Maggie would like to talk to you."

Sam straightened, backed up a step. "Mondays are pretty busy for me."

"Oh, I'm sure she won't take up too much of your time." Michael drained his glass and set it on the bar. "She'll stop by in the morning. Nine o'clock good?"

More murmurs up and down the bar. Everyone was wondering who was the guy with all the questions, and yeah, it looked like I wasn't working. Rumors would be flying as soon as we walked out the door. This place was like Cheers, except here they not only knew your name, they knew all your damn business.

Sam asked, "What does she want to talk to me about?"

"Maggie wants to talk to you about who framed her for Jack Hoffman's murder."

Six

Sam looked so pitiful, at such a loss for words, I almost felt sorry for him. The only thing that prevented any sympathy was the fact that he hadn't stood up for me. That he had turned my scrunchie over to JC in the first place.

"Your comment will surely stir up some shit," I said to Michael as we walked out into the parking lot.

"That was my intention. It'll be interesting to see what happens next." He held the door open for Chris and she jumped into the backseat. Michael and I remained outside the car.

I looked at him over the roof of the car and asked, "What do you mean, Michael? Do you think something will happen?"

"People lie. We all do. Whether it's a little white lie or some huge one, we all lie. I expect them to now try to cover their tracks. Getting you arrested didn't work as planned, so he/she/they/whomever will try something else. Count on it. There'll be plenty of talk."

I glanced over at the building we'd just left and said, "They're all in there right now talking about us. I know from experience how they are. Don't get me wrong, they're good people, but they do love their gossip."

"That's the best way to get information. It'll be your job to weed out the bullshit from the truth. Simply talk to people. Just like we did in there. Think you can do it? I know you can."

———

I woke up exhausted on Monday morning. I'd tossed and turned most of the night, and when I did finally manage to sleep I dreamt about being chased by giant bulls through a large field of weeds. The weirdest part was when Michael arrived on a white horse wearing blinders. The horse was wearing blinders, not Michael. Anyway, Michael scooped me up away from the running bulls and we rode off into the sunset.

I wasn't sure what bothered me more—dreaming about Michael, or losing sleep over these jerks trying to frame me for Jack's murder. For now, I'd focus on getting myself out of this jam, and find out who had set me up. And find out who killed Jack. Piece of cake.

Ooh, cake. I nuked the two-day old coffee cake I'd picked up last night. A special inexpensive treat for myself. I focused on pigging out until it was time to get ready to go see Sam.

For mid-March it was warm, so I put on my favorite jeans and T-shirt. When I arrived at the club, Sam's truck sat alone in the parking lot. Deep sigh of relief. I'd wondered about JC and Dick. They usually were there every morning for "coffee." Yeah, right. Well, JC drinks coffee because he opens his store by ten. They're usually here for a couple hours. Dick's retired, so it doesn't matter if he starts drinking beer this early. Plus he drinks for free. Those two do their planning when no other board members are around. They decide what's best for the club, then round up voting members who'll side with them when the time comes for making decisions. Sneaky bastards.

The bar had that musky smell when I entered through the back door. The smoke eaters were running full blast trying to clean the air. Smoking was still permitted inside veteran clubs as long as there was a unanimous vote among members. At this time of morning, the only lights on in the bar were a few of the neon beer signs. The whiteboard showed me that the daily book drawing still hadn't been won. The place was quiet and kind of spooky. I remembered when I'd first started working here how scary it could be at night after everyone else had left. I had to go around making sure all the doors and windows were locked. Sam told me to make sure no one was hiding anywhere. That scared the crap out of me because I always wondered what I would do if I did find someone.

Since we didn't open until five, I knew Sam would be in the office he shared with JC doing paperwork, counting money—all of the stuff he had to do as steward. Following the twang of country music that Sam always had playing on his radio, I passed Pam's office—the one JC used to have until she decided she needed one. It had taken days for Pam to air it out from all the cigarettes JC had smoked. At home, Pam made JC smoke outside. Now Sam had to put up with it. Poor guy. But Sam always caved in to their demands. I think it had something to do with following orders no matter what. Sure enough, I smelled the nasty cigarette odor and heard Tammy Wynette going on about standing by her man.

"Good morning, Sam." I rapped on his open door. I apologized after he nearly jumped out of his desk chair. "Didn't mean to startle you. May I come in?"

"I didn't hear you." He waved me in and I sat in the other chair. Before I could get too comfortable, he said, "I don't have a lot of time this morning, Maggie. I'll be done with this in a few minutes."

"Okay." I was sure it would take him much longer than a few minutes considering the state of his office. Stacks of manila files, loose papers, and books leaned precariously on two corners of his desk. Brand-new cellophane bags full of gambling tickets were stuffed along one wall waiting to be catalogued, then stored. The other wall housed the copy machine, typewriter, and a small file cabinet. Above the cabinet, a bulletin board was plastered with dozens of colored Post-it notes. He didn't have the greatest memory in the world and constantly wrote himself reminders. Sam, a big guy, must've felt claustrophobic in this room. Funny but I'd never compared him to an animal like I do with most people. He was more like the Pillsbury Dough Boy right down to the blue eyes. I grinned as a mental picture of poking him flashed in my head.

His chair squeaked as he turned to face me. "What's so funny?" he asked.

"Um, nothing. Hey, thanks for working for me last night. I'm all set to come in tonight."

Sam frowned and averted his eyes. Uh-oh. This couldn't be good.

"Here's the thing, Maggie. They want you to take tonight off too." He held up both of his huge hands, and before I could respond, continued, "They think that's best for right now."

I didn't have to ask who "they" were. JC and Dick. But I did have to ask, "What about tomorrow night, and the night after that?"

"Uh," he said, "they're talking about having a meeting. I don't know when, but they don't want you working until then."

I bit my bottom lip hard, which overpowered the pain my fingernails were causing my clenched palms. "What's the meeting for? To decide whether or not I have a job?"

"Pretty much. I'm sorry."

Yeah, you sure are sorry, you miserable son—I stopped that line of thinking real quick. I didn't need Sam to alienate me. He and I had always been able to talk. Sam used me to vent, to rant and rave when they did something he was against. He knew I'd keep my mouth shut.

"Hey, wait. Tonight's your usual monthly board meeting. Why don't y'all just make a decision tonight? Get it the hell over with?"

Sam didn't say a word.

"So," I said, "they're lining up voting members, checking when they're available to meet, and *then* I get fired. They couldn't get enough voting members to be here tonight. They have to set up a special meeting. Is that pretty much it?"

"You know how they are."

Unfortunately, I did. I unclenched my fists so I couldn't slug him for not standing up to them. For not sticking up for me. Speaking of which, that reminded me about Sam finding the scrunchie and turning it over to JC. I asked him about it.

"As soon as I opened Jack's driver's side door, it fell out. I bent down to pick it up and JC saw me. He made me give it to him for safekeeping."

"You mean to turn it over to Bobby Lee in order to frame my ass, don't you?"

"Now, Maggie. Why would JC want that?"

Truthfully? I had no clue. But I could only go on people's actions and past behaviors. JC had a strong sense of loyalty with an even stronger belief in following orders. Probably why I'd never make it in the military—I'd be questioning my leaders all the time. *You want me to storm what hill?* I remembered one night a few years ago JC had come out of his office after getting a phone call. He'd been playing cards with Sam, Kevin, and Dick, and after the phone call, JC had pointed to them and said, "Follow me." Without a word, all three followed him out the door, no questions asked. Later, when they returned, we learned JC's son Scott had hit a deer with his truck and needed help getting the truck out of a ditch. Scott survived, not so the poor deer.

"Okay, Sam." I stood. "Just call me when you guys figure just what the hell you're doing." I turned to leave, then thought of another question. I turned back. "Was there anything gone from Jack's truck? Was his wallet missing? Did it look like he'd been robbed, or that he'd put up a fight?"

"Nope. But I didn't really look for anything. Once I saw all that blood, I knew he wasn't sleeping it off this time."

Seven

Sam's last words stayed in my head as I sat in my car wondering what I should do next. *All that blood.* That's what Bobby Lee had said to me in the parking lot yesterday morning. The reality of Jack's death slammed into me. Only two days ago, he was a living, breathing man. An ornery, grouchy one, but still. Now I wished I'd taken more time to get to know him. I was curious to find out all I could about Jack. What better way than to see where and how he lived?

One night I'd followed Jack home after he told me he wasn't feeling well. He wasn't drunk—I never let my customers get to that state—but his asthma was bothering him and his inhaler had run out while he was at the club. I made sure he got home in one piece that night. I knew his house was close to the club, and I was almost positive I could find it again.

A heavy duty metal gray mailbox with HOFFMAN painted in big white letters stood at the dirt road leading to his house. This detective business might be easier than I thought. I remembered following Jack down the dirt road that night. Bumpy and, since it had been almost one in the morning, very dark. Grateful for the daylight now, I still felt a bit nervous. Slowing down to make the turn, I was surprised to see a car coming out the end of Jack's road.

Crap. A police cruiser. I sped up. That was too damn close. I kept an eye on my rearview mirror and sure enough, the cruiser pulled out in my direction. He was soon right behind me. I recognized the Jacksonville Jaguars cap Bobby Lee wore. I did my best to obey the speed limit—not easy since it was 35 mph and my right foot is made of lead.

A loud *whoop!* from his siren, and he passed me. I was tempted to turn around at the first chance I had and go back to Jack's when a better idea came to me. I followed Bobby Lee all the way downtown back to the police station.

Suddenly feeling brave, I decided to ask the police chief questions that only he had the answers to. First thing I wanted to find out was why he'd sat in front of my house the day before.

He pulled into his reserved spot out front while I parked between two pickup trucks. I remembered how Rob had wanted to get a pickup just so he'd fit in more in this town. They were all over the place it seemed. I never did find out if Rob had been joking.

Bobby Lee was standing at the front counter when I entered the station. He looked up from the pile of mail he was sorting and nodded. "Morning, Maggie. What can I do for you?"

May as well be blunt. "Chief, what were you doing at my house last night?" I kept my hands down at my side pressed against my legs so he couldn't see them shaking. I hoped my voice hadn't betrayed me.

"You know I'm conducting a murder investigation. That's all I'm sayin'."

Whose murder? At one time my house was considered a crime scene. I decided to keep this about Jack Hoffman, so asked, "What about Jack's truck? Was there anything else in it besides my planted scrunchie? Was he robbed? What kind of weapon killed him? Could it have been a carjacking gone bad?"

Bobby Lee stepped back as if my words had actually touched him. "I ain't at liberty to reveal anything. You know that."

I stood my ground, feeling more confident by the second. I was determined to get answers. Maybe if I changed tactics. I softened my voice and said, "Oh, Bobby Lee, it's just that I'm scared I'm going to lose my job. Sam told me they're probably going to fire me over this."

Before I could bat my eyelashes, he smiled and said, "Now, Maggie, I'm sure you don't have anything to worry about." He leaned on the counter and said, "I will tell you this: Nothing else was found in his truck, possibly a knife with a short blade was used, and I'm positive it wasn't robbery or attempted carjacking. I'm only telling you that much so you'll stay out of it. You and Michael Bradley. I don't care how good a police officer he was in Orlando, he doesn't have any right to mess with my investigation."

Ah. Sounded like Bobby Lee had heard about Michael asking questions, and checked up on him. Interesting.

"As far as I'm concerned, the two of you are civilians. You might want to remind him of that." The telephone rang and he reached for it. "And I want you to remember that too. Now, I'd best get back to work."

Clearly dismissed, I left the station and stood on the sidewalk going over my options. Midmorning on a Monday in the downtown square of North DeSoto, there was little car or foot traffic. Any shopping to be done would be happening at the mall out off the main highway. Downtown was slowly dying. On this side of the street stood the courthouse, police station, and post office.

Straight ahead of me was the park. In order to bring life back to the downtown area, several local organizations had united in renovating the town square. Over the years it had become a mess of overgrown shrubs and weeds smack dab in the middle of downtown businesses. The North DeSoto Garden Club was now responsible for upkeep of the beautiful landscape. A small colorful carousel was silent at the moment, and I could see the fountain was flowing. Rather than stroll through the park now, I looked around to get my bearings. Across from the park were a jewelry store, law offices, a realtor, and movie theater. If I turned right, I'd go by the library, an overpriced dress shop, and Sally's, my favorite restaurant in this town. A twenty-four-hour diner and bakery, Sally's was always busy whenever I'd gone in. Rob and I had enjoyed many meals there during those long days and nights of working on the house. My stomach grumbled at the thought of Sally's homemade sausage gravy and biscuits, but it looked like I'd have to really start counting my pennies.

To the left were a closed-up bookstore, a pawn shop, a bank, and JC's hardware store. Oh, joy. I took a deep breath and turned left. Time to see what, if anything, I could learn from JC. My mantra: Be nice, Maggie.

A little bell jingled announcing my arrival when I opened the door to Nelson's Hardware. I had never had any reason to shop at JC's store. Any hardware-type stuff I needed I bought over at the newer big chain store in the shopping center. Nelson's Hardware had been around for over a century, staying in the same family, the same location all this time. I had to move my way around a stack of cardboard boxes to get to the counter.

"Be right with you," a voice called out from somewhere in the back. "Help yourself to coffee and donuts."

I looked around, and sure enough, a little round table near the front counter had a coffeemaker and a couple of Dunkin' Donuts boxes. A handwritten sign told me to help myself.

So I did. I figured this would be the only time I'd get anything good from JC Nelson. I remembered my new mantra. I munched on my glazed donut and wandered around the store while waiting for JC. Strong smells of fertilizer, bleach, and paint filled the air. Not a great mix with my donut, but beggars can't be choosers and all that. I grabbed another donut—toasted coconut this time—and took a bite.

"Maggie! How are you? I'm glad you stopped in. I've been thinking about you, hoping you were doing okay."

I almost choked on my donut, startled not only by his sudden appearance, but his friendly words.

"What can I do for you?" JC moved around behind the counter. "I don't imagine you're here to buy anything."

"Actually, I am. I came in to see if you had a tarp. My poor roof is in pretty bad shape, and the tarp I have now is torn and ragged." I smiled ever so sweetly and popped the last bit of donut in my mouth. "I was hoping your prices were lower than that big superstore. I can't afford their high prices. I'm not even sure I can afford yours, bu ... " *Hint, hint, you sorry bastard for wanting to get me fired and framed for murder.*

"I'm sure I can help you out. Follow me." JC headed toward the newer part of his store. About three, four years ago they had bought the vacant store next door and added on. More strong smells, this time kerosene, sawdust, and the sound of banging.

"Okay, here you go. Different sizes and material. Of course, the thicker, stronger pieces will run you a bit more, but they're worth it in the long run. Any questions?" The banging stopped and I didn't have to shout for him to hear me.

"Yeah. Why are you trying to frame me for Jack Hoffman's murder?" Damn. I forgot my mantra. Hell, as long as I was at it ... "And did you really think that giving Bobby Lee that scrunchie was enough to put me away? There was nothing but that in Jack's truck. Bobby Lee told—"

A clatter nearby interrupted me. What the hell?

"Pam? Honey, are you okay?" JC moved quickly down the aisle and I followed him. We rounded the corner and Pam, sitting on top of a high ladder, came into view. She stared down, then looked at us and pointed at the floor.

"Hello, Maggie," Pam said, sniffing. "Yes, JC, I'm fine. Dropped the hammer. Can you get it for me? I'd like to finish this. I have an appointment."

JC bent to retrieve the hammer and I looked at what Pam had been doing. Along one wall a row of framed newspaper articles hung. I'd seen them before and had received a Nelson family/hardware store history lesson at the same time. Pam was a member of the North DeSoto Historical Society and enjoyed combing through old records. She'd apparently been hanging the most recent one when she dropped her hammer.

"Hi, Pam. A new article?"

"Yes, I found it in the Jacksonville library archives yesterday. That library is so much better than our dinky one." She sniffed again. "Our town library should become one of my projects. It could only improve if I got involved. I'd make sure everything was in its proper place, make things easier to find. Too many times I've found articles in the Jacksonville library that aren't in our own. A disgrace."

JC reached up, handed his wife the hammer, and chuckled. "Pam was in the Jacksonville library all day yesterday. She'd spend all her waking hours in libraries researching if she didn't have so many other responsibilities in the community."

Ah, yes, Pamela Nelson, social butterfly. She belonged to every civic organization in North DeSoto. Rob used to call her a Junior

League Wannabe. He'd softened though when Pam came over with some articles about our own house. The two of them would pore over old documents and photos together. She was the one who told us about our house being a dorm for nursing students starting back in the 1950s. She'd still find papers and stuff and call me. I didn't have as much interest as Rob had, and I cared even less now, but I also didn't want to be rude.

The jingle of the bell over the door announced a real customer. JC said, "If you'll excuse me, Maggie. Let me know about the tarp." He headed to the other side of the store toward his customer, which left me and Pam alone.

Sitting so high above me, I'm sure she thought of me as one of her town peasants. I knew firsthand she didn't need a six-foot ladder to look down on people. Before she could start hammering away, I asked, "Pam, did you overhear Jack say anything at the bar Saturday night? Or maybe Friday night? Anything that might be reason for someone to want him dead?"

She sniffed. The air must be thinner way up there on her perch. I waited.

"I assure you I don't make eavesdropping a habit, Maggie."

I smiled and said, "Of course not. I was thinking more of how easy it is to hear stuff when you're behind the bar. Remarks you don't even realize at the time are important. Anything like that?"

Pam gripped the hammer tighter and opened her mouth as if to respond, then clamped it shut. She shook her head and smiled. "No," she said, "nothing like that. Now, if you'll excuse me, I must get back to this. If I don't do it, it'll never get done properly."

I grabbed another donut before leaving the store. Unbeknownst to her, Pam had given me a great idea and I couldn't wait to follow through.

Eight

The North DeSoto Public Library, a two-story Spanish-style building common in north Florida, was anything but dinky in my opinion. Then again, I'm not one to spend full days in libraries like Pam had the day before. The library's computers should be much faster than the antiquated one I had at the house.

After talking to the reference librarian, I was soon settled at a table ready to find out all I could about Jack Hoffman. Scrolling through old newspaper archives, I came up with two small articles. The first piece, a blurry photograph from 1953, was about Jack's return from the war with his beautiful new Korean bride. The second article was one line listed under Divorces nine years later. So much for that. For the marriage and for my research.

Next up, I Googled "Abby Kwon." Two hits. One was a high school student in Arkansas who had aced her SATs and the other was a real estate agent in Delaware. The search brought up a whole bunch of pages about Nancy Kwan, the actress. I tried "Abigail Kwan" and "Abigail Kwon" and had no luck there either.

I liked the possible connection of Jack Hoffman marrying a Korean woman, and Abby being Korean. Coincidence? I didn't think so. Jack's comment about the bitter-tasting beer that Abby had served him. Abby suddenly leaving town. For shits and giggles, knowing I was wasting my time, I Googled "Abby Hoffman." Yeah, I know.

Then I tried finding Abby through the online Ft. Walton Beach phone book. Nada. Zip. Zilch. Maybe I wasn't cut out for the detective business after all. I slumped in the chair, staring at the computer monitor and wondering what to do next when I overheard whispering behind me. I'd been so involved with my research, I hadn't noticed before, but it sounded like the tail end of a gossipy conversation. I listened closer and heard snippets.

"I heard arrested." "New to town." "Bartender."

I gritted my teeth, not daring to get up or even look behind me. I took a deep breath. Then a few more until I'd calmed down.

Might as well take advantage of the fast Internet connection while I was at the library. I brought up the *North DeSoto Reporter*, the local newspaper, and went to yesterday's issue.

The headline and front page of course were all about Jack's murder. About the only thing not mentioned was the scrunchie found in Jack's truck. Bobby Lee must've withheld that little piece of information for some reason. Abby wasn't mentioned by name, but Bobby Lee was quoted, "We're looking for an important witness, someone who may've seen something." That was probably Abby. I apparently was the "person of interest brought in for questioning, then released."

Terrific. At least my name hadn't been printed. Not that word hadn't spread through town by now. Who was I kidding? Word traveled before Bobby Lee had pulled out of the drive-thru of Mickey D's. In this town if you're heard sneezing, a person will bring you chicken soup, then go tell others you have the swine flu.

Autopsy and toxicology results were expected in a couple weeks. Bobby Lee was also quoted as saying, "It appears nothing was stolen, and the weapon used was a short-bladed knife."

Sonofabitch. He hadn't told me anything I couldn't read in the newspaper.

I scrolled to today's edition and found Jack's very short obituary. Sad, actually, how short it was, and I wondered if the funeral home had written it. Nothing about family members or any survivors. I realized how little I knew Jack Hoffman. He was seventy-eight when he died. The funeral was scheduled for Thursday morning, three days from now. What the hell would I wear? I hadn't been to a funeral since …

Ignoring the rest of that thought, I closed down the computer and pushed back my chair.

"Shhhh!"

Three old ladies, sitting at the table behind me, wagged their crooked little fingers at me. One held a finger to her wrinkled, pursed lips.

"Sorry," I said. I pushed my chair back in under the table, maybe a little harder than I normally would've, and shrugged when it screeched across the wood floor. Mouthing another apology, I left the library. Gossipy old hags.

That made me think of another old lady. Gussie from the house next-door to the club. I'd add her name to my list of people to go talk to, even if the thought made me sweat. Maybe she saw something the night Jack was murdered.

66

As I walked back to my car, I wondered what my next step should be. Going through the list of names, I still needed to talk to Dick and Diane Reid, Gussie, Kevin, and Pete. And somehow track down Abby. I also still wanted to check out Jack's place. As long as the police chief was at the station, maybe I'd be safe in doing that. I peered through the plate-glass window of the police station as I walked by and saw Bobby Lee at the counter with more paperwork.

Time to head to Jack's.

Nine

The narrow dirt road was as bumpy as I remembered, and didn't seem as long in the daylight. My car didn't bottom out once, but I heard weeds scraping the undercarriage. With any luck, the branches of scraggly bushes on either side of the path weren't scratching the car.

Jack's house was surrounded by pine and live oak trees. Normally, I would've stopped to admire the Spanish moss dripping from the trees, but the normally pretty sight seemed gloomy under the darkening sky. I hightailed it across the yard, the pine needles crunching under my sneakers. I moved up onto the porch and came to a dead stop. What? Now I was a friggin' burglar? No way was I going to break into a dead man's house.

Unless there was a key under the mat. I moved past a ratty-looking wicker stand holding a dead plant to lift the front doormat. It was so old and dry, straw flaked to the porch. No key. I walked around it to the front window.

The grimy, black window, its dirty white shutters splattered with love bugs, made me cringe. Leaning in as close as possible without touching the glass, I peered in. I could barely see, but a lamp seemed to be on and I thought I saw something move. A thunderclap boomed, scaring the crap out of me.

Holding a hand against my chest and willing my heart to slow down, I turned away from the window. I moved to the porch steps, accompanied by another thunderclap. Sometimes I really hated Florida and its sudden thunderstorms. Since moving to north Florida, I had also learned a thing or two about sinus headaches. They never bothered me at all in Miami, but the weather was so different here.

The rain burst down before I had a chance to even think about running to my car. I moved back toward the front door to wait it out. Most storms lasted ten minutes or so. I was grateful for the covered porch at least. Looked like Jack's roof was in better shape than mine because the porch was staying dry. My little stoop and doormat always got soaked during these storms. I couldn't decide if I should sit down or lean against the house or stay standing. Nothing felt right, and my skin crawled. I told myself it was the electricity of the storm, not a feeling of being watched. No one was standing out in that rain. After several minutes, the deluge let up enough for me to dash to my car.

By the time I got to the end of Jack's dirt road, the black clouds had parted and the afternoon sun was shining again. I inched my way slowly closer to the main road, hoping I wouldn't run into anyone. All clear.

Since I had struck out at Jack's, I decided to go see Gussie. Unfortunately, there was no avoiding driving by the VFW on my way. Gussie's house sat on the very edge of their property. Her driveway was on the side facing the club, which meant my car would be in plain sight. Nothing wrong with visiting a fellow citizen, though.

A curtain moved on the large picture window above the driveway as I was getting out of my car. A sign on the door next to the window directed people to use the back door, so I scooted around there as well.

"Maggie Lewis. What can I do for you?" A large, older woman with her arms folded stood at the back door, staring me down.

Whoa. That stopped me dead in my tracks at the bottom of the steps. I knew we were on a first-name basis due to all of the noise complaint calls, but I sure as hell didn't expect her to know my last name. I faked it and put on a big smile.

"Good afternoon," I said. "You are Gussie then, I take it?"

"And who else did you expect? Don't be wasting my time, girl, just state your business."

Okay then. "Um, I was wondering if there was any chance you might have seen anything in the parking lot the other night." I pointed over my shoulder toward the club.

"Meaning the night Jack Hoffman got himself murdered?"

"Yes, ma'am." Where'd that come from? I might be a southerner, but *ma'am* and *sir* don't come easily from my lips. There was something about this woman that made me feel inferior.

"I saw that new girl and a man come out together. Jack came out just a few minutes before them."

Who had she seen? Jack, then Abby with either Pete or Sam. Which one? "Those three were the only ones you saw?"

Gussie continued staring. "Isn't that what I just said?"

"Yes, ma'am." Shit. "You saw Jack get into his truck?"

"That's right. And I saw the other man and the girl get into their car and drive away."

I didn't like the way she said *girl*, either about Abby or me. "What about Jack?"

Her gray curls moved as she shook her head at me and said, "Obviously I didn't see him leave, seeing as how he ended up dead."

Somehow I seemed to be asking the wrong questions. I tried again. "What else did you see?"

"Before the man and girl left, he went over to Jack's truck."

"And?" It was like pulling teeth.

"Then he went back to his car and they left."

"The man and the girl left?"

Her expression told me she wasn't even going to bother answering that stupid question.

"Could you see what the man did when he was at Jack's truck?"

"Just stood there for a minute or two is all."

"So, he wasn't at Jack's truck for very long?"

"Girl, what did I just say? The man was there for a minute or two. He went back to his car and they left."

"And you never saw a third man?"

"I saw lots of men that night, just like every other night."

"No, I mean at that same time—when you saw the girl and man leave."

"You didn't ask that, did you?"

I wanted to cry. I felt like a child in front of her. A small, stupid child. I wasn't learning much from this woman. And it seemed like it was my fault.

I smiled at her and said, "Thank you very much. You were very helpful." I turned to walk away, wanting to run back to my car.

"Don't you want to know about the cars I saw later that night?"

Ten

"Ma'am?" I turned back to her. The look on her face made me wonder if she'd been toying with me all along.

Gussie nodded. "Later, I saw a car pull up next to Jack's truck."

"Do you know what time it was? Were you able to see anyone get out of the car? Do you know what kind of car it was?"

"Good questions, girl. Finally." She shuffled over to the porch swing, sat, and pointed to a small wooden chair. "C'mon up and sit."

I felt like I'd passed some kind of test and this was my reward from a forbidding but ultimately fair teacher. I lowered myself to the hard chair, watching her attentively.

"So, let's see. It was too dark to see anything other than the head-lights. What's that tell you?"

I thought about it and said, "It was after two fifteen in the morning because that's when the streetlight goes off." The security light had been installed years ago when bars and clubs were still open until two. One of the past VFW commanders had made the request for the safety of his bartender leaving that late. The light was still set to go off automatically at 2:15 a.m. even though we now closed at midnight.

Gussie blinked slowly. "That's right. What else?"

"You said *cars*, not *car*. You saw more than one. And it sounds like it was two different times. Two different cars?"

She nodded.

"Were you able to see the people who were in the cars?"

"No, it was too dark. Around twelve thirty, Jack came out the front door and got in his truck. Stumbling quite a bit. Five minutes later the man and the girl came out the side door and walked to his car. The girl got in. The man walked over to Jack's truck, then he went back to his car and drove away. Jack sat there for a long time. I've seen him do that, so I wasn't concerned. I once saw Jack drive away just as the sun was coming up. I don't think it's right that y'all allowed that man to drink so much that he had to sleep it off."

I started to object because I never let any of my customers get that drunk, but I had a hunch I'd be wasting my breath. I let her continue.

"A couple of hours later, shortly after the streetlight went out, I saw a car pull in and park next to Jack's truck. I saw the inside light turn on in Jack's truck, but didn't see much else other than moving shadows."

I picked up on that. "Shadows. More than one. Does that mean you might've seen more than one person? But you couldn't tell who they were because it was too dark?"

"Straight to the head of the class!"

I couldn't help my grin. I think I had figured out something else. "You were a teacher, weren't you?"

"Once upon a time," she said with a small smile now. "You just learned how to ask the right questions, didn't you?"

"Okay. So, what else? After that car left, you saw another one come by later? How much later? Was it the same car? The same people?"

"Girl, now you're asking the right questions, but don't you think you ought to give me time to answer them?" She closed her eyes, shook her head back and forth a few times as if she were replaying the scene in her head. I kept my mouth shut and waited.

Gussie opened her eyes and said, "Different car. Smaller. About forty-five minutes, an hour later. The driver got out, went inside the building. Another person got out of the passenger side. Saw the inside light of Jack's truck go on again for minute, then go off. The person got back in the car, sat there for several minutes until the driver came back, and finally drove away."

That may explain the 3:30 a.m. visitor who used my security code. "Could you tell if it was the same two people, but driving a different car?"

The older woman shrugged her broad shoulders. "That'd be my guess, but don't know for sure."

"Thank you, ma'am."

"You're welcome. Now, I'd best get back inside." She stood.

"May I ask you something? Kind of personal?"

"You want to know why I'm always looking out the windows, don't you? Insomnia, girl. I've had it since my husband's passing eighteen years ago. Just can't sleep."

I felt even closer to her. "Thank you again." A hug seemed too familiar, so I stuck out my hand.

"Go on now, girl." She shook my hand quickly and shuffled over to the back door. As I left her porch, she said, "Good luck, Maggie Lewis. God bless."

Delivered in that flat voice, the statement should have made me nervous, but suddenly I had the feeling everything would turn out okay.

Then a loud rumble sounded. Oh shit, not another downpour. Turning, I saw the beer delivery truck over at the club. Man, that *was* loud. No wonder Gussie complained about the noise. Another thought struck me, and I quickly drove around the block to the club's parking lot entrance. Sam's truck was still the only other vehicle in the lot.

I made it to the back porch just as Sam was propping open the screen door so the beer guy could go in and out. I was definitely not the person Sam expected to see.

"Hey," I said. "Need to use the phone. Okay? Thanks." I rushed past him. Knowing I only had five minutes or so while he was busy with the delivery guy, I hurried through the bar and down the hall to his office.

Cool. He'd left his door open. I went straight to his file cabinet and flipped through the folders. Sheesh. Where the hell could it be? His desk? Oh, God. Total unorganized mess.

I quickly looked through one of the paper stacks on the corner of his desk. Aha! Abby's job application. Abigail Quon. No wonder I couldn't find her under Kwon or Kwan. I kept reading. Born in 1987 which made her twenty-eight this year. No other personal information. Even past employer was left blank.

I heard heavy footsteps and I shoved the application back where I'd found it. I plopped down in Sam's chair and picked up the phone receiver. Sam walked into his office.

"Okay, thanks, see you later," I said to empty air. I hung up, swiveled around in the chair, and pretended to be surprised to see him. I stood and said, "Thanks, Sam. I was in the neighborhood and suddenly remembered a very important phone call. Thanks again. I know you're busy, Sam, so I'll leave now. Thanks again, Sam." I moved past him, willing my mouth to shut the hell up.

"Did you find what you were looking for?"

I was really starting to get tired of my feet stopping dead in their tracks. I turned around and faced him.

He leaned over the desk and pointed at the phone. "It usually helps to push one of these when you want to make a call." He pointed at the row of clear buttons on the bottom of the phone base. "So, did you get what you needed?"

Busted. I didn't know how to talk my way out of this one. I stared down at my feet.

"Maggie." Sam walked over to me and pulled me into his arms. Like the Pillsbury Dough Boy, I wouldn't have been able to fit my arms around him if I tried. But I did give in to the hug. Then I pulled away before the blubbering could start.

His arm still around me, he said, "C'mon, I'll buy you a cup of coffee." We walked together to the bar. The delivery guy was bringing cases of beer on his dolly to the walk-in cooler near the back door. We waved at each other. Sam went around to the small kitchen behind the bar. I sat on the same stool I had yesterday when Bobby Lee was questioning all of us. Amazing how one's life could spiral down in a little over twenty-four hours. I put my head down and immediately regretted it. Yuck. The bar was sticky. The club would open in less than an hour and Sam hadn't cleaned the bar yet. Hell, it should've been done the night before. Maybe he'd been too busy. I was never allowed that excuse, but I'm only a peon. Looked like the bottles hadn't been wiped down for a few days either. Friday night, my last night working, was probably the last time they'd been cleaned.

Sam came around behind the bar and handed me a cup of coffee. He'd already fixed it the way I liked it—lots of sugar and milk.

"So. Talk to me." He leaned against the shelf behind him.

I lowered my cup and looked up at him. "Oh, be careful, Sam. Your elbow—" I spoke just in time to save him from knocking over the bottle of Jack Daniels.

He steadied it on the shelf and said, "That was close. Okay, now, where were we?"

The image of Sam running to get that baggie for Bobby Lee made me hesitate. I decided to give a little, as much as the police chief had given me. No harm in sharing that much.

"I found out from Bobby Lee that there was nothing in Jack's truck besides my scrunchie. He wasn't robbed, so I guess that means Jack still had his wallet on him."

"Was the wallet empty?"

Damn. Good question. I shrugged.

"Because," he said, "I'm wondering if the killer could've taken money out but left the wallet behind. He got what he came after and took off."

My shoulders were getting a real workout because I shrugged again. "Good points. Did you see the wallet in the truck? I mean, like on the seat or anywhere?"

"Nope." He sipped his coffee. "What about Jack's notebook? Just thought of that. It should've been in the truck. Did you ask Bobby Lee about it?"

"Wouldn't you have seen it?"

He shook his head, his jowls shaking. "It, um, Jack was lying on his side, so ..." He let his voice trail. Probably didn't want to picture it again, or make me think of how Jack must've looked.

"Excuse me." The beer guy ducked his head around the doorframe. "Hey, Sam, Maggie, I'm all done stocking. You're good until next week. See y'all then."

I heard the back door close and wondered if I'd ever see him again. Depressing thought, so I turned my attention back to Sam. The sooner I figured this out, the sooner I'd get back behind the bar where I belonged. And I had to do it before they had their meeting.

"Okay," I said, "I'll ask Bobby Lee about Jack's notebook and wallet. But he made it sound like there was nothing else in the truck. Nothing but the scrunchie." I swallowed the last of my coffee. I wanted to ask him about what Gussie had said. Why hadn't she seen Sam? Or had she simply missed him? No way could she watch out her window and see *everyone* come and go.

"I should get going. I want to go to the cemetery, then pick up something for dinner before it gets dark." I carried the mug around to the little kitchen and almost ran smack dab into Dick Reid as he was rounding the corner. As much as I wanted to question him, I felt like I'd made enough progress for one day. Getting to the cemetery was top priority.

Eleven

I didn't make it to my car before getting waylaid.

"Yoo-hoo, Maggie!" Terrific. Diane Reid stood at the trunk of their car, a few plastic grocery bags at her feet. So nice of her husband to help her. Then I saw what she was up to. She'd probably told Dick to go on ahead so she could sneak a smoke. He was as bad as Pam when it came to putting the kibosh on smoking.

I waved hello and jumped into my Honda as fast as I could. I wanted to get to the cemetery before dark and I knew talking to Diane would be cutting it too close. When I had more time, I definitely wanted to talk to her.

For a sixty-something-year-old overweight woman, she was fast and suddenly appeared at my window. Her gray spiked hair was matted with perspiration and she used the cuff of her long sleeve to wipe her forehead.

"I'm glad I caught you! So many things to ask!" Diane leaned on my door catching her breath. "Anywho, I wanted to know what you'll be bringing to the funeral reception."

I started the ignition. She didn't move. "Um, I don't know, Diane. I hadn't given it any thought. When is it?"

"Right after the funeral, silly! Here in our hall. What can I put you down for?"

"I don't care. Cole slaw. Put me down for cole slaw. I have to go, Diane. Sorry to be rude," I said, not feeling at all sorry. "See you later."

"Wait, one more thing! Are you still going to clean my house this week?"

"Sure," I said. Thirty-five dollars. Yeah, I'd clean her house. "I'll call you later."

"Okay, and remember—no telling Dick. He thinks I should do it all myself, but what he doesn't know won't hurt him. I don't tell him everything, y'know." Diane giggled. "Men! I wished he felt the same way. He's always going on about how he spends his day when I could care less."

I could've gouged her eyes out then and there. What I wouldn't do to have the chance to hear Rob tell me about his day. I slammed the car in reverse, peeled out of the parking lot, and drove to the cemetery feeling guilty for not visiting Rob the day before.

The North DeSoto Cemetery was small, quiet, and expensive. Sidewalks so white they hurt my eyes in the summer meandered past well-kept gravesites. In the two years I'd been coming, I'd never seen litter or trash of any kind. The grass and shrubberies looked like they were trimmed on a daily basis. I had spared no expense on the grave marker either. The dates of Rob's birth and death were etched in the beautiful black granite, so shiny I could see my reflection. My name was right next to his. Thank God the owners allowed layaway on plots and monthly payments on his funeral and burial. Their compassion led to my decision to bury Rob here in North DeSoto, with me right next to him when the time came.

———

It was just barely light out when I stopped at Winn-Dixie. I opted for the family-size frozen lasagna, which would feed me for five days—six if I didn't pig out—and headed back to the house. Oh, man, what an exhausting day.

Carrying the grocery bag in one hand, my purse and keys in the other, I walked up to the front of my house. Oh, good Lord. No tarp blowing in the wind. No tarp period. My stomach bottomed out momentarily, but... the roof looked okay. As in patched. Fixed.

I ran up the porch steps and rang Michael's doorbell. I hugged him as soon as he opened the door. I couldn't help myself. Oh, hell, who was I kidding? I didn't even try to restrain myself.

"I take it you saw the roof?" He pulled back and grinned.

"Yes, and thank you so much."

"I can't take all the credit. Scott Nelson stopped by and helped."

Afraid of the answer, I asked, "What do I owe you?"

"Dinner. Chris is at her friend Heather's house studying and will eat dinner there too."

"Your timing couldn't be better. Do you like lasagna and garlic bread?" I held up my grocery bag.

He groaned and said, "I love homemade lasagna."

"Yeah? Me too. How do you feel about Stouffer's?"

"I consider that homemade."

"Good answer," I said. "I have so much to tell you about my day. Come on up anytime. I'll go pop dinner in the oven."

"See you in about ten minutes, okay?"

"Great." I unlocked my door and rushed up the stairs. I had less than ten minutes to spruce the place up. No way was I prepared for guests.

While the oven preheated, I shoved the boxes lined along the hallway into one of the rooms and closed the door. Michael knocked on the door as I was putting the lasagna in the oven.

I hollered down the stairs for him to come in.

"You don't lock your door?" He was frowning when he reached the top of the stairs. "That surprises me, Maggie. Anyone could've come in."

"Completely slipped my mind. I don't usually leave it unlocked. Plus, I guess since I knew you were coming right over ..." I let my voice trail off.

"But what if it hadn't been me? You didn't know that. What if—"

"Stop, just stop!" Terrific. Here came the crying jag for the day. I pointed toward the kitchen and said, "Go in there. I'll be back."

When I came out of the bathroom a few minutes later, Michael was sitting at the kitchen table. I sat across from him, took a huge breath, and got ready to tell him the whole story. Because I'd wanted to be truthful to a prospective tenant, I hadn't kept Rob's murder from Michael. He knew Rob had been killed in the small mudroom downstairs and that I'd had it torn down, but I'd never told him everything. Now that he and Chris had been here a few months and we'd gotten to know each other a bit more, I felt I needed to explain.

"Okay, here's the thing. You need to know what happened to my husband."

"Only if you think it's necessary." His voice was soft, as if he were trying to put me at ease.

"You need to understand why I reacted the way I did earlier." I took a deep breath and exhaled. "I'm ready. I just have to get over my—"

My what? My fear? My not wanting to rehash it? A day didn't go by that I didn't think about it. Losing Rob was bad enough; the way he died was so much worse. Time to suck it up.

"Two years ago we—Rob and I—were about done with the renovations downstairs. I was upstairs painting the bathroom. It's the only room we were able to finish before Rob...before he was killed. He was working downstairs. I had my radio playing and I thought I heard him shout out to me.

"I turned down the volume, and it sounded like he was moving furniture around for some reason. I didn't know what he was doing. I was up on a ladder and didn't want to climb down to find out. I would've had to go downstairs, out the front door. The front door to downstairs was locked, so I would've had to walk all the way around to the side door just to see what he wanted. If only I had—"

I lowered my eyes, knowing if I looked at Michael I'd lose it for sure. I took another deep breath. I could get through this.

"Rob was making so much noise, I finally had to find out what he was doing. By the time I got to the side door, I heard the sound of squealing tires. I didn't think anything about it. Not until later. I went inside and Rob didn't answer me when I called out. I—I found him in the mudroom, the back door wide open.

"So much blood. He'd been beaten...he was sprawled on the floor, unconscious. Later, Bobby Lee said he'd been hit over and over with...something. They never did find out what or who did it. He died that night in the hospital. Never regained consciousness."

"I am so sorry, Maggie." Michael moved closer and put his arm around me.

"I had the mudroom demolished. I couldn't stand the sight of it. I moved upstairs and haven't been back since." I gently pushed away from him and said, "And that's why I have a hard time going inside your place. Even with the mudroom gone, the whole downstairs reminds me of Rob. Just hurts too much."

"I'm glad you told me. Thank you."

"Okay, then," I said and stood. I needed to change the subject. "How about a glass of wine since you're not driving?"

"Sounds great."

I was pulling two wineglasses out of the cabinet when Michael's cell phone rang. A normal ring, nothing fancy or musical. He even had an older phone, not one with all the bells and whistles. Go figure. I couldn't help but eavesdrop.

"Oh, yes, Terri, thanks for returning my call. Pizza? I bet Chris loved that." Silence while he listened, then a chuckle. A deep, throaty kind of chuckle that I'd never heard from him before.

Dropping all pretense of nonchalance, I looked at him. Damned if he wasn't blushing. Who the hell was Terri and why was she calling him? Oh, the mother of Chris's friend Heather, of course. Why did it sound like he was flirting? And, more importantly, why the hell should I care?

"Okay, see you in a couple of hours. I'll be waiting out front. Thanks, Terri." He finished his conversation and snapped his phone shut. "Okay, so where were we?"

Guess I wasn't going to hear anything more about Terri. Fine.

I poured the wine and handed him a glass. We spent the next two hours eating and catching up on everything I'd done that day. Except for visiting Rob. And the part about going to Jack's. I wasn't sure how he'd react to that. Something nagged in the back of my brain, but I couldn't figure out what, so I kept it to myself.

"That's interesting about Gussie seeing cars and people," he said. "And I hate to say it, but you will eventually need to talk to Sam about where he was. Suspect everyone. Casual conversation. You don't need to interrogate people, just talk, ask questions. And wait for their answers. I learned long ago that my keeping quiet made them talk."

"Sounds good. I learned Abby's last name is Quon, but little else. I'd planned on checking her out on my computer." I pointed to the ancient desktop on an even more ancient desk shoved into the corner.

"Let's do that now," he suggested. Several minutes later, during which he'd grumbled about my slow connection and small monitor, we were finally online. He hovered over my shoulder while I typed in Abby's full name (properly spelled this time) and "Ft. Walton Beach, FL." Nothing. I tried a few different directories he knew about with no luck.

I leaned back in my chair and my head smacked Michael square in the chin.

"Ouch!" I rubbed the back of my head. "Sorry about that. Are you okay?"

"Man, you have a hard head. Not that I didn't already know that." Michael laughed. "I think you got the worst of it. You okay?"

I jumped, startled when I felt his hand on mine. He quickly pulled it away. I sat there facing the computer wondering who was more embarrassed—him for touching me, or my reaction to it. I felt the heat of a blush on my cheeks.

"Sorry, Maggie, I—"

I waved his apology away. "Oh, no big deal. I'm just jumpy is all."

"Yeah, okay. Um, I think I'm going to go wait outside for Chris. She should be here soon."

"All right," I said, even though we knew Chris wouldn't be here for another fifteen, twenty minutes. I heard him leave the room and sprint down the stairs. I fanned my still hot face. Oh, sheesh. Now I was acting like a southern belle with a case of the vapors. "Why I do declare, Mr. Bradley!" I muttered under my breath.

Enough. Back to work. Work. Sam had said Abby was experienced, that she'd worked as a bartender before. I typed in her name along with "waitress" and "bartender." Whoa. A site popped up linking to a gentleman's club in Ft. Walton Beach. I clicked on it.

A photo came up. A smiling Abby stood between two men, her arms linked in theirs. The caption read, "Dancer Abby with club owner Nicky and bartender Tyler." Nicky looked like the guy from the old "I can't believe I ate the whole thing" Alka-Seltzer commercials. Tyler, on the other hand, belonged on the cover of a romance novel. Drop dead gorgeous with biceps the size of I don't know what. No wonder Abby was smiling. Then I remembered her black eye.

Well, well, well. I leaned back in the chair and immediately thought of Michael. I ran downstairs to tell him what I'd found. He followed me back upstairs.

"Good job," he said after looking at the photo. I noticed he stood a couple feet away. "Jot down the address and phone number. We should go out there this weekend and pay Abby a visit."

I wrote down the information and turned to look at him. I grinned and said, "Oh, I see how it is. You're pretty willing to help when it comes time to visit a strip club."

Score. He blushed. Hell, better him than me. By then it really was time for Michael to go wait for Chris. I told him to come back up with her.

———

"This is so cool, Maggie! I love your house," Chris said. She stood at the overflowing bookshelves, fingering the spines.

"I've never taken time to look through all those books," I told her. "Anything interesting to you?"

"Nope. Just a lot of old cookbooks and medical stuff." She moved away from the bookshelf, plopped back down in her chair. "So, what are we gonna do?"

"Um, are you hungry? I could make some popcorn."

"Yeah, can I help?" Chris jumped up. "Whoa, the floor's wobbly here." She pointed her toes to the carpet under her.

"Be careful. You won't fall through, but the plywood might be coming loose."

"Plywood?" Michael held out his hand to her. "Come here, honey. Be careful."

"It's safe. Chris, I'll bet you don't know what's under the plywood, or behind that wall there." I pointed to where she'd been standing.

"What?" Her voice was a whisper, her eyes wide. "A secret tunnel?"

"Stairs that go down to *your* kitchen."

"Cool! But why are they covered up?"

I placed a bag of popcorn in the microwave and explained the history of the house to her, everything Rob and I had been able to learn thanks to Pam.

"Are there ghosts?"

"Nope, but there's supposed to be a hidden treasure somewhere."

"Awesome! Can we hunt for it?"

The microwave beeped and I shook the popcorn into a big bowl, put it down on the kitchen table.

"What it is? Gold? Money? Jewelry?" Chris scooped a small handful of popcorn into her mouth.

"I don't know too much. Just that there's an old rumor that something very valuable is hidden. Something, somewhere. I don't know." I remembered Pam telling us about the old rumor, then pooh-poohing it. The treasure rumor had been around for decades.

"I bet I could find it. Have you ever looked?"

I thought back to every time Rob and I tore up a floor or insulated a wall. He'd looked out for hidden treasures. He had fallen for the rumor hook, line, and sinker.

After his murder, the rumor had resurfaced, and people said the killer had been looking for the treasure. Bobby Lee always thought it was a home invasion. Considering nothing had been stolen, he called it an attempted burglary gone wrong.

I called it a stupid, useless murder.

The tolling of my grandfather clock shook me out of my reverie. I smiled as Chris counted along with the chimes.

She cried, "Eleven? No way it's eleven o'clock!"

"Subtract three, and you'll get the right time," I said, laughing at their expressions. "The clock came with the house. Never could figure out what's wrong, and it's easier to subtract than get it fixed."

"Totally weird, Maggie," Chris said. "And cool."

Michael stood. "All right, young lady, that means time to get ready for bed. Thanks, Maggie, for the homemade lasagna." He rubbed his belly.

I followed them downstairs, locking the door behind them. Exhausted by the long day and all the running around I'd done, I decided to take a long, hot bubble bath. I had certainly deserved it. While soaking, I planned the next day. Tuesday, my only day off from the club, was when I normally cleaned Pam's house.

I was just getting into my jammies when the phone rang. Since it was after nine o'clock, I knew it wouldn't be a bill collector, so I felt safe in answering. Pam Nelson's southern drawl twittered in my ear.

"Maggie, JC just told me the dreadful news. Bless your heart. How horrible for you!"

That was her way of saying, "How horrible to *be* you." Something I'm sure she thought on a regular basis.

"—and I told her that I would phone you. She wants to hear from you too. Of course. When I told her I was calling you, she immediately said she would also. It's like she can't think for herself, always doing what I do. I swear, if my son wasn't married to her daughter..."

I'd missed some of what Pam said, but I knew she was talking about Diane Reid, the Pam wannabe. Oh, how Diane envied Pam. Pam didn't have to work; she was active in the community; her husband treated her like a queen, yadda yadda.

"Maggie? Are you there?"

"Yes, Pam. I'm listening." Barely. Hurry up. I wanted to go to bed.

"So, you'll clean tomorrow as usual? I can expect you at ten?"

"I'll be there." For fifty-five bucks, I'd polish her shoes. Maybe. Who was I kidding? I definitely would.

"I have meetings all day tomorrow. I'll leave the key in the usual place, and your payment on the gathering island." Only Pam would call it a gathering island, such a fancy high-class term for a big chunk of butcher block.

In a hurry to end the call, I said, "Sure, see you tomorrow." I hung up the phone.

Whoa. Wait a minute. What dreadful news?

I reached for the phone to call her back and ask when the damn thing rang, scaring me. Probably Diane. Sorely tempted to not answer at first, I figured I may as well find out what I could from Diane. I picked up the receiver ready to hear her whiny voice.

"Back off, bitch." Click.

Twelve

The next morning I slept in until nine. I'd had trouble falling asleep after the phone call (fortunately no others had followed), but I had struggled trying to figure out who it could be. The husky voice wasn't one I recognized, and I couldn't tell if the caller was male or female, disguising it or not. I'd shrugged it off as a prank, but in my gut ... well, I'd deal with it later. Now here it was later, and I was no closer to figuring out anything. I started to roll over and go back to sleep when I remembered I had to be at Pam's at ten. I dashed around like a mad woman and ran down to the car. Which refused to start. Not even a little growl from the battery. Dammit. I slapped the steering wheel a few times.

I hated to keep relying on him, but I needed Michael's help again. Twenty minutes later he pulled up to Pam's house. It usually takes me ten minutes to get to Pam's, but he stopped at every damn yellow traffic light along the way. And there were a lot of them. Whatever. I was grateful to get a ride. Michael said to call when I was finished and he'd pick me up.

Dodging fat raindrops, I unlocked the front door, slipped the key back under the mat, and quickly stepped inside. I went through the foyer, then the living room to the kitchen/family room. I tossed my purse on the leather couch.

"Hello?" I hollered just in case someone was home. No answer. Good. I could get straight to work. I pulled the bin of cleaning supplies out from under the kitchen sink. A note was taped to an emery cloth. "PLEASE FOCUS ON FR FP TOOLS. YOU MISSED THEM LAST TIME."

Ma'am, yes, ma'am. FP of course stood for fireplace. They had two. One in the master bedroom, the other in the family room (FR). The first time I'd seen them I wondered who'd need one in Florida. That was before our first winter here when temperatures had dropped to 28 degrees. Fortunately, Rob and I had our fireplace cleaned and ready to use.

Damn, Pam was right. I brushed away cobwebs from the poker, tongs, and andirons. Solid freakin' brass, those tools were heavy. I used the emery cloth to polish them, remembering how casually Pam had mentioned what they'd cost. Rob had laughed when I told him. I smiled now, recalling how we had mimicked Pam and JC that night. We'd pretended our Hamburger Helper was prime rib, and we drank cheap beer out of champagne glasses. Rob had used the glass with the chip because he wanted only the best for his queen.

Good times. Grateful for the many years I'd spent with Rob, I lifted my head to send up a silent prayer of thanks. I giggled at the skylight above me. Glad I didn't do windows. A big old mess of bird poop was splattered on the glass.

I dusted the knick-knacks and silk flowers on the mantel and moved on to the next task: the bathrooms. All three. Why the Nelsons needed a four-bedroom, three-bath home was beyond me. Scott was their only child, if you could consider him a child. I know from stories I've heard there are times he acts like a child instead of a man in his late twenties. Before he married one of the Reid girls, he'd been quite the rebel. From what I gathered, he'd straightened up and now worked nights in his father's store full-time.

Rob liked Scott, treated him like a younger brother. Rob had played on the VFW's softball team with Scott, Pete, and Kevin. Scott had helped Rob with lots of work on the house, which reminded me I needed to thank him for helping Michael patch the roof.

Fortunately, two of the bathrooms took little time, and I concentrated on the master bath. Not wanting any more notes written in all caps, I made sure it was spotless. Pam had more silk flowers in the bathrooms and I dusted them too. Maybe I could get some since I can't be trusted with keeping live plants. I had to laugh when I thought back to the time I overwatered Diane's plants. She has dozens of them and I think I killed half of them. She was pissed for a month.

Dusting and vacuuming done, the kitchen was the last room to do. Since Pam used her kitchen as often as I used my own, I was finished in no time at all. I called Michael and he said he'd be right over.

Crap. No envelope on the gathering island. The rich bitch was going to stiff me. I went through the kitchen drawers looking for it. Nothing. Her office maybe? I hadn't seen it when I was cleaning in there earlier, but I'd check.

Pam's office was gorgeous and if I ever had one, I'd design it after hers. I snorted. Yeah, right. Her desk alone would probably pay off two of my creditors. Speaking of pay, no envelope in sight.

Her briefcase leaned against the bottom desk drawer and I moved it. I rifled through the desk drawers, stacks of papers, and found nothing. Now I was pissed. I turned, ready to storm out, and promptly stubbed my toe on the stupid desk leg. Now I was pissed and in pain.

I kicked Pam's briefcase and sent it flying across the room. It landed by the door. Stupid desk. Stupid briefcase. Stupid Pam for not paying me. Stupid me for not looking for the envelope before doing all that work.

Okay, breathe. Flipping out would get me nowhere. I strode over to the briefcase to put it back where it belonged. Something stuck out from behind the door. Pam's tri-folded cardboard D.A.R.E. display.

Pam Nelson had been instrumental in getting the police department to implement the D.A.R.E. program in the school system. She felt the county was behind the times and needed to "save our children from the dangers of drugs." Pam was very vocal about her own history with drugs and she visited all of the schools to spread the word, carrying this display with her.

I checked to make sure I hadn't damaged it during my little tantrum. Crap. The doorknob must've hit and punctured one of the small baggies taped to the cardboard. A cloud of white powder poofed in the air. The label beneath the baggie read *Cocaine*.

Really? I dipped a wet fingertip in the powder, tasted it, and waited for my tongue to go numb. Flour. Regular, ordinary flour. I quickly replaced it with a new baggie and buried the ripped one in the trash. Hopefully, Pam wouldn't catch on to what I'd done.

I heard a car horn and looked out the front window. Michael, my hero. I dodged raindrops as I sprinted to his car.

"I want to swing by the school and pick up Chris," he said as I buckled up. "I don't want her walking from the bus stop in this rain."

"Sure, no problem." I thanked him for coming to get me. "I really appreciate all the help you're giving me, Michael."

"Glad to do it. Besides, I was starting to feel a little bored from not working. We're helping each other out." He backed out of the Nelsons' driveway. "Oh, and Maggie, speaking of helping each other out—and don't worry about paying me back—but I went ahead and got a new battery for your car."

Wow. All that in one breath. "I'll start running a tab for what I owe you, okay? And thanks."

"There's more," he said. "The battery wasn't dead, it was missing. Stolen."

"What? Stolen? Who would steal a battery? And why? And how?"

"Probably no way to find the thief, for parts, and if you left your car unlocked, they simply released the hood. The mechanic said it didn't look like the car had been broken into. Was it locked?"

"Of course it was. I always lock—well, I think I did." I vaguely remembered having my hands full the night before. "I was carrying the grocery bag with the lasagna and … well, crap, I don't remember locking the car door. Damn." Could last night's prank phone call be connected? I hadn't told Michael yet about the call, and now wasn't the time as we got closer to the school.

Michael pulled into the long line of waiting cars outside the elementary school. The kids were just coming out. Michael jumped out of the car. He whistled and Chris came running over, sliding into the backseat.

"Hi, Chris," I said. When she didn't respond, I turned and looked at her. I repeated my greeting. Still nothing.

"Chris, Maggie's talking to you."

"Hi," she mumbled, her head turned toward the window.

I had no children, but I recognized a pissed-off kid. And I was looking right at one. I shrugged it off, figuring even ten-year-olds can have bad days.

Michael dropped me off in front of the house and I ran up to the porch while he pulled into the driveway. I reached into my mailbox and pulled out a stack of envelopes. Even with the newly patched porch roof, the soaked doormat wasn't up to its purpose, but I made it inside without tracking in wet leaves or mud.

Only one new message on my answering machine. Maybe it was Pam apologizing for forgetting to pay me. I pushed the button and heard Sam's voice.

When would I learn to stop listening to my messages? This must've been the dreadful news Pam had been talking about last night.

Thirteen

Suspended for five days. Then a meeting to determine my future with the VFW scheduled later. Meanwhile, they wanted my keys ASAP.

Oh, and no pay while on suspension, of course. Rat bastards.

Sam's voice was so curt I figured someone was standing nearby while he made the phone call. Otherwise, I'm sure he would've been more gentle, sympathetic.

Yeah, right. A quick picture of him running to the kitchen to get that damn baggie for Bobby Lee reminded me how loyal Sam was. What could I expect, really? Sam was only looking out for himself. Hell, he needed his job.

Yeah, and so did I.

Whoa. Enough of this. All this back and forth garbage berating then defending Sam was making my headache come back.

I rubbed my temples and started to go upstairs when someone knocked on the front door. I peered through the peephole, saw Chris, and opened the door.

"Hi, Maggie, I apologize for my rude behavior earlier. It'll never happen again. I promise."

Wow. Nothing like a rehearsed grown-up apology. I smiled at her and said, "So, what's up? Still mad at me for whatever reason?"

Chris bit her bottom lip, tears welling up. Oh, man. Now what? I am so not used to kids. I wanted to give her candy or ice cream or anything to make her not cry. Totally out of my element. Normally I'd tell a joke to defuse an awkward situation. For the life of me I couldn't think of one clean enough to tell Chris. I ended up just hugging her.

"I really am sorry," she mumbled against my shoulder. "I'm not mad at you. It's just—just that …" She pulled away from me. Her little face was red and wet from tears. "Somebody at school called me a liar 'cause she didn't believe me when I told them about your treasure."

"Oh, honey, I'm sorry. What can I do?"

Chris shook her head. "I dunno. But I'm not a liar."

"Of course you aren't," I said. "Hey, go ask your dad if you can come in for a while to visit. I bet I could find some ice cream. That always cheers me up."

"Okay! I'll be right back."

After quickly getting out of my damp jeans, I prayed I had some ice cream in the freezer. Sure enough. I scraped enough to fill two small bowls when Chris came up.

"Hope you like strawberry." I pushed a bowl toward her and we sat at my kitchen table.

"It's my third favorite after Rocky Road and Moose Tracks." She grabbed her spoon and dug in. I followed suit, concentrating on eating because I sure didn't know what to talk about with a ten-year-old.

I needn't have worried. Once she started talking about school, her classes, and friends, there was no stopping her if I'd wanted. I learned all about her best friend, her favorite teacher, and more.

A lot more. Stuff I'm sure Michael wouldn't want her talking about. How he and her mom still fight over the phone, why they moved to North DeSoto, and how much she missed her mother. As curious as I was, I knew I had to be the grown-up and change the subject.

I was saved by the bell—literally—when Michael called for Chris to come home. We hugged again and she thanked me. I set the bowls in the sink with the other few dishes I'd let pile up, and wondered what to do with myself. This time of day I'd usually be on my way to the club.

Five more days without work. And then what? No guarantee I'd have a job after their meeting. Why were they waiting anyway? Why not hold the meeting now, get it over with?

What the hell was I going to do? Maybe there was another job out there for me. Considering it a luxury I couldn't afford, I'd dropped my newspaper subscription months ago. The online edition did just fine.

While waiting for the computer to boot, I went to my bedroom closet and searched for something to wear for a job interview, should I get lucky. Finally I came across a black blazer that would go with my black slacks and gray sweater. I could wear the outfit to Jack's funeral too. I set the blazer aside and went back to read the classifieds. Nothing suitable. Damn.

Damn Pam. More than ever, I needed the fify-five bucks she owed me. I knew I'd find her at the club, and I was supposed to turn in my keys, but ... I dreaded going in that place. Plus, let the bastards wait for their keys. But I needed money. This wishy-washiness was driving me nuts. My head felt like it was about to explode. Or would that be implode? I needed to do something constructive.

I decided to catch up on figuring which lucky creditors would get money from me this month. Two deposited paychecks—measly as they were—and half my tips would pay the cemetery, plus the phone and electric companies. Visa and the water company were paid last month, so I skipped them this time around. I felt like a friggin' juggler. The rest of my tips would get me some food and my monthly box of wine. Not having a job to drive to would save on gas money. Oh, joy.

I played a game of Solitaire, then Free Cell. I switched over to Hearts, changed the players' names to JC, Dick, and Bobby Lee and slammed their asses. This passive-aggressive side of me was starting to be fun.

It also wasn't getting me anywhere. I needed to go in there, demand my money from Pam, and throw the keys down on the bar. Yeah!

Yeah, right. What I needed was for Michael to go in there with me, interrogate the hell out of everybody, find out who's framing me, and get my job back. I pushed the chair away from the desk and headed toward the phone to call Michael. After a few minutes of talking to him, I felt better. I told him I'd appreciate his moral support because I had a bad feeling. We agreed to meet at his car at six, drop Chris off at her friend's, and then go to the club.

———

An hour later, Chris lugged her backpack into the backseat while Michael explained that she had another study date with her friend Heather. We'd have a couple of hours to spend at the club before Heather's mom brought her home.

Oh, right, good old Terri. *Stop*, I told myself.

"Looks like most of the regulars are here," I told Michael when he pulled into the VFW parking lot. "Pete will be on the road, and Scott works nights at the hardware store, but it looks like everyone else is accounted for."

We were greeted with a loud chorus of "Hey, Maggie's here!" Word of my definitely being suspended had apparently gotten around because no one asked about it. I wondered about the ratio of truth to bullshit in the rumors going around. I was once again amazed how fast news traveled in this place.

Michael and I walked through the dining room to get to the bar, passing Dick, Diane, and one of their daughters sitting at a table with JC. Terrific. Where the hell was Pam? She was the one I really wanted to see. They all nodded in greeting. I nodded back. I'd make nice as long as they did too. I stopped to hug Kevin and sign the daily book, then we grabbed a couple of empty stools at the bar.

Sam came right over and took our order. Michael stuck to his usual soda since he was driving. Sam brought it and my beer over and set them down in front of us. "On me," he said, pushing my money back to me. "How are you, Maggie? Been worried about you."

"I'm just hunky dory, Sam." I met his eyes. He might care, but I wasn't handing over the damn keys until he asked for them.

"Good, good," he answered.

Michael said, "I suppose you'll be working a lot of extra hours? Late nights, early days."

"Yeah, well, a man's gotta do what a man's gotta do. I'll probably close up early tonight."

I took a quick gulp of my beer to keep myself from commenting. Yeah, sure, now that it wasn't me back there, they could go ahead and close early. Do whatever the hell they wanted and not get in any trouble for it. Must be nice. I sipped more beer.

Someone tapped me on the shoulder and I turned. Diane Reid stood next to me. "Oh, Maggie, I'm so sorry about what happened. Dick feels just awful about it. He told me to leave you alone, but I had to come over and say something."

"Thanks, Diane, I appreciate the support." It hurt to make nice, but I was determined. I trusted this woman about as much as I trusted her husband and all of his old cronies. I smiled at her, and said, "It was nice of you to come over and talk with me." The little voice inside my head screamed *Liar!* Another long sip of beer drowned it out.

"I also wanted to make sure you weren't going to drop out of the Ladies Auxiliary. Your membership is very important to us, y'know. We do so much…"

As treasurer of the Ladies Auxiliary, I knew Diane was really only interested in getting my money each year for dues. More beer. Before I knew it, I'd drained my glass. I waved it at Sam and he immediately refilled it. This time he took my money.

My membership. Hell, for only twenty-five bucks a year it was worth a shot at winning the daily book one of these times. I said, "Yes, Diane, as of now I plan on keeping my membership. Thanks so much for your concern." Good thing my words weren't made of sugar. My teeth would rot.

"I'm so glad to hear you say that. I'd hate for there to be any hard feelings. Dick and JC were just talking about it, and Dick mentioned how he was the one who told Bobby Lee not to handcuff you. Darlene said it was just like her daddy to be so thoughtful. You remember our Darlene, don't you? She's the one who married into the Nelson family."

Married into the Nelson family? Sheesh. Who talks like that? A southern belle wannabe, that's who. "Oh, yeah, sure, I remember her. Nice girl." I thought of Darlene as a whiny little mouse of a girl, just like her mother. Another sip of beer. If I didn't watch it, I'd soon be drunk.

"I'd better get back over to the table before Dick spends all our money trying to win that knife. He's been playing that gambling board like crazy."

My ears picked up on that. "Knife? The one on the gambling board?" I glanced at Michael to make sure he was listening. He sat facing the bar and not looking at us, but he seemed like he was on alert. Just like a loyal German Shepherd.

"Yeah. JC said it's been on there for a while now, and nobody's been playing for it. He and Dick are having a fun little competition over who wins it."

"Funny, but I've never known Dick or JC to ever gamble on any of the games," I said. "I know that knife board has been up there for a few weeks, but they never showed any interest in it before." As president of the club, Kevin shopped a few times a month, buying stuff to put on the gambling boards. The boards are actually cardboard sheets with paper tickets we sell for a buck each. When all the tickets have been pulled off, the bartender hands over the prize to the holder of the winning ticket. Since most members own at least one knife—hell, even I have Rob's knife in my purse—this board had been sitting for a long time. Members had been complaining about the lousy prizes lately. In the past, fishing equipment, gift certificates for Nelson's Hardware or the local meat market, and camping gear had been popular prizes. Kevin seemed to be slacking off on buying quality stuff.

Diane lowered her voice and moved closer to me. "JC said it's been up there too long. He said you never pushed the gambling and that'll change now that you're gone."

A long-ass gulp of beer. I used both hands to hold the glass to keep myself from decking her.

Michael turned at that point, smart man that he is. "Hi, I'm Michael Bradley, a friend of Maggie's. I couldn't help but hear your conversation."

Diane smiled and said, "Oh, you're Maggie's tenant, aren't you? I forgot you were a landlady, Maggie."

She said it in a way that sounded dirty, low-class. I turned away from her and Sam stood there with a fresh glass of beer for me. I swallowed the last of mine and took it from him.

"That's right, my daughter and I live on the first floor."

She nudged me and said, "I don't suppose you have a connecting door between bedrooms, do you? Oh, that was so naughty of me!"

Dick must've heard that last comment because he suddenly appeared at Diane's side. He latched on to her wrist. "C'mon, Diane, why don't you leave these good people alone and come sit back down at our table."

"Oh, now Dick," Diane whined, "I'm just talking."

Dick yanked her wrist. "I said now." He offered an apologetic smile and pulled her away from us.

I simply drank more beer. We hadn't even been there fifteen minutes and I was already in the middle of my third beer. I excused myself and staggered into the ladies' room. And there Pam Nelson stood before one of the mirrors, using her professionally manicured nails to finger comb her hair. Even on a night out at the VFW, she was dressed to kill.

"Maggie, I'm surprised to see you here!" Pam didn't bother turning, instead she talked to my reflection.

"I've got to pee," I responded, my voice slurring.

"Really, Maggie." She frowned and said, "No, I mean here at the club. I figured you'd never show your face again after the humiliation of being suspended and God forbid, arrested."

"Not arrested, just questioned." I blinked, tried to focus. Too much beer in a short time on only a little bit of ice cream. "Suspended…oh well, shit happens. Now, if you'll 'scuse me," I said and wobbled past her into one of the stalls. I closed and locked the door and tried to mind my own business. Too bad Pam couldn't—or wouldn't—do the same.

"All I know is everyone's talking about it. How they found evidence pointing to you in Jack Hoffman's truck. And how the stab wounds weren't very deep and that it was obvious a woman could've killed him. Of course, you're the only woman who could've done it."

Man, I had never heard Pam talk so fast. What the hell? She acted like she needed some Ritalin. I hoped the sound of peeing would either stop her from talking, or drown out her words. But, no, of course not. She continued.

"We all know how it's just men who are here into the wee hours at the bar, and that you're the only woman here with them." She sniffed. "That is, used to be the only woman. I understand that's about to change, and Sam will be the bartender. Not paying him a salary will save us a lot of money. Of course, that's how it should've been all along."

I couldn't help myself. That last remark was way too weird to ignore. "How what should have been all along?" I asked.

"Why, having a man behind the bar. I mean, you're not that much to look at, but after our husbands have been drinking all night, you must surely have been appealing."

Good thing my jeans were draped around my ankles. Otherwise I would've gone barreling through that door.

"Oh, I hope that didn't offend you, dear. I certainly didn't mean that the way it sounded. I really should get going. Bye now." I heard the door open, then, "Oh, and please don't forget to wash your hands."

Fourteen

I shoved the door leading out of the bathroom and ran into a wall. Well, a wall of Dick Reid. He blocked my path to the bar, to the dining room, to Pam. Seemed like I kept running into him.

"Excuse me," I mumbled and tried to go around him. Michael, carrying my purse, was headed in my direction.

Dick moved closer to me. He said, "I want to talk to you, Maggie."

"And I'm sure she wants to talk to you, but it won't be right now. We have to get going." Michael, once more to my rescue, handed me my purse. "C'mon, Maggie, time to go." I simply grabbed my purse and followed him mutely. I had nothing good to say to anybody in that place.

The cool night air did nothing to sober me up. Michael helped me to the car, even buckled me in. I leaned against the headrest and closed my eyes. When I opened them minutes later, Michael was pulling into the drive-thru of Steak 'n Shake.

"Neither of us ate dinner," he said.

My stomach grumbled in confirmation and I told him what I wanted. When the food came, he handed me the bags and I held them on my lap. We got back to the house and decided to eat out on the patio because Chris would be getting back fairly soon.

Rob had installed a partial six-foot privacy fence that hid our cozy little patio from the street but still gave us access to the driveway. We'd splurged on a nice wrought iron table and four chairs. The verdigris lamp post cast soft light over the patio. Empty flower baskets hung from hooks Rob had attached to the fence. He had been the gardener. Shoot, I still needed to help Chris plant those flowers.

Michael and I settled ourselves at the table and dug in. Considering how this man had seen me at my absolute worst the past couple of days, I made no pretense as to how hungry I was. I scarfed my double bacon cheeseburger and milkshake.

"Feel better?" Michael asked. He held out his half-eaten sandwich. "Want some of mine?"

I laughed and shook my head. "I'm stuffed, and yes, I feel much better. Thanks."

And I did feel much better. Most of the beer seemed to've worn off and my tummy was happy. Warm and fuzzy, that's how I felt.

Wanting to share the warmth, I reached across the table to take Michael's hand. He jerked away, a really weird look on his face.

"Uh, Maggie, I—" A car pulled into the driveway, and he practically jumped from the table. "That must be Chris."

The warmth faded quickly. Not quite true: my face suddenly felt very warm. What a stupid move. Why the hell did I do that? Maybe the beer hadn't actually quite worn off all the way. Yeah, that was it.

No, that wasn't it. I had no *feelings* for Michael. If he had let me finish, I would've been able to tell him how much I appreciated his friendship. That was all.

Yeah, you keep telling yourself that, Maggie.

Enough. Sheesh. How many voices did I have in my head? And when had I started arguing with them? I shook my head to clear it and realized Michael was talking to me from where he stood at the car's driver side door.

"And this is my landlady, Maggie Lewis. Maggie, this is Terri, Heather's mom."

A very attractive, tall blonde stood next to him, her nicely manicured hand draped around the shoulder of a little girl.

"Nice to meet you, Maggie," said Terri, then she turned to Michael. "And I really enjoyed seeing you again, Michael. I hope we'll see more of each other." He didn't jerk away from her when she reached for his hand. She shook his hand, and it sure seemed like a long time before they released.

———

Every time I opened my eyes the next morning, my head let me know it was not time to get up. I listened to it and finally rolled out of bed in the early afternoon. I dragged myself to the kitchen, made coffee, and slumped over the counter to watch it drip slowly, so damn slowly, into the pot. I gulped down the first cup, then poured another.

I went to my desk, found my legal pad and pen, and added to my lists and notes. I spent a good few hours doing this and impressed myself with my results. I came up with a list of people to talk to—who I'd already talked to and those I still needed to go see. Feeling pretty clever, I added specific questions I wanted to ask each person. I wanted to know more about the night Jack was killed.

I knew from the conversation Bobby Lee had with us all at the bar Sunday morning that Pete, Sam, JC, Dick, and Kevin had all been there Saturday night. And Abby. JC and Dick said they left just after the news, and Kevin about the same time. No mention of their wives, but Pam and Diane didn't usually stay much past ten o'clock, so that sounded right.

We knew Sam was working with Abby. But Gussie had only seen Abby and probably Pete leave at closing time. She must've missed Sam leaving. Pete was hanging out because of Abby. He was her ride, but he would've been there anyway, just like any other weekend night. Same with Kevin. Sometimes Scott hung out with his parents and in-laws after work.

Motive. Why did Jack get murdered? Why wasn't his notebook in his truck? What had he said or done? When had he said or done it? I wish I'd been there that night. Instead, the person who could've heard something left town. What was that all about? Did Abby leave because she didn't like it here? Didn't like Pete? How had he talked her into coming here, leaving Ft. Walton Beach? She had sure looked happy in that website photo, but who knows how long ago it had been taken. How did she get that black eye? Did she have family that she left behind? Was there a connection between Abby and Jack? How long had Pete and Abby known each other? Did she really leave town on her own?

Oh, this was good stuff. Great questions. Now all I needed were answers. Before I could decide who to tackle first, someone knocked on the front door. *Shave and a haircut. Two bits.* That could only be one person, and I ran downstairs to eagerly swing open the door.

"Brenda! Come in, come in."

Brenda Blackwell, my best friend, hugged me, then held me at arm's length. "Where the hell were you at eleven o'clock?"

"My appointment! I'm so sorry, I forgot."

"You're forgiven, now turn around." She fingered my ponytail and said, "Looking good. Another couple of inches and we can send it in."

Brenda, my only real friend since Rob died, was also my hair stylist. Several months ago she had talked me into letting my hair grow, then when it got to at least ten inches, she'd cut it off and donate it to the Locks of Love foundation. Every eight weeks or so, Brenda spends the day in her Jacksonville salon (she owns three in the northern part of the state) and she trims my hair. I had missed my scheduled appointment.

I grabbed a couple of beers out of the fridge, and we got comfortable at the kitchen table. I really needed to start thinking about getting some decent living room furniture. I'd had more company in the last forty-eight hours than almost all last year. I was too ashamed to let anyone see the ratty-looking loveseat in what should be the living room. Easier to just close the door on that room.

"So, what's going on? I called the club a half hour ago and some guy answered, so I hung up. Why aren't you at work?"

I took a long sip from my bottle before answering her. Once I started talking, I couldn't stop. God love her, Brenda didn't interrupt me once as I told her about the last four days of my life.

"Finish your beer, then let's go. I'm taking you out for dinner. Nowhere fancy, so you're fine the way you are." She draped her arm around my shoulder and squeezed. "Hell, you're always fine. Straight up."

No wonder she's my best friend. A liar with a good heart. I told her as much. She chucked me on the shoulder she'd squeezed and gently pushed me out the door.

"We'll take both cars because I need to get to West Palm tonight. I'll leave right from the restaurant. If I get on the road by eight, I should get there by midnight. No big deal."

Her little red Miata convertible looked nice, really nice, in my driveway. I was even more grateful my poor little Honda had a new battery. He would've felt bad otherwise. As we got into our cars, Brenda shouted, "Just follow me. Try to keep up. Okay?"

I let my mind wander as I followed Little Miss Lead Foot. Rather than dwell on the murder investigation, I thought about the good things in my life. My blessings. Brenda was on the top of that list. We had the kind of friendship where months could—and often did—go by without us seeing or talking to each other. We always seemed to pick up right where we'd left off.

I remembered the day we'd met. Not too long after Rob died, I'd gotten in my car and drove with no destination in mind, just wanting to get away. I pulled off in Jacksonville and wandered aimlessly through some mall. Up one side, down the other, over and over again. Normally, I despise going anywhere near a shopping mall, but on that day I needed the busy noise of others around me to deflect the quiet numbness overtaking my body and mind.

"You don't need the exercise, but you could use a shampoo."

It had taken me a second to realize someone had spoken to me. I stopped and turned. A tall, slender brunette woman leaned against the doorjamb of one of the shops. She smiled and said, "I've seen you pass by my salon at least a dozen times today. I could do wonders with that gorgeous red hair of yours." She stepped forward, her hand outstretched. "I'm Brenda Blackwell, owner of Blackwell Hair Salon. Catchy, huh?"

I shook her hand, mumbled it was nice meeting her, and started to move on my way.

"Hey, today's my birthday and I'm giving away a free shampoo and cut. You're the lucky recipient." She pulled me into her shop and I spent the next couple of hours being pampered. It was truly the beginning of a beautiful relationship. Two years later, and here she was again being my savior. So, yeah, Brenda was definitely on the top of my list of blessings.

My trusty little Honda kept up just fine, and I pulled in right next to her at the seafood restaurant she'd chosen. We ordered our meals and decided to split a carafe of wine. Brenda poured generous amounts into each of our glasses, then leaned forward and said, "Okay, tell me all about this Michael Bradley. Last time I'd talked to you, he had just moved in. Bring me up to speed."

"Michael? He's just a tenant. He has a little girl named Christina, she's ten. I know he's divorced, but I don't know for how long or why. He's a former police officer, soon to be a private investigator." I sipped my wine. "Nice guy who's agreed to help me out on this whole bum rap deal I'm in. So, what do you think of that whole situation? Pretty crazy for anyone to think I'd kill somebody, huh?"

"Nice try, hon. Don't change the subject. I want to know more about Michael, and if you're getting any."

Embarrassed, I looked around to make sure no one nearby had heard. I looked back at Brenda. "You're bad, you know that? Michael and I are really just friends, nothing more." I sipped more wine, then remembered my decision to not get drunk in public again. "So, tell me about what you've been up to."

She held up her hands in resignation. "Okay then, we'll talk about something else. Actually, I do have some exciting news. I'm planning on opening up my fourth salon later this year. That's why I'm going to West Palm Beach. Time to work on the blue-haired, blue-blooded rich old ladies."

"That is exciting news. Congratulations!" We clinked glasses. "Does this mean you've met your goal of toning down all the big-hair gals of north Florida?" I remembered how I'd laughed when she'd told me that was her plan. She felt an obligation to work on the local good ole girls by showing them how to use mousse and hair spray properly. After opening her first one-chair salon in Fernandina Beach, where she still lived, she expanded to one in Gainesville geared for the university students, and then a few years later, another in Jacksonville, which is where we met. And all before she turned thirty-two. Amazing. Especially considering the horrific childhood she'd survived.

"You've done pretty well for yourself, Brenda. I'm proud of you."

"Damn straight."

Our food arrived and we dug in. For dessert, we splurged and split a huge piece of ice cream cake. I felt full, warm, and happy. It reminded me of the night before when I'd felt that way and reached for Michael's hand.

"You okay, hon? You're all flushed."

No way in hell would I tell her what I'd just been thinking. "Too much wine, I guess."

"No such thing as too much wine." As if to prove her point, she drained the remaining wine from the carafe into her glass and finished it. She grabbed the check and said, "Shall we? I'll be in West Palm for a few days, then I'll drop by your place on the way back up. Okay?"

"Sounds good to me. Thanks so much for dinner, Brenda," I scooted my chair back and stood. "Whoa." I put my hand on the table to catch my balance.

"Maybe for you there is such a thing as too much wine. You okay to drive?"

"Sure," I said. It came out slurred. Terrific. A bartender who couldn't handle two glasses of wine without getting sloshed. "But maybe you could follow me part of the way?"

"I'll follow you all the way, hon. It's practically my fault you're a little tipsy."

Arm in arm we walked out to our cars. The cool night air seemed to help considerably, but I was still glad she was going to be behind me. I used to laugh at my mother when she complained of driving at night. Now I knew what she was talking about. Dammit.

I pulled out first and Brenda stayed with me. Instead of getting on I-95, I took a back road, which I knew would take us longer, but also no state troopers would be hanging around. I stuck to the speed limit, and I'm sure there were several times Brenda wanted to pass me, but she didn't. She flashed her lights, and I sped up to appease her. When she did it again, I looked at my rearview mirror wondering what her problem was. Going a few miles over the limit had to be good enough because I wasn't going to risk it. No cops, but there were plenty of deer in this neck of the woods and surely she knew that. No streetlights, and the night was so dark animals could dart out with no warning. Her tiny Miata certainly couldn't take on a deer without causing heavy damage. For that matter, neither could my Honda.

Brenda flashed her lights a third time and having no place to pull over, I was tempted to slow down and let her go around me. That's when I saw the vehicle behind her. Because of the lowness of Brenda's car, the other guy's headlights shone right into my car. He was right on her ass. Had Brenda been alone, I'm sure she would've turned it into a race with this clown. And she probably would've won.

I lightly hit my brakes a couple of times, hoping that would signal her to let the guy go around us. Big mistake. I felt the tap on my bumper and my whole car swerved. I grabbed tightly onto the steering wheel and sped up a bit.

Another tap. Now the guy's high beams flashed on, and stayed on. His lights practically blinded me, and I took one hand off the wheel to move the rearview mirror. Just as I did that, the jerk roared past Brenda and came up beside me. A big ugly ass pickup truck. I expected the jerk to zoom in front of me and I'd gladly let him.

Instead he moved to the right, inching his way closer to me. I slammed on my brakes to get out of his way, praying that Brenda wouldn't plow into me.

Some prayers aren't answered the way we want. Metal crunched and glass shattered as I screeched to a stop.

The guy laid on his horn, pulled over into my lane, and hauled ass. I watched his red taillights fade.

I jammed the car into park and sat there shaking.

Brenda. Oh my God. I pushed open my door and ran to her car. The Miata's front end was pushed up under my rear fender. I smelled burned rubber and oil. Glass crunched under my shoes as I rushed to the driver's side door and pulled it open. Brenda's body nearly fell out of the tiny car.

Screaming her name, I pushed her upright and held on tight. Before I could make sure she was alive or not, I heard her trying to speak.

Thank God. Still holding on to her with one hand, I gently pushed her back a ways to check for damage. She raised her head and mumbled something.

"Shhh, Brenda, not now. Talk later."

She shook her head, then winced. "Now." She lifted her arm an inch or so and said, "What the—"

Then she passed out.

Fifteen

Hospitals everywhere must buy their disinfectant in bulk from the same supplier. North DeSoto General Hospital smelled like any other hospital I'd ever been in. Bright lights, beige walls, muted sounds as hospital staff walked up and down the hallway outside the ER waiting room. The ambulance had brought a conscious and fairly alert Brenda in over an hour earlier and I still sat waiting to hear word on how she was. I'd been checked out at the accident scene and the paramedic decided I was okay enough to follow the ambulance in my car, which thankfully had suffered little damage. Compared to Brenda's car, mine looked gorgeous. I was also grateful for the driver who stopped and called in the accident. A nonlocal, he'd taken off before I'd had a chance to really thank him.

Other than the accident itself, the worst part was that it happened in Bobby Lee's jurisdiction. Then again, if it hadn't, I'd be sitting in a hospital in an unknown town. One of North DeSoto's officers had taken the report then promptly left.

Just when I decided to go to the nurse's station to find out anything about Brenda, Kevin Beamer walked into the waiting room. Startled to see him, I jumped up from the chair.

"Maggie, are you okay? I heard about the accident on my scanner." He hugged me, then held me at a distance, looking me up and down. "You seem to be okay."

"I'm fine, Kevin." I filled him in quickly on what happened. "I'm about ready to go check on Brenda."

"I'll go with you." He carried his motorcycle helmet under his right arm and wrapped his left one around my shoulders.

Together we walked up to the U-shaped desk where a couple of nursing staff worked. One looked up and smiled at us. Rather, she smiled at Kevin. I glanced over. With his dark hair, blue eyes, and dressed in his black leather jacket and gloves, he was easy on the eyes.

"Hi, I'm wondering if there's any word yet on Brenda Blackwell. She was brought in an hour or so ago."

"The car accident victim." The nurse rifled through some papers, pushed a few keys on her keyboard, then looked up again. "She's being discharged right now. Should be out in a few minutes."

Relieved, I thanked her. To Kevin I said, "Sounds like Brenda's okay." The relief and utter exhaustion weakened my knees, and hot tears welled up. Here came another crying jag. I was afraid one of these days I'd start crying and wouldn't stop.

He took my arm and led me back to the waiting room. Without a word, he seated me back in the chair and sat down next to me. Having him close brought comfort, and I was grateful he had a scanner and had been listening to it. I closed my eyes and silently we waited.

Brenda finally came out a half hour later. Kevin helped me get Brenda into my car and announced he'd follow us back to my house. I felt rattled getting behind the wheel again and was grateful for his steady light behind me. Once we got there, he again helped with Brenda. I waited to make sure she was settled and sleeping in my bed, then Kevin and I went back out to the hallway.

"Can I get you a beer?"

He smiled, shook his head. "Now's not the time to be playing hostess, Maggie. You need to get some sleep. You're about to drop, aren't you?"

I didn't argue with him.

As soon as Kevin left, I checked on Brenda one more time. She snored softly and, afraid of disturbing her, I left. I curled up on the lumpy loveseat and pulled an afghan over me. Just before falling asleep, I wondered what kind of information is transmitted over scanners.

———

I woke the next morning to the smell of coffee, and to the clock chiming twelve. Nine o'clock. I rolled over and nearly fell off the loveseat.

"Smooth move there, Maggie. Or should I call you Grace?" Brenda sat on the arm of the loveseat, coffee mug in hand. "Good morning. Coffee's ready."

I sat up and stretched, minor aches and pains shouted through my body. I followed her into the kitchen, and while I loaded my coffee with sugar and milk, asked her how she felt.

"One hell of a headache," she said and sat down at the kitchen table. "So, who tried to kill us last night?"

"Bobby Lee told me on the phone last night, and I quote: 'Some good ole boy out for a good time trying to scare y'all.' End quote."

"Asshole."

I didn't disagree with her. I'd already told her about the threatening phone call, and I brought it up again, wondering if there was a connection.

Her eyes widened. "Phone. Where is mine?"

"I couldn't find it last night to call 911." I bit my lower lip. "Damn. Do you suppose it's still in your car?"

"Could be. I don't remember much after that jerk sped by me." She rubbed her forehead and winced.

"I got your purse and suitcase out of your car before the tow truck took it away. It's no big deal, is it? I mean, you can always get a new one."

"Yeah, it's just that that one was important."

"It's only a phone. You'll just have to enter all the data you had in it to a new one." I didn't understand why she seemed to be so concerned. I didn't even have a cell phone. Just another expense I couldn't afford.

"The thing is, that phone might have a good picture of the sonofabitch who nailed us."

Sixteen

"What? You got a picture of him? How—When—"

"Quit yelling." She rubbed her head again. "When you said *phone*, I remembered. And not a picture of him, just his license plate. I'm pretty sure I got a clear shot of it as he sped by."

"Well, come on, let's get dressed and go find it! It must be somewhere near where the crash was." Brenda followed me into the bedroom. I started pulling clothes out of my closet when I came across the black blazer I'd set aside a couple days ago.

Jack's funeral. I had nearly forgotten about it. My bedside clock told me the funeral was in less than an hour. Damn. No time to look for the phone.

"Hey, feel like going to a funeral with me?" I quickly explained.

"Sure," she answered. "I mean, I didn't know the guy, but I'll go. We can look for my phone after the funeral."

"Um, there's a reception after the funeral. Oh, damn, I forgot to get the cole slaw. We can get it on the way to the reception. We'd better hurry."

"Okay, so our plan is funeral, grocery store, reception, look for my phone. Let's do this."

———

Both sides of the street were lined with cars, and we finally found a spot to park a couple blocks from the funeral home. Brenda and I walked arm in arm down the sidewalk and when we reached the steps of the building, I heard my name. Michael stood by the door looking handsome in his dark suit.

"Brenda, this is Michael Bradley. Michael, my best friend, Brenda Blackwell." They shook hands, and we moved inside so we weren't blocking the entrance.

The funeral home was more packed than I thought it'd be. I don't know exactly what I expected, but practically every lined-up folding chair was taken. This being the small town it is, I recognized nearly everyone. Whether they were friends or just curiosity-seekers, I didn't know. A good majority of the people in attendance were members of the club. Sam, Pete, Kevin, and a few other active members, dressed in their Honor Guard uniforms, were huddled together near a side exit. I knew they'd be leaving to go to the cemetery before everyone else. As members of the Honor Guard, they'd be ducking out before the service was over to stand near the gravesite. Their way of honoring the dead. It was a very solemn ceremony that consisted of the flag draping the casket being folded and Taps playing hauntingly in the background. I cried every time I heard Taps played.

Dick, JC, and their wives sat in the first row of chairs. I guessed that row wasn't reserved for family this time. I remembered wondering if the funeral home had written the obit, so I still didn't know if Jack had family. He never talked about anyone, but then again, I usually listened to him with only one ear. Maybe if I'd listened closer, I'd have a clue to who killed him and why.

"Hey, let's go talk to Pete. I'm glad he's here, now I don't have to wait until tomorrow to ask him about Abby." I started heading toward the group of uniformed men, but Brenda pulled me back. "What?"

She shook her head. "Now's not the time, Maggie. Let's sit down."

I wanted to smack myself for being so inconsiderate, so thoughtless. Of course the funeral wasn't the time or place to question people. Eager to resolve this whole situation and get my butt back to work at the club, I'd forgotten my compassion.

We found three seats in the back, and when the funeral home director approached the pulpit, others around us settled in their chairs. I recognized the man standing next to him—the chaplain from the VFW—and after a few brief words, the director introduced him.

The chaplain made no mention of murder while he spoke of Jack. Instead he talked about him as if he were a fallen comrade, very patriotic, and I felt the lump in my throat forming. I realized I missed the talk at the club, the way the vets could go on and on with their war stories. Of course, after working there for as long as I had, I heard a lot of the same stories. Sometimes they were retold verbatim, other times the stories were embellished. Maybe it had something to do with how much beer was consumed. With so many members, over two hundred that came in regularly, I'd learned not all of them liked talking and reminiscing about the war. Seemed most of them just liked the idea of belonging to the VFW because of the unspoken camaraderie.

A final prayer was given, and it was time to view the casket. I hated this part. While we waited our turn, I noticed the differences between this funeral and Rob's. Today there were no flowers, no photographs, no soft music playing. No sobbing family members.

When our row was up, Michael stood first, and Brenda and I followed him up to the open casket. Jack had never looked better. Weird, but true. He seemed content, peaceful. No scowl or frown, no worry lines marring his face. An almost healthy color in his cheeks. Amazing what a little makeup could do.

———

The hot sun blasted us when we got outside. Cars were lining up in the street for the funeral procession. Was the big ugly ass truck among them? Brenda looked at me, cocked her head as if asking if I wanted to join them.

"I don't think I want to go the gravesite. Do you?" I asked Michael.

He glanced at his watch. "No, doesn't look like I'll have time. I'm meeting Terri in a half hour."

"Oh. Okay." I turned to Brenda. "How about you?"

She shook her head and said, "Not really. Let's go to Publix, get the cole slaw, and head over to the reception."

We said our good-byes and Brenda and I walked to my car. "So, who's Terri?" Brenda asked while buckling her seatbelt.

"The mother of Michael's daughter's best friend," I answered.

"And what does she mean to Michael?"

"Beats me." I shrugged, pulled out onto the road. I looked at the dashboard clock and said, "The kids are in school, but it's close to noon. Maybe they're meeting for lunch. No business of mine."

"Uh huh, if you say so."

We made a quick trip of our errand and soon pulled into the parking lot of the VFW. On the drive over, Brenda and I talked more about the accident and decided to watch as people arrived. Maybe we'd see the truck. Long shot, but maybe worthwhile.

I wondered again if this was connected to that threatening phone call. Had whoever told me to back off also tried to run us off the road last night? Did they also steal my car battery? Was any of this random?

"Who do you think it was?" she asked. "Who all have you talked to? Where have you been?"

"Let's see. Sam, Gussie, Pam, JC." I ticked the names off my fingers while I spoke. "Where have I been? Um, JC's store, Gussie's house, the library, the club. Oh, and of course, outside Jack's house. And I talked with Bobby Lee at the police station. I should've talked to Kevin last night at the hospital while I had the chance, but I was more concerned about you."

"I sure wish I hadn't been so out of it when you two brought me back to your place. I don't even remember him. That must've been some drug they gave me." She rubbed her temple. "Truthfully? I still feel out of it. Spacey. Blech."

"You were pretty banged up. I'm just glad that guy came along when he did, and that Kevin showed up at the hospital."

"You don't think that's funny, as in funny weird? How'd Kevin know you were at the hospital? How'd he know about the accident? Does he drive a truck, by any chance?"

I opened my mouth and closed it. Good point. But, Kevin? "Hmmm. He said he'd heard it on his scanner. And he does have a truck, but he only uses that to deliver the stuff he gets for the club, and in inclement weather. What information goes out on scanners, do you know?"

"One of my brothers had one and his gave out all sorts of stuff—victim's name, their address, even their date of birth."

"For an accident? All that?"

She nodded. "Of course, this was several years ago, and I don't know if it's still that way. Any chance it was just a coincidence? Who would know where we were last night?"

"Maybe we were followed. Hell, I don't know." I shrugged my achy shoulders.

"But why you? Why are you involved? Why'd they plant your scrunchie?"

"Pam more or less said a woman could've done it, and I'd be the most likely one."

Brenda snorted. "Ridiculous. You should've reminded Pam that since she's a woman, she could've killed him."

"She'd be too afraid of breaking a nail," I said. A few cars had started pulling into the parking lot. No trucks yet. I wondered if we were wasting our time.

"So how do we prove you weren't involved?"

I grinned. "You want to be my sidekick? Help me solve the murder?"

"Sure, Nancy Drew, I'd love to play Bess or George. Looks like I'll be in town for at least one more day. Oh, hey, want to go car shopping tomorrow? I called my insurance agent before you woke up. They'll need the official reports, but from the description of what happened, my car is totaled. I need a new one ASAP."

"Are you feeling well enough to drive, especially the four-hour trip to West Palm?"

She waved away my concerns. "I'm fine. Just a little headache." She chuckled. "Guess I should get a Miata with an airbag this time around. Maybe a nice brand-new model. I might have to cut down on some expenses for the new salon, but I'll be getting a check from the insurance company. Oh, and I need a new phone."

"Maybe not. We should go look for your old phone right after the reception. It'll be dark in a couple hours."

"Actually, Nancy Drew, I have a better idea. But for now, let's head inside."

Everyone must've gone straight to the reception because the bar was pretty empty, but I stopped briefly to say hello to the few people who were sitting there. I didn't recognize the man behind my bar.

Brenda and I strode into the reception hall, one of the annexes attached to the back of the main building. The hall was built to hold receptions such as this. Considering the number of World War II vets and the rate at which they were dying, having this hall was one of their better ideas. Hell, even the number of Korean War veterans was dwindling.

The hall was filled to capacity, but I didn't see Pam Nelson anywhere. I hadn't forgotten she still owed me money. Diane Reid stood behind one of the long food tables and we walked over to her. I handed Diane the plastic grocery bag.

"Finally." She sighed as she pulled the container out of the bag. "Store bought?"

Brenda pulled on my arm and broke the awkward beat of silence. "So, introduce me to some folks, Maggie. People you think are worth meeting." She coolly looked Diane up and down, and we sashayed away.

I nudged Brenda with my elbow. "You're bad."

"It's why you love me."

"True, very true."

"What's with her clothes? It's hot as hell today and she's wearing long sleeves and a high collar."

"I noticed that at the funeral, but look at me with the blazer. I should've left this in the car."

Lots of people sat at tables. I recognized every person in the room, and I felt disappointed. I had hoped some family member would've shown up, but no luck. Sam, Pete, and Kevin, still in their Honor Guard uniforms, stood off to one side. We walked over to them and I made the introductions. Amused, I wanted to tell Sam to stop drooling. Another reason why I loved Brenda—she doesn't know how beautiful she is. I also wondered if Sam was okay. His eyes were red, as if he'd been crying. I'd never known for Sam and Jack to be friends, but I remembered how it looked like he'd been crying the morning he found Jack's body. I also remembered him speaking up for Jack when JC and Dick badmouthed him on Sunday morning. I'd talk to him if we got a moment alone together.

"I should have bought drinks while we were in the bar. Didn't think about it. Brenda, you stay here and I'll be right back." I started to walk away, then as an afterthought, said, "Behave yourself while I'm gone."

Sam sputtered, "I will."

"I was talking to Brenda." I winked.

Since the bar was still pretty empty, I got a stool right away. Unfortunately, I didn't get waited on as quickly. The new bartender, down at the end of the bar stocking the cooler, didn't see me. Rather than create a scene, I waited quietly, hoping he'd eventually realize he had a customer. At least the bar itself was clean, and my hands didn't stick to it like the other day. Even the bottles on the back shelf had been dusted and were lined up in the right order again.

"Hi, there, what can I get you?"

"Hi," I answered and ordered my beer and Brenda's gin and tonic. I pulled out three dollars knowing that would include a decent tip.

He set the drinks down in front of me, "That'll be $2.50."

I blinked. "Are you sure? I mean, I know you're new here, so you might not know all the prices."

"Yeah. A buck for the beer, and a buck fifty for the drink."

"Since when?"

"I don't know." He eyed the three bucks on the bar, and I could tell he wondered if I was going to add to it.

I took the drinks, slid off the stool, and said, "Thanks. Have a nice day."

Brenda was still standing where I left her, and I handed her her drink. "When did you guys raise the prices? Sheesh. Almost three bucks for these."

Kevin had the decency to hang his head, and Sam said, "It wasn't our idea. We were out-voted at the meeting Monday night."

"Yeah, it really sucks," Pete said. "I sure was surprised. Now I know why the place is so dead this afternoon."

Sam shrugged. "We couldn't do anything about it. Apparently, there's going to be lots of changes. They—"

Kevin spoke up. "Uh, Maggie, Brenda, how are you feeling? I was concerned about you two last night after I left."

"Thanks again, Kevin, for following us back to the house. We're both fine." I looked at Sam and asked, "What were you about to say? What kind of changes?"

Before he could answer, Kevin said, "I don't think we should be talking about what goes on in the meetings. No offense, Maggie."

"None taken." I tried to get Sam's attention, but he didn't look at me. I figured he'd tell me later what had gone on in their meeting. Plus I had to wonder if Kevin was a little put out that I was interrupting the attention Brenda had been giving him when I walked up. My stomach rumbled.

"Hungry, Brenda? You want to go eat?"

"Sure." She looped her arm through mine. "I hear the cole slaw is out of this world, can't wait to try it."

Seventeen

"Are you sure we should do this?" My clammy fingers clutched the steering wheel. "What if we get caught?"

"We won't get caught." Brenda reached for the passenger door handle. "Listen, you made a good start by coming out here the other day. Now it's time to follow through."

"Yeah, but what if someone comes along? What if—"

"C'mon, we need to do this before it gets dark," she interrupted me. "Everyone's at the funeral reception. Besides, this place is pretty remote."

Remote was right. A half-mile off the main street, we'd bounced our way down the rutted dirt road to where Jack's place was tucked away. We both closed our doors quietly after getting out of the car. I stalled by taking a moment to really look at Jack's house.

A light gray stucco one-story, the house sat on a small dirt lot covered with pine needles. Slivers of weak sunlight flitted through the tall, scrawny pine trees. A green lizard, basking in what little sun there was, skittered away from us. After the rain we'd had, the air smelled musty, dank, and the temperature felt fifteen degrees cooler. At least that's what I blamed my shivering on. It didn't explain my pounding heart, which I apparently could hear because of the damn deathly silence. Skulking along across the spongy, muddy yard, I followed Brenda to the steps of the sagging covered porch.

"Stop acting so suspicious," she said. "Just act like you belong here."

"Too bad we don't have a clipboard. I've heard carrying one makes you look official, that you can go anywhere with a clipboard." I was rambling and I knew it. I also knew that I was scared this time because I hadn't gotten caught the other day. I figured I couldn't be lucky twice.

Brenda simply shook her head at me and climbed the steps. "C'mon."

Looking over my shoulder instead of watching where I walked, I stepped into a puddle under the wicker plant stand. We both wiped our muddy shoes on the dry and fairly clean doormat.

I whispered, "Do you think anyone's inside? I thought I saw something move when I was here before."

Brenda shrugged. "Only one way to find out." She knocked on the screened door, rattling its metal frame.

Nothing.

She tried the front doorknob. Locked.

I started to turn away. "So much for that. We tried."

Brenda grabbed my arm yanking me closer. "C'mon," she said and led me over to the window beside the front door. She cupped her hands against the grimy glass and peered in. "Damn, I can't see anything." She pushed on the window. It didn't budge.

"Well, that's that," I said. "We gave it our best shot."

"Don't wimp out on me now, doll." Brenda looked around, then lifted the dead potted plant and held up a key with a wide grin. She wiped it on her pants and said, "Voila! See how easy that was?"

Terrific.

She pushed the key into the doorknob, and it turned easily. The hinges creaked, but we were inside within seconds. I peeked outside once more making sure no one was creeping behind us, and then closed the door.

The smell of stale beer and, I hate to say it, urine attacked my poor nostrils. A worn vinyl easy chair with long strips of duct tape that looked like racing stripes faced an old television set. A TV tray next to the chair held a remote control, small lamp, an inhaler, and a coaster. Flimsy pea-green curtains were drawn across a window next to the TV, specks of dust swirling in a weak ray of sun. Dark-brown paneling matched the thin, stained carpet.

No other furniture. How very sad. No couch, not even another chair for company. With all the time Jack spent at the club, I imagined he wasn't home too often, and when he was he didn't have people visit.

"Okay, let's be quick," I said. I not only didn't want to get caught in a dead man's house, but the stink was really getting to me. I wiped my clammy palms across my slacks. "We're looking for a spiral notebook, like the kind you would've used in school."

I winced as I lifted the chair's cushion and looked underneath. Nothing but a couple of coins, crumbs, and what looked like white animal hair. I let the cushion drop back down. No notebook on the TV tray. I peeked under the chair and came up with nothing.

Brenda finished looking around the TV stand and curtains and came over to me. "No luck," she said. "Now where?"

Straight ahead of us was a swinging door that I assumed led to the kitchen. To our left, a short hallway with a doorway on either side. Bedroom and bathroom?

I wanted to get out of there, so I quickly moved on, Brenda right behind me. I elbowed the swinging door open. Something brushed my leg. I shrieked and let the door swing shut.

"Shhh! What happened?"

A loud meow answered her question. A flash of white hightailed it under the living room chair. Turning back to the swinging door, I gingerly pushed it open again and we stepped into the kitchen. And I was glad to see that the overpowering stench of urine came from the kitty litter box shoved up against one wall in the kitchen. What I hoped were bits of dry cat food lay scattered on the floor next to a full water dish. Or were they rodent droppings?

I turned to Brenda. She held her nose, her eyes watering. I asked, "Should we bother looking in here?"

"Let's look in the bedroom first. Seems more likely we'll find it in there."

I said, "How about we save time and split up? You take the bedroom, I'll check out the bathroom."

"Deal," she answered.

We moved down the short hall and went our separate ways. Immediately, I regretted taking the bathroom. Mold and bleach smells hung in the air. Green-tiled walls with a dingy white sink and bathtub sans shower curtain, and a toilet that ran worse than mine. The tank lid leaned against the wall behind the toilet. A pile of towels and clothes heaped on the cracked linoleum floor. Cigarette burns marred the Formica vanity where a can of Gillette shaving cream and a gunky razor with dried up blobs of shaving cream and little black and gray hairs sat.

I opened the vanity door and peeked inside. No way was I putting my hand in there. I shivered, imagining the rodents that had probably taken residence. A quick look told me there was nothing in there but Ajax, rolls of toilet paper, and folded towels. I flipped through the towels. Nothing in the medicine cabinet either. I kicked the pile on the floor just to make sure the notebook wasn't there.

"Hey, Maggie, come here."

I joined Brenda in Jack's bedroom directly across from the bathroom. The curtains in the bedroom were also drawn, and the room was dusky. A full-sized unmade bed, a dresser, and a night stand. A door across from the bed, which I guessed to be a closet.

"Look at this." She pointed to the night stand.

A clock, a pen, and a framed photograph sat on the night stand. Using the hem of her shirt, she picked up the photograph. "Is this Jack?"

I looked at the photo. A man and woman stood side by side, the woman holding an infant wrapped in a yellow blanket. The man wore orange overalls, the woman a flowered housecoat. Behind them was an old blue Ford sedan.

"Well, is it?" she asked.

I looked closer. "It could be Jack. I know he was once married to a Korean woman, and she's definitely Asian. Take it out of the frame, see if there's anything written on the back."

As soon as she loosened the cardboard backing, another photo slipped out. I reached down and picked it up. Dated 1958, it was a close-up of the man in the first photo. Across the left breast of his overalls, a name etched in white. Jack. Same buzz cut, but dark hair.

"Son of a gun," I said. "It is him." I looked up at Brenda. She had turned over the other photo. "Can you read what it says?" I asked.

"No," she answered. "It's in pencil and really faded."

"Let me see." She handed it to me and I tried reading what had been written. "I can make out Jack's name. Is the second name Joon? June? And the third name looks like it starts with a G. Has an L and a Y. Maybe an A."

"Gayle? Do you think that could be it?"

"Maybe," I said, handing the photos back to her. "Yeah, that makes sense. So, Jack must have a daughter some—"

"Shh. You hear that?" Brenda's fingers fumbled as she shoved the photos back into the frame. Her eyes wide, she whispered, "I heard something. Go look."

"You go look," I whispered back. I stepped out into the hallway, Brenda right behind me pressed up against my back. Slowly, we moved into the living room. Neither one of us had time to go anywhere to look. Or to hide. Instead, we stood frozen as the front door creaked open.

Eighteen

"**M**aggie?"

Damn. I recognized that voice. Bobby Lee. Before I could say a word, Brenda shoved me forward and raced into the kitchen. The front door opened wider and in stepped the police chief.

"Hey, Bobby Lee, how you doing?" A clipboard wouldn't even have helped at this point, and I acted as nonchalantly as possible. I think my voice was steady, but my knees sure were wobbly.

"Saw your car out front. What are you doing in here?" His beady little eyes squinted at me. "How'd you get in, Maggie?"

"Hey, Maggie, I'm almost done in here," Brenda called out from the kitchen. The expression on Bobby

Lee's face was priceless and I almost laughed. When his hand reached for his holstered gun, I straightened up real quick.

"It's okay, Chief—" I started.

Brenda came out of the kitchen carrying a white plastic bag. "We'll throw this out back in the garbage can. Oh, hello," she said, "glad to see the police force are on the job, doing their duty." She shifted the garbage bag to her left hand and reached out with her right hand. "I'm Brenda Blackwell."

Bobby Lee seemed taken aback, but he shook her outstretched hand. Then he looked back at me. "Maggie?"

"Sir, would you please close the door? We'd hate for the cat to get out," Brenda said.

"Uh, sure, of course," he said and pushed it shut.

"So, Maggie, you ready to go? Jack's cat should be fine for another day or so until you decide what to do. Meanwhile, I'll prop open this door so it can get to its food. Okay, Maggie?"

"Oh. Yeah. I'll ask around at the club to see if anyone wants it. I'm glad I remembered Jack had a cat and thought to come check on it."

"Yeah, good thing Jack once told you about the key being in the planter." Brenda flashed Bobby Lee a dazzling smile. "I'd hate for anyone to think we broke into the place."

She hoisted the garbage bag out in front of her. "We should get going. This bag is getting really stinky." Brenda moved by Bobby Lee, opened the front door, and stepped out onto the porch. She made a show of returning the key to where she'd found it.

I quickly followed her, saying over my shoulder, "Bobby Lee, you coming? Please make sure the door's locked." I rushed to join Brenda out in the yard.

"Now, you two little ladies hold on one dang minute here."

Damn. Busted. So close to getting away. Brenda and I stopped and turned. "Yes, Bobby Lee?"

He shuffled toward us, pointing to the bag in Brenda's hand. "I reckon it's the gentlemanly thing to do to take care of that for you."

Brenda handed him the bag. "Why, thank you ever so much, sir. It's right kind of you."

———

Later, when we sat in my kitchen, Brenda and I were still giggling. My knees had shaken as I drove, but I was able to get us back to my house in one piece. Well, two pieces since there were two of us.

"I thought I'd die laughing when you said that! 'Right kind of you.' I'm surprised you didn't bat your eyelashes at him."

She chuckled. "Oh, I would've, I definitely would've if it became necessary. The little southern belle in me comes out when I want something. Or when I want to get out of something."

"I guess so. Oh, and I loved the drawl."

"Yeah, that comes in handy too sometimes."

"Bobby Lee was putty in your hands. He never stood a chance." I shook my head in awe. "Amazing. Beautiful."

"I had to turn the situation around. We both know what kind of trouble we could've gotten ourselves into. I'm just glad you caught on so quickly."

"Really! I was clueless for a few seconds there, though. I'm glad you're so quick on your feet. You knew exactly what to do. Had I been alone, I'd probably be in jail right now for breaking and entering. Or at the very least for trespassing."

"It was the only possible way to get out of there. All about choices. Straight up, hon."

Her tone had grown serious and I didn't want that to happen. I smiled at her, and said, "So now what?"

"What have you got to eat around here?" She rummaged through the fridge, then my cabinets. "Stale coffee cake, one serving of lasagna, and strawberry ice cream. Typical," she said. "How in the world do you manage? How can you not cook? Unbelievable."

"What can I say? You know I hate to cook." I pointed at my phone. "Anything I want is right there. Delivery just minutes away." And a large pizza would feed me for three nights.

"And I suppose they're all on speed dial?"

"But of course." I grinned. "Hey, my mom hated cooking. I got it from her, I guess."

"I had no choice growing up. If I didn't cook, we didn't eat. Being the only girl in a family of six sucked in more ways than one."

"Straight up." I said it to let her know I understood. Even though I could never truly relate to all she had gone through, I could let her know I understood.

"Stealing my lines now, huh?" She tilted her head. "Thanks, hon, I appreciate that. Now, back to eating. Any suggestions?"

———

Only one place I could think of and soon we sat in my favorite booth at Sally's Diner, the one overlooking the town square. I remembered the first night Rob and I spent in North DeSoto. A whole new world compared to Miami. We had walked the streets of downtown, and we'd laughed because it turned out to be a whole fifteen-minute journey.

"Thinking of Rob, hon?" Brenda must've caught the smile on my face as I reminisced.

"Yeah. Our first night in this town." I told her about the walk. "We ended up coming in here to eat dinner, even sat at this table. We always tried to get this booth when we came in. The square is really pretty at night."

"And the food's not bad either," she said, shoveling in another mouthful of mashed potatoes. She wagged her fork at me across the table. "These are real! Imagine—made from potatoes, not flakes."

"Wait'll you see their desserts. Made from scratch. They have a little bakery display case up front."

After dinner, Brenda wanted to test the fifteen-minute walk. Most of the offices and some of the shops were closed at eight o'clock, so we passed a lot of dark buildings. The county courthouse, post office, and library were also closed.

"Not much activity, even for a Thursday night."

I agreed. "It's a shame, business started dying when the mall was built a few years ago. My favorite bookstore moved there right before Christmas. And with Wal-Mart and Lowe's nearby, a lot of people have stopped coming downtown."

We approached JC's hardware store. Lights were on and a few customers could be seen. "This is owned by one of the guys I told you about."

"Was he at the funeral today? One of the ones I met?"

"No, one of the assholes. I steered as far away as possible from him and Dick today. You met Sam, Pete, and Kevin."

She nodded. "Yeah, that's right. Nice guys. Handsome in their uniforms. All those ribbons. The one guy had an impressive assortment."

"Really? I've never noticed."

"It's probably because of my oldest brother—the only one I keep in touch with—he once told me what the different medals and ribbons represented. He's still in the Army and I always get teary when I see him in his dress uniform. So handsome, just like those guys today."

"And that ends our tour of downtown." We arrived back at Sally's and my car.

She pushed up her jacket sleeve to look at her watch. "Seventeen minutes. You were close."

"If we hadn't stood in front of the hardware store for an extra minute, I'd be even closer." Nelson's Hardware was directly across the square from Sally's Diner.

"I didn't realize how big it was up close. His store looks twice the size as the shops around him," Brenda said.

"He built on a couple of years ago. They bought the building next door and doubled his space."

"Must be doing pretty well for himself."

I shrugged. "Not according to what he says. JC always bitches about Lowe's taking away a lot of his business. Only his most loyal customers still buy from him."

Brenda wrapped her arm around my shoulder and squeezed. "Loyalty is a good thing."

"Don't I know it?" I squeezed back and kept my mouth shut. No way in hell would I tell her that Pam Nelson still owed me money. There's such a thing as misguided loyalty, and knowing Brenda, she'd have no problem demanding that Pam pay me. It wouldn't be pretty.

Brenda hadn't stopped talking about how good her dinner was until we were back at my place. Since we were going car shopping the next day, we decided to do some searching on the Internet ahead of time.

While I booted up the computer, she dragged a chair from the table to sit next to me. She asked, "Are there many car dealers to check out?"

"I know of a few. Let's see if they have websites."

An hour later, Brenda had a list of dealers she wanted to visit. I was surprised when she showed interest in an Escalade instead of another sports car.

"I don't want something that can be smooshed. I want something that can run over other cars."

"I'm sure we'll find you the perfect vehicle." I shut off the computer and slid my chair back. "We'll leave first thing in the morning."

"First thing will be breakfast. I took a look at Sally's breakfast menu and my mouth is watering for a mushroom and Swiss cheese omelet. Lord knows I won't find anything to eat in your kitchen."

"Hey! I do have coffee, y'know." I stretched my arms and stood. "I'm beat. Are you ready to call it a night? I figured we'd share the bed tonight, if that's okay with you."

"Sure. Just keep your hands to yourself." She followed me into the bedroom.

"I promise to only use them to punch you when you start snoring."

Her mouth dropped open. "I don't snore."

"Yeah. You keep telling yourself that." I pulled back the covers of my bed and slid under them. I picked up the novel on my night stand. "You want a book to read?"

"No, thanks, I'm exhausted. Do me a favor, though?"

"Of course."

She rolled over onto her side and said, "Don't read one of those sexy romances. It'll only make you horny and I'll just have to fight you off of me."

I smacked her. "Keep talking like that and people will get the wrong idea."

"Uh-uh. Not everyone has gaydar as strong as mine."

"Gaydar? What's that?"

"The signal that tells me when I meet someone gay." She yawned and mumbled something else.

"What did you say?" I asked.

"Hmmm? Oh, like that guy at the funeral today."

"What guy?"

"The good-looking one." She yawned again.

The only guys she met were Sam, Pete, and Kevin. And I highly doubted she'd consider Sam good-looking. He was about fifty pounds overweight and balding. Pete was our handsome Casanova, but I thought Kevin was adorable in a cuddly kind of way too. I didn't think either of them were gay. Never really thought about it. Maybe she met someone else while I was getting our drinks.

"Brenda? Who all did you meet today?"

Her answer was a soft snore.

Terrific.

Nineteen

"That was an excellent breakfast," Brenda said pushing her plate away. "I'm glad this place is open twenty-four hours, so we could be here early. We'll have time to go look for my phone before you drive me around looking for a new car."

"Have you decided on looking only at the Escalades?"

"Yeah, I think so. A black one." She reached for the check. "Um, hon, how are you set for money? Need a loan, or will you be okay until you find another job?"

"I'm fine. Plus, I'm planning on going back to work at the club once we find Jack's killer. Don't worry about me. Thanks, though."

She squinted at me. "Do you think that's a good idea—going back to work there?"

"Sure. I'm already familiar with the place, the people. Pretty good money too." I frowned, then said, "It was, anyway. Now that they've raised the prices, business may die. I don't know. I'm not worried." It practically killed me to lie to her, but there was no need to tell her how pathetic my bank balance was. She called it a loan, but I had a hunch she'd refuse any attempts at paying her back. I'd get by without becoming more indebted to anyone.

"Can you at least let me pay for gas since you're playing chauffer today?"

"Deal," I said.

I filled up the gas tank before we headed out of town. We had a pretty good idea where the accident happened, and sure enough, saw the skid marks. I pulled over onto the side of the road as far as I could and parked.

We crunched our way through the broken glass sparkling from the morning sun. Brenda and I split up, her taking one side of the road and me the other.

"Here!" I heard her shout. Bent over, Brenda was combing the high grass.

I rushed over. I looked at what she held in her hand.

"I can't believe I found it! The poor thing looks worse than my car probably did."

I had seen her car and knew better, but I didn't say anything. "Well, that was a lost cause. But at least you found it. Maybe you can use it as a shoe horn."

She snorted, then slugged me. "It might be salvageable. I'll have somebody look at it."

We spent the rest of the day driving to car lots. At the last one Brenda found what she was looking for. We hugged good-bye, she promised to check in when she reached West Palm Beach, and off she drove in her shiny black Escalade.

My stomach rumbled, reminding me I hadn't eaten since breakfast at Sally's. I sat in my car pondering my choices. Brenda had already established my cupboards were bare, so eating at the house wasn't an option. Not that it usually was an option.

The club. Tonight was the Spaghetti Supper and I knew I could get a decent meal for a really cheap price. The hell with my pride. I was hungry and could afford a cheap meal. I checked my wallet and found two tens. I'd spend one of them on the meal, one beer, and a decent tip. Depending on who waited on me.

The bar was quiet and after signing the book I grabbed my usual stool in front of the mirror. The same guy was working, and he came over to me. "Hey, I remember you from yesterday. You were with that funeral group. What can I get you?"

I bet he did remember me considering I'd left him a fifty-cent tip. "A glass of Coors Light, and I'll take one dinner. Okay to eat here at the bar?"

"Sure," he said and went off to place my order and get my one allotted beer. I nodded and smiled at the few people around me. When he served my beer, I thanked him and asked, "What's your name? Do you like working here?"

"I'm Cody, and this is just a temporary thing."

Damn straight it is, I wanted to tell him. Give me and Michael a little more time, and my butt would be back there where it belonged. Hopefully before the big meeting that would decide my fate.

"I'm an officer over at the Third Street Vets, and fill in when other clubs are shorthanded. The steward here was needed in the kitchen tonight, so they asked me to help." Someone called out to him at the other end of the bar. "I'd better get to work. I'll bring your dinner out when it's ready, should be a few minutes."

Good. Cody hadn't been hired to replace me. That was a relief, I had to admit to myself. My job would be waiting as soon as all of this was over. He came back over with silverware wrapped in a napkin and a paper placemat to put in front of me.

Even with my back to the dining room, I could watch from the mirror. Pam and Diane were running from table to table taking orders, serving food, and bussing tables. I was surprised to see Pam playing waitress. She usually sat at a card table near the door collecting the money and schmoozing. Then when the time came to clean up, she busied herself by counting the money. This wasn't the time to ask her for my money. Way too busy.

Our monthly spaghetti dinners were open to the public and they came in droves. Alcohol wasn't available to non-members, but the crowd we got didn't usually care. Mostly senior citizens, they were there to get a good meal at a great price. As expected, the dining room was jammed with customers at five o'clock. With the exception of the one small table. My eyes teared up thinking of the story behind the POW/MIA table.

The table cloth was white, symbolizing the purity of their intentions to respond to their country's call to arms. A red rose was placed in a vase to remind people of the families and loved ones who awaited their soldier's return. The red ribbon tied to the vase represented all those who demand a proper accounting for our missing. A lit white candle is reminiscent of the light of hope that lives in our hearts to illuminate the missing soldier's way home. The table was set with a piece of lemon on the bread plate to remind those of their bitter fate, and salt for the tears of their family members as they waited. The glass was inverted because they couldn't toast with us tonight, and the chair was empty because they are not here.

"Here you go," Cody said. He placed the plate of spaghetti and meatballs in front of me. "Ready for another Coors Light?"

My glass was nearly empty. Damn. I'd let my mind wander. "Um, no. How about a glass of water instead?"

"I'll buy Maggie a beer."

I looked over at the person who'd spoken. Phil, one of the woodies, waved at me. The daily book must be getting high again for him to be here.

"How are you doing, Maggie? Good to see you. I'm glad you didn't let the bastards get you down."

I swallowed the last of my beer and slid the glass toward Cody. "Thanks, Phil. I'm doing just fine. Appreciate the drink and the kind words."

"Sure thing." He lifted his empty glass. "I'll take another wine, Cody."

That's when it hit me. Brenda must've met Phil yesterday when I was out of the room.

We'd been so busy today that I'd forgotten to ask her who she thought was gay, and now it made sense. There had been gossip about Phil over the years since he'd joined the club as a social member. The way he talked, some of his mannerisms, the way he didn't talk about himself so we knew very little about him. A lot of speculation from the older members—the same ones who bitched about women being allowed in the military.

I dug into my meal, savoring every bite. Someone in the kitchen had been kind and given me an extra meatball. Unless it was a mistake. That seemed more likely. Didn't matter to me as long as I ate and someone else had done the cooking. And the cleanup.

Phil moved from his stool and sat on the one next to me. He leaned closer and whispered, "Have you heard the latest?"

Terrific. Just because he'd bought me a beer he felt he could drag me into gossipy conversation. I was tired and hungry and all I wanted was to eat my dinner. Then I remembered I should be on the lookout for any information. I answered, "No. What?"

"There's talk that the gambling board knife is the one used to kill Jack." He jerked his head toward the kitchen. "A couple of people were really anxious to win that knife. A couple of people who usually never gamble."

"JC and Dick? Yeah, I saw them with that knife board the other night. So?"

"It's weird that Bobby Lee hasn't found the murder weapon yet, and everyone's saying how that knife was used, then cleaned and put back on the board." He leaned back in his stool, crossed his arms, and watched me.

"No, I don't think so. Besides, Bobby Lee said it was a knife with a short blade."

"I don't know. Seems mighty suspicious to me."

It was his sing-song way of speaking that made some members think he was gay. I remembered that now as I listened to him. I shook my head again. "I don't buy it. Not after what Bobby Lee said."

Phil snickered. "Like we can trust him. He's probably in on it with them. That would explain why there hasn't been any arrest yet." He gasped. "Oh! Except for you, of course."

Catty bitch. "I wasn't arrested, Phil. Bobby Lee just wanted to talk to me privately."

"That's not what I heard."

I finished my beer, wiped my mouth, and tossed my crumpled napkin on the empty plate. I refused to get into an argument with this guy. Let him and anyone think what the hell what they wanted.

"Well, Phil, you heard wrong." I put a ten-dollar bill down and scooted from my stool. "Now, if you'll excuse me, I need to get going. Thanks again for the beer."

My hands were shaking when I unlocked my car door. The gall of that little shit. I'd forgotten how malicious the gossip could be in the club. I'd listened to it night after night for years. How the hell could I

147

have so easily forgotten? Probably because it'd never been directed at me before. Or maybe there had been gossip about me and I hadn't known. I remembered what Pam said about wanting a male bartender. They could've been setting me up all along, and Jack's murder just sped things up for them.

I took a few deep breaths before I started the ignition. My right leg shook so badly I was afraid to drive. I hadn't felt this angry since … since I don't know when. Maybe when the assholes suspended me. Or Pam stiffed me. Or I caught the chief of police watching my house. Or how about getting run off the road? A few more deep breaths. Oh yeah, and what about being accused of murder? Screw it. Time for big changes. I'd said it before, and this time I meant it. The time had come to kick some serious ass.

First thing to do would be to show the bastards how much I didn't need them. Even if they came begging, crawling on their hands and knees, no way in hell would I ever go back to work at that place.

Time to move on.

Twenty

On my way back to the house, after visiting with Rob and ranting to him for a while, I splurged on a newspaper. Way past time to find another job. Easier said than done, it turned out. I searched the few classified ads and by the time I finished, I felt completely under-qualified to do anything. Definitely not good for my ego.

Wanting to hold on to the anger and not wallow in self-pity, I sat at the kitchen table and grabbed the pen and legal pad still there from the day before. I wrote down everything that Phil had said. I wanted to make sure I remembered it all so I could tell Michael.

Michael. I hadn't seen or talked to him since the funeral yesterday. Since his date with Terri. I wouldn't be surprised to hear he and Terri had run off and gotten married. Oh, sheesh. Now I was being ridiculous.

I needed a plan. Who could I go talk to? I looked at my list of names. All of them, with the exception of Abby and Pete, were busy with the spaghetti supper. Right about now they'd probably be cleaning up. I could go back in and casually talk to them, all friendly-like.

Yeah. I couldn't see that happening with JC or Dick. But I could probably get Pam to pay me. That could be my excuse for going back in. I'd just have to make nice, even if it killed me. And I'd stay the hell away from Phil if he was still there.

The VFW parking lot was nearly empty. Damn shame for seven o'clock on a Friday night. One week ago exactly the place had been jumping and I'd been complaining about being tired. Be careful what you wish for.

I climbed out of my car and heard Pam's voice before I saw her. I stood there listening.

"No, I will not stay and help clean up. It's bad enough I had to wait on tables tonight, JC. You should be grateful for that."

I couldn't hear JC's response, but I did see them on the front stoop. I slowly, quietly closed and locked my door, waiting to see if anything else happened. Pam turned and walked down the steps. JC went back inside. I made a beeline toward Pam, catching up to her just as she got to her car.

"Hi, Pam, glad I caught you. I know it was an oversight, but you didn't pay me on Tuesday." I smiled ever-so-sweetly.

She almost hit me with her car door she swung it open so fast. "Oh, Maggie, I don't have time for this now. I'm late for an appointment."

And with that, she was gone.

I don't think so.

In mere minutes I was two cars behind her, stopped at a traffic light. I stayed on her tail for a few miles when it became obvious she was heading home. Sure enough, she turned down her street, then pulled into her driveway. I parked a block away and waited. I figured she'd be right back out and on her way to her appointment. I watched, ready to resume following her as soon as I saw her car again.

Fifteen minutes later, I was still waiting. And I had to pee. I wondered how Jessica Fletcher managed when she was on stakeouts. That thought only made it worse. I started the car, drove to Pam's, and parked behind her car. I walked quickly and carefully to the front door.

I lost track of how many times I'd pushed the doorbell when she finally opened the door. The look on her face was priceless, but I didn't take time to enjoy it. Not caring about rudeness, I brushed by her and said, "I need to use your bathroom. Thanks." I rushed down the hallway.

Pam, her arms crossed and a foot tapping, leaned against the hallway wall when I came out. I smiled and said, "Sorry about that. I was in the neighborhood and suddenly had to go. I knew you wouldn't mind."

She pushed herself away from the wall and walked toward the spotless kitchen. I was right behind her. Her purse sat on the gathering island right next to what looked like a stack of library books, and she pulled out her checkbook. Her hands were shaking and I wondered if it was a sign of anger, the same reaction I have sometimes. Too bad, so sad. Let her be angry. I shouldn't have had to wait three days to get paid.

"Here," Pam said, holding out the check. She rubbed her nose and sniffed. "I'm sure you can see yourself out."

I made it a point to study the check in front of her, then looked up at her. Interesting. I pointed to the sprinkle of white powder on her shirt. "Been baking, have you?"

I thought her eyes would pop out of her head. She brushed the powder away, and glared at me. I'm sure she wanted to lick her fingers. Sure was a waste of good cocaine. Appointment, my ass. I must've interrupted her little party, probably even rushed her by ringing the doorbell so many times.

I showed myself out. I practically skipped to my car. I could get used to this assertive side of myself. Man, it felt good.

Since some of my bills were paid, I could use part of the check for groceries. I drove to the store close to the house, knowing they'd have no problem cashing the check. I bought my usual supply of frozen dinners and popcorn. Toilet paper, toothpaste, deodorant and I was good to go for another month.

Both sides of the house were dark when I parked in my driveway. Michael's car was gone and I wondered where they were. I lugged the groceries upstairs, put a bag of popcorn in the microwave, and put everything else away.

I was ready to veg out for the rest of the evening with my Lehane book and a bowl of popcorn. I set the microwave timer and went into my bedroom to get my book. A beeping noise startled me. And smoke, I smelled smoke. Oh, crap. Now my microwave was on the fritz?

I rushed to the kitchen and my microwave was humming along nicely. Where the hell was the beeping come from? And I still smelled smoke. Damn! It was the smoke detector in Michael's apartment.

I called 911, grabbed my keys, and flew downstairs to Michael's front door. The doorknob wasn't hot and I unlocked and opened the door. And froze.

No. *Grow the hell up. Move. Now.*

"Michael? Chris?" I shouted and stepped into the living room. No smoke in there, but the kitchen in the back of the house looked foggy, hazy. I couldn't see any flames. A stench of burning…something. Plastic? I pulled up the collar of my shirt to cover my mouth and nose, rushed forward. Sirens in the distance. Very hot in the kitchen. My eyes watered. The smoke detector screamed. I yanked the side door open.

Thick fog shifted, rolling with me as I went out the door. Cool air hit me.

People across the street were shouting, pointing, running. One woman came over to me, pulling my arm. We stumbled our way to the other side of the road.

"Anyone else in the house?" she wanted to know. I shook my head. More sirens wailed, and an ambulance and police car rounded the corner. A man ran over to me and the woman.

"Is she okay, honey? Everyone out of the house? Firemen went in through the front door. One of them outside needs to know if the house is empty." All this rushed out of him.

The woman spoke, "She seems fine and says everyone's out. Here comes a paramedic and the police chief."

Forcing my gaze from the house, I turned to look. Sure enough. Bobby Lee and another man carrying what looked like an oxygen tank ran toward us. I don't think I've ever seen Bobby Lee move so fast. He was panting by the time he reached us. Bent over, his hands pressed against his knees, he fought to catch his breath.

Pointing at the tank, I told the paramedic, "I think the chief needs that more than I do."

Twenty-One

My popcorn was cold by the time we were allowed back in the house. Bobby Lee, Michael, and I sat at my kitchen table. Chris was at my computer, grumbling about its slowness. For the third time I told Bobby Lee what had happened. Time for him to answer our questions.

"What caused the fire, Bobby Lee?"

He scratched his head, and looked from me to Michael. "A pot had been left on the lit stove. I'm surprised at you, Bradley."

Michael shook his head. "I'm surprised too, sir. I know I didn't do that before I left the house." As if he knew the question was coming, he said, "We left here at three to meet with my daughter's teacher and principal. Chris and I ran a few errands, had dinner, and we got home about nine. Just as all the excitement was dying down."

"Is there any chance Chris might've done it?" I really didn't think so, but what were the alternatives? Besides a sudden onset of dementia for Michael.

"I don't see how. Or why. Or, hell, even when she could've done it. Chris knows better than to use the stove." Michael rolled a popcorn kernel back and forth in front of him. "I don't even like her using the microwave when I'm not close by."

"Well, Bradley, somebody started it."

"Bobby Lee, what kind of pot? And was there any food?"

The police chief flipped through his little notepad. "A Dutch oven. Yellow. No food." He looked at Michael again. "Did you start to boil water, then forgot about it?"

"No, sir. I'm positive. Was there any sign of a break in, forced entry?"

Bobby Lee snorted. "You think someone broke in, started to cook, and then left? That this was some sort of prank?"

Saying it like that did sound kind of silly. But weird things had been happening, so why not? I said, "Both doors were locked."

The look on Michael's face told me he just realized what I'd done. How I had come into the first floor of the house. I shrugged and smiled. He smiled back.

"If no one broke in," Michael said, "how we do explain what happened? Maggie, does anyone else have keys?"

"No, definitely not. I have mine and I had one made when I listed the apartement." I highly doubted it, but asked, "Does Chris have her own key?"

Michael shook his head.

"So, no sign of a break-in, and you and Bradley have the only sets of keys?" The smugness in Bobby Lee's voice grated on my nerves.

155

"As far as I know, Bobby Lee. I was still in Miami when Rob had the closing. I could always ask the hospital administrator if you want. Actually, I think I will. It'd be good to know if there are other keys floating around." Not very likely, and I really wanted to prove Bobby Lee wrong. I just knew someone had to have broken in, and that it wasn't due to carelessness on Michael's part. Bobby Lee needed to know how serious this was. Sticking to what he did know for sure, I asked, "What kind of damage did the fire do?"

"The pot's a total loss. Also, the dish towel that had been next to it. Other than that, not too bad. Soot on the wall behind the stove, but that can be cleaned up." The police chief pushed his chair back and stood. "I reckon painting the kitchen might be in order."

"Which I'll take care of, Maggie," said Michael.

"Thanks. And tomorrow I'll see if I can talk to the hospital administrator. I wonder if I'll have to make an appointment to see him."

Bobby Lee pushed his chair back in and said, "Oh, I don't know, Maggie. North DeSoto ain't like big cities. Mr. Jacobs will be in his office in the morning before he goes out to the golf course. That's what he does most Saturdays. You best get there before eight."

A little jab telling me he knew the goings-on with his town. I was a city girl, not a local, still an outsider. Just like at the club. I was the only true outsider since most of those people had grown up in North DeSoto and have known each other for years.

"I'll see myself out, Maggie." He put his hat on and tipped it at me. "Y'all stay out of trouble."

"I'll walk out with you, sir. Be right back, Maggie."

After the day I'd had, I wanted nothing more than to soak in a hot bubble bath with a glass of wine and my novel. Instead I went over to the computer to see what Chris was up to.

I watched Chris play a spirited game of Hearts for several minutes, then Michael joined us. "Chris," he said, "I need you to call Heather and then I want to talk with her mom."

"Sure, Daddy. Can I finish playing this game first? Only be a couple minutes."

"Okay." He glanced at his watch. "Tell her it's important and apologize for calling this late. Let me know when her mom's on the phone. Maggie and I will be out in the hall." He handed Chris his cell phone.

"So," he said, "besides the fire, how've you been?"

Where should I start? With Brenda and me breaking into Jack's house and finding the photograph? Finding the crushed phone? What Phil had said? What was important? What didn't matter?

I ended up telling him everything. Even down to looking for a car for Brenda, and how we'd eaten dinner then breakfast at Sally's. I even included the walk we'd taken downtown after dinner, our entire conversation.

Exhausted after dumping all that, I leaned back and waited.

"Wow. You've been busy."

All I could do was nod.

"I can't believe you broke into Jack's house. And that you got away with it." He grinned. "Too wild."

"How's this for too wild?" And I told him what Brenda had said about one of the guys being gay. "At first I thought she meant one I'd introduced her to, but then I figured she must've met Phil while I was out of the room."

"You're saying it can't be anyone else? Who did she meet while you were with her?"

"Sam, Pete, and Kevin."

Michael frowned. "Hmm."

"What are you thinking?"

"I'm still wondering about motives, and now I'm thinking a gay man in a military club might be one hell of a secret," he said. "One he wouldn't want known."

"Oh, you're right about that. There was lots of gossip about Phil when he first joined as a social member. It died down after a while when it became obvious he was a woodie, and not a regular. But a lot of the older guys have a real problem with gays. Jack Hoffman had been one of the loudest complainers. If Jack knew for certain, yeah, I can see it definitely being a motive."

"I have no doubt you'll figure it out. I just hope you do it legally. Don't break into anyone else's house." He grinned again.

I shrugged. "It was all Brenda's idea. She made me do it."

"Yeah, right." He rubbed his hand across his mouth, then said, "I'm glad she was here. I haven't been much help the past couple of days."

I reached for his hand, then stopped. Didn't want to make that mistake again. He saw it, and instead of backing off, he reached for my hand and held it in his.

"Thanks." He patted my hand, then pulled back. "And now I'll tell you what's been going on with my darling daughter. Chris was suspended yesterday and today for pouring ketchup on another girl's head. Can you believe that? Ketchup."

I bit my bottom lip to keep myself from laughing. "Um, why?"

"Why?" He stared at me. "What the hell does it matter why she did it?"

"She must've had a reason. What did she say?"

"Something about this girl took her friend's boyfriend away." Michael shook his head. "A ten-year-old has a boyfriend? Christ."

"Sounds about right. Thing is, the boy probably doesn't even know he's involved. Girls that age have crushes on boys who still hate girls. So, what did Chris do?"

"They were at lunch when this other girl apparently said something to Chris's friend. She started crying and Chris got mad. Went over and poured ketchup on the girl."

"Seems harmless enough. I mean it could've been worse, I suppose. They could've had an actual fight. Chris was just sticking up for her friend."

"Now you're defending my daughter? You think what she did is appropriate?"

I shook my head. "No, not at all. I'm just saying it could've been worse, and that Chris was trying to be a supportive friend." I should've just kept my mouth shut. Nothing worse than a childless person telling a parent what to do. Hell, I couldn't even keep a houseplant alive, but that didn't stop me. Maybe I could go at it from a different angle. "Was the little girl hurt?"

"No. Just needed a shampoo."

A loud laugh burst from me. I clamped my hand over my mouth and looked at him. Fortunately, I saw a glint in his eyes and he grinned.

"I know it's not funny, and I don't want Chris to go around doing stuff like this, but ..."

I agreed. "She was being a loyal friend, that's all, and that's a good thing to be. As long as no one was hurt, no harm done. Just a little prank, a nuisance. Hey, speaking of nuisances, why did you walk out with Bobby Lee?"

"I wanted to ask him about your car accident the other night, and if the toxicology reports on Jack Hoffman came in yet."

"Daddy, Heather's mom's on the phone!"

We walked back to the kitchen. Michael took his phone call with Terri out to the hallway, and I got busy rearranging my notes at the table. I turned to the page where I'd written down all of my questions, and wrote down some more.

What did I remember from the last night I worked? Jack had bitched about women joining and ruining the place, how they never should've allowed women in. What else had he said that night? Something about loyalty, working together, and him being a past Commander. How things were done right back when he was in charge. Then he'd mumbled something I didn't catch. Damn. But I bet someone around him had heard. Who all was there that last night I worked? I closed my eyes to concentrate.

Pete had sat at the table with Abby. Kevin in his usual place at the end of the bar, near Jack, Pam, and Scott. Diane flitted around between cleaning the kitchen and sitting at the bar. JC and Dick were in their office most of the night, and Sam wasn't there at all. Unless it was the next night when he was training Abby. Something nagged at the back of my brain and I couldn't think now what it could be. Maybe I'd remember later.

For now, I wanted to focus on Abby. We still hadn't talked to her, found out what her story was. Michael hadn't seemed as excited about the scenario I'd dreamed up. The fact that Jack had married a Korean woman, they had a child, and that child's name was probably Gayle. Abby. Abigail. I didn't think it was too much of a stretch. Of course, the age was all wrong, but maybe Abby was Jack's granddaughter. And maybe she … I rubbed my temples, trying to ward off a huge tension headache. So much to think about, keep track of. What else did we have to do?

We had to find out who all had been in the club Saturday night when Abby worked. Probably safe to assume Kevin, JC, and Dick. Sam might remember, but maybe not. How could I find out who was there that night?

The book! The daily book, of course. Whoever was there that night had to have signed in. Except that may not completely help. Damn.

People like Sam, JC, and Dick who come in before the club opens sign the book, so their names are on the top of the page. But since they're usually in every night, there's no way of telling what time they came back. Then there are the ones like Phil, the woodies who come in only to sign the book when the pot's high. To be fair, Phil had stuck around and had at least two glasses of wine. Yeah, but—

"Maggie, you okay?"

I opened my eyes. "Yeah, why?"

Michael laughed. "You were sitting there with your eyes closed, moving your head and hands around. Like some little dance."

My face felt warm. What the hell was going on with me blushing so much? "I was concentrating, trying to picture the last night I worked. I guess I forgot to open my eyes when I started thinking of other stuff."

He sat down. Chris was still concentrating on the computer, and I saw earbud cords trailing down the sides of her head and connecting Michael's cell phone sitting on the desk. "And what did you come up with?" I told him and he said, "Let's plan on going to see Sam tomorrow and take a look at the book. We'll see who was there the night Jack was murdered." He leaned back in his chair and frowned. "Did you really think you'd go back to work at the club once this is all over?"

"Yeah, I did. I wasn't looking at it realistically. Somehow I thought they'd decide to keep me once the suspension was over and they had their meeting. Total denial on my part, I guess. But that's over now."

"You can always raise my rent until you find another job."

"Hey, you better not be joking. I might have to. So, what did you find out from our illustrious chief of police about my accident and the toxicology reports?"

"He's not a bad cop, Maggie, not really. The chief doesn't share his investigation with civilians, and"—Michael raised his voice a little—"he is still investigating Rob's murder."

"Yeah, he told you that?" My eyes stung and I blinked tears away. *Not now.*

"He did. The chief says it's an ongoing investigation. And I believe him."

I had no intention of getting into a battle with Michael. I knew how I felt about Bobby Lee's incompetence, and that was that. I crossed my arms tight against my chest. "Okay, so what else? Anything?"

"He checked out the tire treads left at the accident scene. Said they're very unusual and he was interested in them. But, and this is the most curious part, the tox results came in and—"

"Already? The newspaper said it'd be a couple weeks."

"I told you the police don't share everything in an ongoing investigation." He arched an eyebrow. "Anyway, Jack was stabbed twice, yes, but that wasn't the cause of death."

"What?" Talk about making me sit up and take notice.

"Jack Hoffman was poisoned."

Twenty-Two

"Poisoned? It was the green beer, wasn't it? Jack said it tasted bitter, but I didn't believe him." I jumped up, twirled around, not sure what to do first. "We need to talk to Abby. Can we go see her tomorrow? Ask your friend to babysit Chris. I'll drive, no, we'll take your car. We can—"

Michael grabbed my arm. "Maggie, calm down. Breathe. Yes, we'll go see Abby tomorrow." He dropped my arm. "There's more to tell you, but not until you sit down."

"More?" I sat. "Okay, what else? I'm listening, I'm calm." My feet tapped in rhythm with my pounding heart. I tried to keep still. I blew out a deep breath. "Okay, now I'm ready."

"Here's the thing. Doc Shenberger did the autopsy and he discovered something suspicious near one of the knife wounds. A small needle mark. The initial drug screen didn't show anything other than the alcohol level in Jack's system. While the level was high, Doc knew it wasn't high enough to cause death, so he ran further tests, which came back today and he called the chief immediately."

Damn. Not the green beer.

"Wait. How'd you get Bobby Lee to tell you all this? One cop to another type of thing?"

He shook his head. "Not really. The chief knew I'd be able to get the information anyway, so he shared it with me once I reminded him of that. Anyway, let's plan our day for tomorrow." Michael slid the pad of paper closer to him and wrote while he talked. "While you're at the hospital talking to the administrator, I'll map out our road trip, make hotel reservations, gas up my car. Heather's mom said Chris can stay overnight. We'll drop her off on the way to the club to find out what we can about the book."

Finally. I felt like we were making progress.

He continued, "It's a six-hour drive to Ft. Walton Beach, so we could leave in the early afternoon. The website said the first show where Abby works starts at eight."

I pictured a smoky, dark place with scantily clad women sliding down poles. Topless waitresses serving drinks. Back rooms down dark hallways that provided a more personal type of entertainment. What the hell would I wear to a place like that? Be nice if I could lose forty pounds and grow six inches taller by morning. That'd be nice anytime. Since that wasn't going to happen, I got up to get a beer, and offered one to Michael.

"Sounds good, thanks," he said. He took a long drink from the bottle, then set it on the table. "We still have to talk to Dick, y'know."

I groaned. "I know, but I've been doing my best to stay away from him. Him and JC. Although I am surprised how nice JC was to me at his store a few days ago. Will we need to talk to him again?" I really hoped not. He was nice that one time and I didn't want to push my luck. I told Michael as much.

"We might. I don't know yet. A lot of this is winging it. What one person says will lead us to another, and so on and so on." He chuckled and said, "You found that out on your own."

My phone rang and I got up to answer it. "Oh, hi, Diane." I rolled my eyes, making Michael grin. "No, I'm sorry I won't be able to clean this weekend. I'm going out of town. Yeah, just a little trip. How about I call you early next week?" We spoke for a few more minutes and I hung up. "I suppose you gathered that was Diane Reid. Okay, now, where were we?"

Instead of answering, he rubbed his hand across his mouth. A sure sign he was apprehensive. "What is it, Michael?"

He looked back to check on Chris. She didn't turn around. "I'm not sure what to make of something. It's only happened a few times, but I think someone has broken in. Nothing's ever missing, but things are moved around, weird stuff." He squirmed in his seat then chuckled. "Chris thinks we have a poltergeist."

"And what do you think? Why didn't you tell me this before, when it happened?"

"It's been silly stuff, not worth mentioning. Like a glass of milk left out on the kitchen table. I don't drink milk, and Chris swore she hadn't done it. Another time a book I'd been reading was in the refrigerator. Once an umbrella I've never seen before showed up on the couch."

My mind flashed back to last month when I thought I'd misplaced my umbrella. I kept it in the umbrella stand by my secretary desk, and one day I couldn't find it.

"A Daffy Duck umbrella?" I asked.

He blinked several times, and I figured I had my answer. "What the hell? I'm definitely going to see the hospital administrator tomorrow. These sound more like pranks, though."

Michael said, "I agree. Like I said, silly stuff and nothing taken."

"Except for Daffy. And he was just moved to another spot in the house."

"And he—I mean, the umbrella—then later disappeared. I never saw it again," he said.

Poltergeist?

"I brought this up now because I think you need to use more caution with telling people you'll be out of town."

My phone call with Diane. Damn.

"Okay," he said, "let's get back to planning tomorrow's trip. We'll figure out the rest of the weekend after we've talked to Abby. We—"

"You really don't think Abby did it, do you? But it makes so much sense."

He shrugged and said, "We have to be open to all possibilities. We still have to talk to Kevin, Pete, Sam, Diane, and Dick. I think it's obvious at least two people are involved, considering what Gussie told you about the cars she saw that night. We'll see what we find out, if anything, from Abby. Then we'll go from there."

"Okay. And this Sunday will be good because we can find all of them at the club. The fourth Sunday of the month they have a brunch, so Pam and Diane should be there working with their husbands. Pete doesn't leave to go on the road until Monday. Kevin's off that day too. And we'll talk to Sam tomorrow." As soon as I said Sam's name, whatever was nagging me flashed through my head. Damn, I wish I could figure it out.

"Something's bugging me about Sam, but I can't put my finger on it," I said. "And since two people are involved, it doesn't make sense that Sam's one of them. He simply doesn't hang out or socialize with anyone when he's not at the club. But, still … I wish I could remember what he said."

"Are you sure it's something he said? Maybe you heard something from someone else, or maybe you saw something?"

"I don't know." I took a good long swig from my beer bottle. "How about we focus on what we do know? Is there anyone we can rule out?"

"Not at this point," Michael said. "I left someone out—what about Scott Nelson? Have you talked to him?"

"Scott? I hadn't even considered him. But, again, we're talking about two people. So who would be with Scott? His father? His mother? In-laws?" I laughed at that. "Somehow I can't picture Scott and Dick doing anything together. They don't get along real well. Dick's so stuck on the military and hates it that Scott wasn't part of it. He also hates that Scott smokes. Hell, all of them hate that. That was one time Dick didn't get his way. Active members voted on whether to ban smoking in the club. Without JC to help, Dick couldn't get enough guys to show up to vote their way. Man, he and Pam were pissed. The ones who did show up to vote were heavy smokers, couldn't quit if they wanted to. After the meeting that night, they all came to the bar as usual. Jack bitched about the non-smoking rule not being passed, and Scott deliberately blew smoke in Jack's face. He denied it was intentional, but I told him to knock it off and make sure it didn't happen again. Jack made a big deal out of having to use his inhaler that night."

"His inhaler? Jack had asthma?"

"Oh, yeah, really bad. Of course that night, he made it seem even worse—made a big show." I swallowed the last of my beer and considered having another when Michael glanced at his watch. I wanted to pick his brain some more, so kept talking. "This isn't getting us anywhere. What about motive? We still haven't figured out *why* Jack was murdered."

"Some of the more common motives are money, jealousy, fear, crime of passion, mental illness, hate crimes, elimination. I saw just about everything when I was a police officer. People will kill for the stupidest reasons. Makes perfect sense to them at the time. Then there are the ones who accidentally kill. A crime gone wrong, for instance."

"Like Rob's murder."

"Yes. Bobby Lee says it was most likely a robbery that went wrong. Maybe the killer thought no one was downstairs and Rob surprised him."

"He was supposed to be upstairs with me painting the bathroom. I had told people about our painting plans. The same people who knew Jack Hoffman." I blinked hot tears from my eyes, took a deep breath, and said, "Tell me more about the poison that killed Jack."

"Have you ever heard of propranolol?"

I shook my head. "Pro—what?"

"When I finished making arrangements for Terri to watch Chris, I did a quick Google search. Propranolol. It's used to treat angina, high blood pressure, migraines, hypertension. Patients shouldn't drink alcohol while taking it, and it can be harmful to people with asthma. Even fatal."

"So someone injected this drug into Jack knowing what it would do since he was asthmatic and had been drinking." Damn. "Who would have that drug? I don't know of anyone who takes it. I'm assuming this stuff is prescribed? Doesn't sound like something you could get over the counter. Hell, you can't even get some cold medicines that way anymore."

"That's true." Michael laughed. "I have to ask the pharmacist for Coricidin. As far as who? You'd know that better than I. Does anyone have a history of heart problems? Anybody make it a point to not drink alcohol?"

"Pam and Diane. Pam has a history of drug abuse, but I don't think alcohol." I told him how Pam helped with the D.A.R.E. program in the school district. I also told him about the powder on her shirt. I couldn't be sure it was really coke, but the expression on her face was priceless. If nothing else, she was embarrassed to be caught unkempt. Oh, the horrors!

"It's no secret that she was once addicted to pain killers. I think she considers herself some type of hero now that she's clean. So she just stays away from alcohol now, as does Diane. Oh, oh! Dick has a heart condition. Diane doesn't drink because of Pam and she says Dick shouldn't drink because of his heart condition." I almost jumped out of my chair again. "It must be Dick's medication!"

He laughed again, but this time at me. I didn't care. I bounced in my chair.

"Don't hurt yourself, Maggie. You really want to jump up and down, don't you? Now, before you do, ask yourself why Dick Reid would want Jack dead."

Damn. My shoulders slumped making me feel like a deflated balloon. Michael had gone and ruined what I thought was a good clue. Truthfully, I didn't know why anyone would want Jack Hoffman dead. I said as much to Michael.

"Sorry. I didn't mean to burst your bubble, but we have to always think motive. Why was he murdered? What did he know? Or what did the killer think Jack knew?" Michael stood and put his empty beer bottle on the counter. "Keep thinking along those lines and we'll get there. You surprised yourself by remembering that Dick Reid has a heart condition. Bits of what may seem like useless information could be the key. We'll have plenty of time to talk more tomorrow on our drive. Right now Chris and I should get going. It's been a long day for all of us."

"Yeah, it has." I tossed both beer bottles in the recycling bucket. "Chris can keep the computer on. I'm too keyed up to go to bed just yet."

"Will do. But don't stay up too late. You've got an early day ahead of you tomorrow."

"Yes, dear," I mumbled. I followed them downstairs. I flipped on the porch light and opened the door.

Damn. One of North DeSoto's finest sat in his cruiser across the street. If Michael saw him, he gave no sign. We said our good-nights, I locked up, and headed to my computer.

One e-mail from Brenda letting me know her phone was beyond repair, so no photo and she was really sorry. I wondered about what Michael had said regarding tire treads and Bobby Lee's interest. Could he track down the driver by looking at tire treads? I supposed nothing was impossible. I knew they did it all the time on those TV crime shows. Yeah, and all within an hour.

My computer dinged and another e-mail from Brenda popped up. This one had a link, and nothing else. No explanation or anything. Brenda must think it's important, relevant to the case though, so I clicked on it. A website for an organization run by a group of veterans. What the hell? Why hadn't she included any text? Maybe she was in a hurry, wanted to send it when she had a quick chance?

I scrolled down through the site reading bits and pieces. All of the articles were about men who'd been caught lying about being in the military. Buying fake medals and ribbons over the Internet. Dozens of men (funny how no women were mentioned) whose lies were revealed because of inconsistencies. Actual veterans, members of VFWs and American Legions, telling stories of listening to alleged war heroes. How you can tell a true vet by how little he speaks of his time in the military, not the boasting. Ask the right questions of these lying bastards and the truth will come out. Only a true vet knows.

I leaned back in my chair, stared at the computer screen. What was Brenda saying? All she'd done was send the link. No suspicions, no names. Narrowing it down to who all she'd met, I came up with Sam,

Pete, Kevin, and Diane. Oh, and probably Phil. Was she saying one of them was lying about being in the military? According to the site, the maximum penalty for wearing medals never earned, a misdemeanor, is six months in jail and a fine. Not to mention the humiliation and embarrassment. Someone would not want that lie to be revealed.

Is this what Jack Hoffman knew and had he written about it in his notebook? And why the hell did Jack write stuff down in his damn notebooks?

Notebooks. Plural. Yeah. He had to have more than one. The five years I'd known Jack he'd been writing in them. No way in hell could it be the same one over and over. So where were they? The only place Brenda and I hadn't checked in Jack's house was his bedroom closet. Bobby Lee had shown up and interrupted us. There could be a whole stack or boxful of notebooks in that closet. Unless he threw them away, but I didn't think that was possible. Sam had told me the notebook Jack had brought to use against the Reids was months old. Only one way to find out if there were any notebooks lying around.

Damn. Did I have to break into Jack's house again? I'd gotten away with it once already. If Bobby Lee or anyone caught me, I could just say I was there to feed the cat. Oh, the cat. Sheesh. I really should do that. How many days could an animal survive without food or water? Definitely have to check on the cat. I'd tell Michael in the morning that I wanted to stop by Jack's to feed the cat, then I'd slip into the bedroom real quick and look in Jack's closet.

I'd decide later whether or not to tell Michael my plan to snoop. I felt a little twinge of guilt, but knowing Michael, I'm sure he wouldn't be crazy about contributing to me snooping. He seemed to've found it humorous that Brenda and I had done it, but I didn't think he'd want to be an accomplice.

The clock chimed twice. Eleven o'clock already. Time to turn in. I closed the website, turned off and unplugged the computer, and climbed into bed. I set the alarm clock for too early. Exactly one week ago this time, I was working with an hour to go on my shift. Dead on my feet and wishing the clowns in charge would hire someone else.

So, instead of having a job to go to tomorrow, I would be talking to the hospital administrator about house keys, Sam about the daily books, snooping in Jack's closet, and riding across the state to visit Abby in a strip club.

Gussie said she saw two people and two cars. Were they the same two people each time, but in two different cars? Four different people? Was this another *Murder on the Orient Express*? Except in that case, it was one murder weapon and several killers. Murder weapon. Add poison to the mix. Why was Jack stabbed *and* poisoned? And where was the knife?

Twenty-Three

The next morning I checked the online newspaper's job ads. Oh, well, maybe I'd have better luck with the larger Sunday edition. I showered and dressed, and because it was such a beautiful morning, I decided to walk to the hospital.

The automatic doors swooshed open and I walked over to the switchboard operator to ask for directions to the administrator's office. The woman at the desk made a phone call and told me where to go. Maybe that would be a good job for me. I'd get paid for telling people where to go. Cool.

I stepped into the elevator, pushed the button, and got off on the third floor. As soon as the door opened, the wonderful smells of bacon and coffee hit me. My stomach grumbled then stopped when the strong odor of Ben-Gay overpowered the pleasant aroma of breakfast.

Nurses and aides bustled, pushing elderly patients in wheelchairs and assisting those with walkers to a large room that obviously was the dining room. I'd ended up on the nursing home floor. One nurse stood behind a semicircle desk near the elevator watching the activity around her. The woman was huge, like an Amazon queen or a bouncer, and I went over to her. She towered over me.

"Excuse me, I'm looking for Mr. Jacobs's office."

"Oh, sure, he's—just a second, please," she said, left the desk, and walked over to the elevator. "Miss Pearl, time for breakfast. Please go on into the dining room with the others. Come on, dear, don't argue with me. It's time to eat."

I turned around to see who could possibly argue with this woman. Oh! That little old lady who gave Chris those flowers. What was her name? I didn't remember it being Pearl.

"I'm sorry about that," Amazon Queen said when she came back to the desk. "Mornings are pretty busy around here. Mr. Jacobs's office is down this hall, the last door on the right. I know he's in."

"Thanks so much," I said. "That lady you were just talking to. What's her name?"

"You mean Miss Pearl? She's a handful, that one. Sweet as pie when she's lucid, but oh boy, when she's confused…"

"Does she take walks around the neighborhood? I could've sworn I met her, but the name Pearl doesn't seem right. Maybe it's not her."

"That's what I mean about being a handful. She'll slip out without any of us seeing her. I've been after administration to get some kind of lock or passkey system on the elevator, but…" she said, shrugging her shoulders in a *what can you do?* way.

The name suddenly came to me. "Dottie! That's what she said her name was."

Amazon Queen paled, lowered her eyes, and then looked at me again. "Um, who did you say you were?"

That came out of left field. I frowned and answered, "I didn't. I live in the neighborhood and have a question for the administrator about my house. My husband bought it from the hospital."

"Oh. Like I said, his office is right down the hall. Have a nice day." She abruptly left me and walked into the dining room.

Alrighty then. That was strange. I walked down the hall and found Mr. Jacobs's office. The door was open and I introduced myself to the man behind the desk. He strode toward me with his hand outstretched and a big smile. Bobby Lee had been right. This man was certainly dressed for a day of golf.

"Mrs. Lewis, how nice to meet you! I'm Fred. What can I do for you?" He gestured for me to have a seat in one of the comfy chairs in front of his desk.

"Nice to meet you. I'm a little pressed for time, but I need to know if I have the only set of keys to my house."

He sat down behind his desk. "I'm sorry for your loss. A terrible tragedy. Your husband was a fine man."

"Thank you. Now, about the keys?" I explained about the fire and why I was asking.

"A fire? I'm so sorry." He cleared his throat. "I thought your husband had planned on replacing the front doors. I recall him telling me as much, or at the very least replacing the old doorknobs. You never did that?"

Damn. No, we hadn't. It seemed like a waste of money at the time when we had so many other expenses. We eventually were going to get new doors, hardware, kick plate, even a new mailbox. "I'm afraid not," I said.

"Well, there you go. To the best of my knowledge, you have the only keys. We turned over the ones we had." He glanced at his watch and stood. "Is there anything else I can do for you, Mrs. Lewis? I don't mean to be rude, but I'm needed in the dining room to say grace for our morning meal."

"No, and thank you," I said and rose from my chair. We shook hands and walked down the hall together.

The same little old lady who Amazon Queen had called Miss Pearl stood at the elevator waiting for the doors to open, a rolling shopping cart next to her. And with what looked like my Daffy Duck umbrella sticking out of it.

"Dottie!" I said.

"Oh, shit," Mr. Jacobs muttered. He blushed when he realized I'd heard him. "Oh, sorry, Mrs. Lewis. Um, would you mind waiting here a minute? I'll be right back." He approached the elderly woman and spoke softly to her. She nodded and grabbed hold of her little cart. He took her gently by the elbow and they went into the dining room.

Amazon Queen looked away when I saw her staring at me. What the hell was going on here? Something told me I'd be wasting my time and breath by asking her, so I waited for Mr. Jacobs, who emerged a few minutes later.

The smile on his face wasn't as big as when we'd met in his office. He ran his fingers through his hair and punched the elevator button. "We'll talk on the way down."

The doors opened and we stepped in. As soon as the doors closed and he pushed the first floor button, I turned to him and said, "Okay, what's the deal?"

He looked like he wanted to cry. Or run away. Be anywhere else but in that elevator with me. Whatever he had to tell me was big and unnerving the hell out of him.

"Okay, here's the situation. Pearl lived in your home when it was the nursing dorm." He glanced at me. "You do know the history?"

"Yes."

A huge sigh escaped his lips and he continued. "Pearl was the house mother and cook for years. The woman loves to cook. Still does. We let her lead a cooking class as one of the weekly activities here."

The man was starting to ramble. Time to rein him in.

"And ...?"

"And she refuses to hand over her keys."

"That's exactly what I just asked you, and you said no! She has keys to my house?! *My* house?"

"I'm afraid so. But, really, she's harmless. I'm sure she never gets in."

His expression told me he was sure of no such thing. And he knew that I knew. I kept quiet, remembering what Michael had said about letting the guilty speak. Eventually they gave themselves up by offering too much information in the uncomfortable silence.

"Okay, okay," he said.

Damn. It worked.

"Pearl is a very sweet lady who was suffering from the early stages of Alzheimer's at the time we sold the house to your husband. In order to not agitate her, we let her keep her keys. She put up quite a fuss every time we asked her for them."

"Why didn't you tell my husband all this?"

He rubbed his hand over his mouth again. "Your husband said you wanted to replace the doors, that it was going to be one of the first things done." The forlorn tone of his voice and the puppy dog expression got to me. I actually felt sorry for the man. He was right. Rob and I had planned on getting new doors. We had always meant to.

"Okay, Mr. Jacobs, I think I understand."

"Oh, Mrs. Lewis, thank you." He placed his hand on my arm. "Thank you so much."

"We—my husband and I—met Dottie once while we were taking a walk around the neighborhood. She was weeding her garden ... Oh. I guess it wasn't her garden?"

He shook his head slowly. "I'm afraid not. That house you're talking about is very close by. We usually catch Miss Pearl before she gets as far as your house."

The elevator doors opened. He followed me out into the hall. The big smile was back on his face. He reached into his back pocket and pulled put his wallet.

"Please allow me to pay for the damage to your kitchen. It's, um, quite possible that it was Pearl. She, uh, was unaccountable for awhile yesterday afternoon." He handed me a hundred-dollar bill. "Is that acceptable?"

"That'll be fine, Mr. Jacobs." I shook the hand he held out to me. I smiled and said, "Don't worry. I'll keep an eye out for Miss Pearl from now on. I should probably get your number so I can call you next time she's 'unaccountable.'"

He pulled a business card out of his wallet. "Yes, please do. And I'm so sorry again, Mrs. Lewis. Thank you for understanding. Bless you and have a good day."

I turned to leave, then thought of something. "Mr. Jacobs? When I met Miss Pearl she introduced herself as Dottie. Can you explain?"

This man would make a lousy poker player. His face practically crumbled. "It's somewhat embarrassing, Mrs. Lewis, and quite, um, unprofessional."

Now I was really curious. I tried the good old trick of keeping quiet again.

"I'm afraid Pearl heard one of the nurses call her that, and in her confused moments she thinks that's her nickname."

My lack of understanding rattled him.

He looked around and mumbled, "You know—dotty. As in dotty in the head?"

"Ah, I get it, Mr. Jacobs. And, yep, very unprofessional." I couldn't stop the smile from spreading across my face. "But in a fun sort of way. Maybe?"

I thought the man would wet himself he looked so relieved.

———

Michael and Chris were out on the patio when I got back to the house ten minutes later. Chris had packed an overnight bag and Michael tossed it in the backseat next to her, and we were off to Terri's house. I couldn't wait to tell Michael what I'd learned from Mr. Jacobs, but I didn't want to say anything in front of Chris. Instead we listened to her excited chatter about their plans, and going to church the next day with Heather and her mom. Michael seemed to sense something because he kept glancing over at me. It felt like it took forever to get to Terri's.

I waited in the car when we finally got there. Terri and Heather stepped out onto the porch after Michael rang the doorbell. I carefully watched for any signs between Michael and Terri. Once she did put her hand on his arm and I noticed he didn't pull away. I also noticed she kept it there for a little too long. Talk about aggressive. Sheesh. Some women.

I went over in my mind the conversation I'd had with Mr. Jacobs. I wanted to make sure I didn't forget to tell Michael any of it. What the hell was taking Michael so long? We had work to do and I wanted to get going. He and Terri were still on the porch, but the girls must've gone inside. At least she didn't have her paws all over him anymore, but this was ridiculous. Let them flirt on their own damn time.

I tapped the horn. Not being used to Michael's car, what should've been a friendly toot to nudge them along became a loud blast. Both of them turned and looked over at me, neither very happy. I wanted to crawl away and die.

Surprisingly, Michael didn't slam the car door when he got in. At least not as hard as Terri closed her front door. Too bad, but I wanted to get this show on the road. Still, that was a pretty loud horn and I'd manage to embarrass all three of us.

"Michael, I'm sorry. The horn ... I didn't think ... well, I'm sorry."

A curt nod. He continued staring straight ahead, knuckles white on the steering wheel. The news that our break-ins were fairly benign could wait for another time, I decided, keeping my silence.

I never thought I'd feel as happy about seeing the club as I did then. Since Michael and I hadn't arranged a meeting with Sam ahead of time, I wondered what kind of reception we'd receive. Sam wouldn't be expecting us, and I hoped he'd still let us in to look at the book.

Fortunately, Sam was in a cooperatively great mood, and let us in with no problem. I explained why we were there and he led us back to his office. Getting better at identifying country singers, I recognized Gretchen Wilson singing about how great it was to be a redneck woman. I couldn't disagree with good ole Gretchen. Coming up from Miami to this small north Florida town was like moving to the real south. We lived so close to the border it was like living in south Georgia. I'd learn to "yeehaw" like the best of 'em. My mother would die if she knew that.

Michael and I sat side by side at one of the tables outside Sam's office while he went and got the book pages for last Friday and Saturday—the last night I worked and the night Jack was murdered.

"I made copies of these for Bobby Lee, but I don't see any problem with showing them to you," Sam said. He handed me the pages and sat down across from us.

I'd worked at the club for so long the names were easily and quickly identified.

"What the hell are they doing here?"

180

I spun around. JC Nelson. And he definitely wasn't in a great mood or cooperative. Sam scrambled out of his chair and turned to face him. Just past JC, I saw Pam come out of her office. She leaned against the doorjamb, a smirk on her face.

"Sam? What the hell's going on?" JC pointed a finger at me. "Get her out of here. She has no business being in the club before we open."

Poor Sam sputtered, "Aw, c'mon, JC, she's—"

"No, I don't want to hear it, Sam." JC glared at me and Michael. "Neither one of you have any business in here. Especially coming in this time of day unannounced." He shoved by Sam and stormed into their shared office, slamming the door behind him. Shania Twain got cut off in mid-sentence when he apparently turned off the radio. Pam did an about-face back into her office, closing the door softly behind her.

I didn't know who I felt sorrier for. JC for being such an asshole, or Sam for bearing the brunt of his assholedness. I guess I leaned more toward Sam, then I became worried when I looked up at him. He hadn't moved an inch, but his body shook, and his face was an ugly shade of purple. I rushed to him.

"Sam?" I whispered, careful to not let JC hear me. "C'mon." I took his arm. Michael jumped up and took Sam's other arm. Together we led Sam up to the bar and helped him onto one of the stools. Michael stayed with him while I hurried into the kitchen for a glass of water.

Sam's color seemed to be returning to normal after a couple more minutes. He sipped at the water I'd handed him. The shaking also had stopped.

"Whew, you scared me there for a second, Sam. You okay now?"

"That sonofabitch." He eyed the closed door of his office. "That miserable, good for nothing mother—"

"Whoa, Sam, don't let yourself get all riled up again." Silently, I agreed with Sam and happily would join in on his rant, but his physical reaction scared me. I patted him gently on the back. "You okay now?"

"Yeah, thanks." He took another sip, then put the glass down on the bar. Still looking at the office door, he said, "It's been hell around here lately. They're making all these damn changes … making me work two jobs … You guys better go. If he comes out here—"

"Okay, Sam, not a problem. Maggie, let's go." Michael took hold of my elbow and started to lead me away. I glanced once more at Sam to make sure he was back to normal. He seemed to be, and I eagerly went with Michael.

"Can we just sit here a minute?" I asked once we got settled in Michael's car. "I don't care if JC does see us out here. He can't complain if we're outside."

"Sure," Michael said. "Besides, it'll give me the time I need to look over these."

I looked at him to see what he was talking about. "Oh, sheesh, Michael! Are you nuts? Those belong to the club. If JC knew—"

"Calm down." He shook the sheets of paper. "I'll just say I slipped them into my jacket pocket when it looked like Sam needed medical attention. 'I did it without even realizing. I'm sorry.' How's that sound?"

I'd never seen his devilish grin before. Cute in a bad-boy kind of way, and I wasn't sure how I felt about it. Then again, it was much better than the stormy look I'd gotten earlier.

"Let's just look at them real quick and we'll give them back to Sam later. JC will never know what happened." He handed me the pages and I immediately went to the last page for Friday night. I was right in remembering who was there at closing. And it looked like the same guys were there at closing the next night when Abby worked.

"Damn. This wasn't at all useful. The same people are in the same time every night." I looked out the windshield at the building where I'd worked these past five years. The place where I'd made friends. And enemies. The place I'd felt welcomed, secure, and, for the most part, happy. It was more than just a paycheck. It was a friggin' reason to get out of bed every day after Rob died.

"That didn't help at all, and now we've managed to piss off JC. And did you see the smug expression on Pam's face?"

"Why was Pam there?"

"She goes in every Saturday morning to go over the Ladies Auxiliary books and paperwork."

"But, I thought Diane was the treasurer," Michael said.

"Yeah, but as the president, Pam has to control everything. You should've seen her at last year's Ladies Aux bake sale. After another lady had arranged and organized who was bringing what, Pam went right behind her back and called them all over again."

"Funny how JC just appeared. I didn't hear him, did you?" Michael asked.

"No, and JC's usually the noisy one, not like Dick who suddenly seems to show up."

Turning my eyes away from the building, I repeated, "Damn, I can't believe all this is happening. Oh, hey, I forgot to ask you if we could stop by Jack's. It's been a couple days since the cat's been fed."

"Sure, it's close by, isn't it?"

I gave him directions and stared out the window as he drove the few minutes to Jack's rundown little house. When we got there I told him I'd be right back. I sprinted across the yard.

Happy to find the key still under the now dead plant, I got in with no problem. The cat made a brief appearance when it heard the sound of dry food hitting its plastic dish. I rinsed out, then refilled the water bowl and emptied the litter box. That out of the way, I needed to be quick and check Jack's closet. I peeked out the front window, saw Michael still sitting in the car. I rushed to Jack's room and swung open the closet door. A dozen or so shirts and slacks on hangers, a few pairs of shoes on the floor. The shelf above looked bare, but I had to make sure.

I dragged a chair from the kitchen, climbed up, and sure enough, the damn shelf was empty. I climbed down off the chair and brought it back to the kitchen. The notebooks had to be here somewhere. Sam once told me Jack had been writing in them since he'd known him, forty years or more. Plus, the notebook Jack had brought to the meeting when he accused the Reids of cheating on the daily book was old. I felt certain Jack never threw them out. And the one he was writing in more recently—what happened to it? I know he had it on Friday night, the last time I saw him. I closed my eyes. He had it on Saturday too when I picked up my paycheck.

I went back to close the closet door. The cat had jumped up on the bed and lay curled up on Jack's pillow, softly purring.

Under the bed. One hand on the bed, I knelt down and looked. Nothing. The cat stretched, got up, and came over. It brushed its cheek against my hand. I'd have to call the SPCA in the next day or so and let them do something about the cat. No way could I take it. I couldn't even get a grip on my own life let alone take care of something else. This was not the time.

Terrific. Here came today's tears. The cat nuzzled closer. I scratched its ear and let the crying take over. Then I jumped a foot in the air when a voice sounded just a few feet behind me.

"Did you look under the mattress?"

Michael stood in the doorway. I caught my breath and wiped the tears off my face as I scrambled to my feet.

"What?"

"I asked if you'd looked under the mattress. You were taking so long, I figured you were up to something." He came over to me. "You'd be surprised at how many people think that's a good hiding place. You take that corner." He gently shooed the cat off the bed and we lifted the mattress.

Sonofabitch. A curled up red spiral notebook. I grabbed it.

"Now, let's get out of here."

I locked the door, replaced the key, and followed Michael to the car, clutching the notebook the whole time.

"What are you going to do about the cat?" Michael asked.

I shrugged. "Probably call the SPCA. Do you want it?"

"Sorry, Chris is allergic. Why don't you keep it?"

Could I? I shook my head at the thought. I couldn't even get through a day without crying. I wondered what would happen to it if I did bring it to the pound. And that of course brought on another onslaught of tears. I closed my gritty eyes and turned my head toward my window so Michael wouldn't see.

Twenty-Four

"I need pie," I told Michael after we'd driven in silence for a few minutes.

"Pie? It's not even ten in the morning."

"I don't care. I want pie. Let's go to Sally's Diner. She's probably pulling fresh blueberry, or apple, or peach pies out of the oven right now."

"Sally's it is."

I hadn't opened my eyes, but I knew he was smiling at me. I heard it in his voice.

My favorite booth wasn't available and I resisted the urge to kick out the people who'd dared to sit in it. Saturday mornings must be the day for the whole town to be out and about. I'd never seen Sally's so busy. A scrawny busboy hopped from table to table, piling dirty dishes into his tub, wiping down the tables as he went. A waitress with bright green hair, plates stacked on her arms, served customers as fast as she could. She reminded me of myself twenty years ago. I checked out the bakery display case. Michael and I waited close to ten minutes for two stools to open up at the counter.

Sally herself waited on us. If Bobby Lee was the Michelin Man, Sally was Mrs. Michelin. Short strands of gray hair poked out from her black hairnet, and she pulled a pencil from behind one ear to take our order. She rattled off the daily specials and scowled when I asked for a slice of banana cream pie and coffee. Her frown deepened when Michael just ordered coffee.

"Have y'all eaten breakfast this morning?" Sally asked.

I shook my head and Michael told her he'd had toast.

"Nope." Sally shook her head and poised her pencil on the pad she held in her chubby hand. "That ain't breakfast. Now, what'll y'all have?"

Michael and I both ordered the egg special. She seemed happy with that and went off to place our order.

He chuckled and said, "Guess we're having breakfast."

I giggled. "Looks that way." I reached for the sugar and dumped some in my coffee mug. Michael drank his black. In a matter of minutes, Sally set two plates heaping with fried eggs, bacon, home fries, buttered toast, and unasked-for grits before each of us.

"That looks good," I said. "I didn't realize I was so hungry."

Sally smirked and topped off our coffee. I savored each and every bite. Michael and I ate and drank in silence. I scraped the last remaining egg off of my plate with a last bite of toast. Sally whizzed by, grabbed my plate, and plopped down a piece of banana cream pie.

"Now, you can have some of my pie. You earned it."

I groaned.

"Shoot, sugar, a little thing like you can do it." She winked at Michael and asked, "And what about you, handsome? Can I get you anything else? Or do you reckon she'll share some of that pie with you?"

"I can only hope, ma'am, I can only hope," he said.

"Ooh, manners. I like that—being called ma'am, and from a Yankee no less." She smiled at him. "Ain't that sweet? He blushes too." Sally moved on down to wait on another customer.

"How'd she know I'm a Yankee?"

"You're kidding, right?" I licked some whipped cream from my fork. "Say 'shit.'"

"Shit."

"Yankee. Say it with two syllables and you'll have a chance at becoming one of us."

"I'll work on it."

I laughed and felt a lot better than I had an hour earlier. "So, now what? Time to—"

"Shh," he answered.

Huh? Having learned a thing or two about him, I did as he said and shut up. Sure enough, I overheard Sally talking to another customer a few stools down from us.

"Well, I still say it's a shame. No matter how mean or ornery he was, he didn't deserve to go and get himself murdered like that."

The man Sally was talking to shook his head and said, "Of course he didn't deserve it, Sally. All I'm saying is I'm surprised it took someone so long. Hell, you know how he was."

"I knew Jack Hoffman all my life. It was only the last fifty years or so that he turned mean. And, hell, who can blame him after what happened?"

"Yeah, yeah, I guess you're right."

"I'm right about most things, Hank. Best you remember that. Now, you want more coffee?" Without waiting for his answer, Sally filled his cup then moved on down the counter.

"Interesting," I said quietly to Michael. "We need to ask her some questions."

He simply nodded.

"Well, call her down here." I was ready to jump up and flag her down myself. Sally knew Jack, according to her, all her life. Michael just sat there and sipped his coffee. God, the man was infuriating sometimes. How could he sit there so calmly, so damn quietly when the answer could be right in front of us?

"She'll be here in a minute. Be patient."

I growled at him and before I knew it, Sally stood before us. She refilled our mugs and handed Michael the check.

"Thank you, ma'am." He pulled his wallet out of his pocket and put a twenty on the counter. "Keep the change."

"Ooh, Yankee, you're gonna win my heart over yet. Manners and money." She looked at me, winked, and said, "Good combination in a man, sugar."

"I was wondering if you could help me," Michael said.

Sally leaned forward on the counter. "Yankee, I'd do just about anything for you right now. What is it?"

"I couldn't help but overhear you talking about Jack Hoffman. I take it you knew him pretty well?"

"Shoot, me and Jack practically grew up together. Course, he was a number of years older than me, but yeah, I knew him real well."

"I know this isn't any of my business, but what did you mean about after what happened to him? If you don't mind telling me, ma'am."

"Oh, it ain't no secret. Jack Hoffman was a good man. Fought in Korea when he was just seventeen. He brought Joon-Lee home with him, and they got married soon as he came home. Life seemed real good for them."

"Did they have any children?" I asked. "A daughter, maybe? Named Gayle. Or Abigail?"

Before she could answer, the telephone rang. "Be right back."

"Damn." I bounced on my stool and watched her walk away.

Under his breath, Michael muttered, "Patience, Maggie, patience. Here she comes."

"Damn kids. What's wrong with 'em nowadays? When I was young, I was grateful to have a job. Showed up on time every day, worked late when I needed to. Shoot."

"What happened?"

Sally waved her arm at the phone. "Oh, that dang night girl. Lazy as all get out. Calling off sick again. Second Saturday night in a row—can you imagine?"

"That's a shame. It's obvious how hard you work to keep this place going."

I wanted to kick him. The hell with all this. Let's get back to Jack and his story.

She looked at me and said, "I hear you're out of work, Maggie. You want a job? Night shift, five to five, weekends, Friday, Saturday, and Sunday nights, minimum wage, no benefits. All the food you can eat for free."

My mouth dropped open. "Waitressing here? I'd love that."

"Nope, I just hired a waitress for day shift, and my girl on nights has been with me for years. I'm looking for a cook."

"Oh." I wanted to kick something. "I can't cook."

She shook her head at me. "Damn kids."

I think she was referring to me.

"Shoot, I may have to stop being open twenty-four hours if this keeps up. No way I can work another double like I did last weekend. Too hard on this old woman. Not to mention how I almost missed church." She shook her head again. "And the Lord always comes first."

"Amen."

"You making fun of me, Yankee?"

"No, ma'am, not at all. Of course not," Michael stammered out the words.

I wondered if *he* felt like a damn kid now. I planned on keeping my mouth shut.

"Least it wasn't a total waste. I got some good cleaning done Saturday night in between customers."

"Business good on Saturday nights?" he asked.

"I reckon. Mostly drunks, but they didn't stay long once they seen I was working. I won't put up with rowdiness and they all know it. Still, I was glad to see JC was close by if I needed a man to help me out."

"JC?"

Sally nodded her head toward the front of the restaurant. "Now, I know you know who I'm talking about, sugar. I don't reckon his store was open, but he was in there that night."

Michael asked, "Saturday night? What time?"

"Since it was after all the bars closed, I suppose I should say Sunday morning. About two thirty or so. I seen the lights go out about ten, fifteen minutes later. No idea what the man was doing there that time of night, but it's his store and I reckon I don't have a say in the matter."

"Have you ever seen him in his store that late before?"

"Now, Yankee, I already said I don't usually work nights, so what makes you think I'd know a thing like that? Shoot." She turned to me and said, "Okay, sugar, what were you asking about Jack?"

"Did he have a daughter named Gayle?" I wanted to keep my questions short to lessen any chances of being scolded. She was reminding me of somebody.

"Naw, Jack and Joon, they had a little boy." She pursed her lips and seemed deep in thought. "Can't rightly remember the child's name. Joon-Lee up and left after what happened. Nearly broke the man's heart. Terrible thing. He never was the same after that."

"That's so sad. Why'd she leave?"

"Oh, that's right, you're new here." Sally winked at Michael and said, "You too. Well, seeing as how it was all over the news way back then, it won't hurt to tell y'all now. Wait. It just came to me. The child's name was Daryl. Yeah, that's it." She tapped the side of her head with an index finger. "Sharp as a tack, this old mind of mine. Watching *Jeopardy!* every night with my sister keeps us both sharp. Course after *Jeopardy*'s over, there ain't much worth watching. Thank goodness for TV Land and good old wholesome television. Oh, shoot, I'll have to call and tell her I won't be home tonight. Damn kids." She looked from us to the people waiting for seats, then shuffled over to the phone, refilling coffee mugs along the way.

"Do you think we'll ever find out what happened to Jack and his wife? What's the terrible thing that happened?" I asked Michael. "Hey, you have a pen? I want to see something." I pulled a napkin out of the dispenser and wrote down *Gayle* and then *Daryl*. Yeah, it was easy to see how Brenda and I had come up with Gayle. Damn. So much for my theory of Abby being short for Abigail. Not that it made too much sense to me now, considering it would've had to've been Abigayle. Whatever. This detective work wasn't easy. I crumpled up the napkin and handed the pen back to Michael.

He glanced at his watch and said, "We'd better get going. I still have to pack a bag. How about you? Are you ready?" He slid off his stool. I reluctantly followed him. We waved at Sally on our way out and Michael said, "Thank you, ma'am, for the great food and the hospitality, and have a great day."

"They're all great days, Yankee, Lord willing."

"What were you writing down?" Michael asked once we got in the car. I explained about the Daryl/Gayle idea.

"Okay, but didn't you say Abby's in her late twenties, early thirties?" He pulled out into the steady stream of downtown traffic. "Even if Jack did have a daughter, Abby would be too young."

"I know, but so many other pieces seemed to fall in place. I wanted to make it fit. It's stupid now, but after I saw that photo of Jack with a

Korean woman and baby, I thought maybe the baby was Abby. Jack complained his beer tasted bitter, and the way she left so suddenly made me suspicious of her." Grateful Michael wasn't laughing at me, I went on. "I thought maybe she'd come back to town, looking for her father. Maybe she found him, and he rejected her, so she killed him. Or maybe she hated him all these years and tracked him down. It was the way Pam had said a woman could've killed Jack, that's what made me start wondering all that about Abby. Too bad Jack had a son. I wouldn't have wasted all that time thinking along those lines."

At that Michael smiled. "No time wasted. It's good to brainstorm, to play 'what if.' The way you kept thinking 'maybe this or maybe that' is good. Same as what if. What if Jack's kid, all grown up now, came back to kill him? What if Jack knew something about someone and that person killed him? What if Jack owed somebody money and that person murdered him because he wouldn't pay or couldn't? See? You were headed in the right direction."

"Maybe Abby was Jack's granddaughter? That could work. Couldn't it?" I groaned. "Sheesh, this is so hard. Are we ever going to get on the right track?"

"We will, Maggie." He cleared his throat. "Sure as shee-it, we will."

"What the hell?"

"I'm practicing. Didn't that sound better?"

"Damn Yankee." It felt good to laugh. Too bad it didn't last long. We turned the corner to the house and saw one of North DeSoto's finest cruisers, lights flashing, parked near my driveway.

Bobby Lee waddled over to us as we rushed toward the driveway. "Now, little lady, just hold on there." He put his arm out blocking me going any farther. I looked over his shoulder and couldn't see anything wrong. No smoke, no fire, nothing. I glared at him. If he called me little lady one more time, I was going to slug him.

"What's happened, Bobby Lee? Is someone hurt? Is my house okay?"

"No one's hurt, and your house is fine. And, uh, I hope your car insurance is up to date, little lady."

Michael grabbed my arm as I was swinging it back to belt Bobby Lee.

Twenty-Five

"Not a good idea," Michael said in my ear. He held a firm grip on my arm, making sure I didn't assault the chief of police. Sure way to visit his holding cell.

"I'm sorry, Bobby Lee. You know I never would've really hit you."

He looked at me as though he knew no such thing. I tried a smile, and he seemed to mellow a bit even as he kept both eyes on my hands.

"Really, I'm sorry. You know the last couple of days have been pretty rough for me."

"Oh, that's all right, little lady."

Michael grabbed my other arm and held on tight. Smart man.

"Can you please tell me what's going on?" *Before I completely lose my mind, you stupid idiotic moron of a man,* I wanted to add.

"Seems there was some trouble at your place a little while ago. Neighbor called it in." He turned, gestured with a nod for us to follow him to my house. "Some petty vandalism, not too much real damage."

"What happened? Who called it in?" My words rushed out in one breath.

"More of a nuisance, I think." Bobby Lee pointed to a man wearing a jogging suit standing nearby talking to another uniformed cop. Sheesh. Looked like the whole North DeSoto police force was out. "He's the one who called it in."

I vaguely recognized the man. I looked at him carefully. Was he simply a jogger, or something more sinister? Had he been casing the joint?

I told myself to get a grip. The man was an ordinary guy out running. I had seen him plenty of times before in the neighborhood.

Almost afraid to ask, I turned to the police chief. "What about my car? You said something about my car."

He glanced at my arms, then at Michael. "It ain't pretty, so be prepared."

Michael still held one of my arms, and with my legs feeling like lead, we walked around to the driveway.

Windshield wipers twisted, bent at angles. Two slashed tires. A long scratch the length of the car. My poor little trusty, paid-for car.

Good thing Michael was still holding onto me because my legs buckled. He led me to the patio table and into one of the chairs, Bobby Lee not too far behind. Michael sat next to me holding my hand, but for comfort now more than restraint. I started to speak and the lump in my throat stopped me. I tried again, and this time managed a weak little squeak, "Who? Why?"

"Oh, I reckon it was just a couple of boys out looking for something to do," he answered. "Y'all know how these good ole boys can be."

"You really think that, Chief?" Michael asked. "This was some kind of random act?"

"Well, sure. We see this a lot. Boys out driving around, smashing mailboxes with their bats. Happens all the time. This here's a bit different, but still some harmless fun."

That did it. I sprang from the chair and got as close to Bobby Lee as I could stand. "Harmless fun? Good ole boys? Petty vandalism? Are you nuts?"

He backed away several steps. "Now, I didn't mean it like that. Of course, it's not harmless. Or fun for the owner. But now, Maggie, it's not like someone cut your brake lines or rigged the thing to explode. Not like someone set out to hurt you. Car sitting out like this, you're lucky the damage was visible to a passerby. You've had quite the run of bad luck as of late, little lady. Perhaps you ought to be more careful."

A chill raced up my spine, and the fear made me angry. I closed in on him. "What are you going to do about this? Or are you going to screw this up just like my husband's murder investigation?"

He reached for his handcuffs on his left side, and his gun on the other.

Michael suddenly appeared at my side. "Maggie, why don't you go upstairs and pack? I'll take care of things down here. Okay?" He put his arm around me and pulled me away. "I'll meet you on the front porch in fifteen minutes. We need to get on the road soon."

The road. Yes. "Okay." I gave Bobby Lee one last dirty look for good measure and walked away. By the time I got to my bedroom, I'd calmed down a bit. I'd let Michael handle the situation downstairs while I focused on packing. First things first. Prioritize.

What did one wear to a strip club? Particularly a short, middle-aged, slightly chunky woman. Boas and spandex immediately came to mind. Spiked heels? Low-cut top with a mini skirt? Push-up bra? Hell, I wasn't performing, and I felt pretty sure that clean jeans and a nice

197

blouse would do. Good thing too, considering I had none of the other items in my wardrobe. Deciding on sleepwear was easy. I pulled one of Rob's T-shirts out of the drawer along with a pair of socks and tossed them into the bag. Toiletries out of the bathroom and I was ready.

Michael had gassed up his car, mapped out the directions ahead of time, and we were all set to go. He said he called a local mechanic and my car would be towed later in the day.

I thought about what Bobby Lee had said about brake lines and explosions. What was to stop someone doing those things once I had the car back? What was to stop someone from doing something else to hurt me? Someone planted that scrunchie to frame me, and I hadn't been excessively sneaky about all the questions I was asking.

We had a six-hour drive ahead of us, and I had my pen, legal pad, and Jack's notebook stacked in my lap. Normally, I hate reading while riding because it's too jiggly, but I couldn't just stare out the window for such a long stretch of time and I truthfully couldn't wait to get started on Jack's notebook.

I flipped it open to the first page. It read like a diary, a journal of sorts. Dated November 20, 1962. Man, this was a really old one. Jack had written in pen, and his handwriting was surprisingly legible. I soon got lost in the words in front of me.

> Joon left today. Can't blame her. We tried to make things work, but we both knew it was hopeless. Just a matter of time before she hated me enough she couldn't stand the sight of me anymore. She said she didn't really hate me, but how could she not after what I did? It's best this way. Joon said there were too many days she'd forget and go into his room to wake him up. Then she'd remember and it hurt all over again. Some days the hurt didn't go away at all. She couldn't stand the thought of him not being here for Thanksgiving.

Maybe she wouldn't have left if I told her more. If I talked more. All those times she wanted to, but I couldn't. All those nights of her laying there crying. Then sleeping in his room. Boxing up his stuff. Clothes. Toys. All those damned stuffed animals. Too much and too soon. Should have let her pack them away for when she was ready.

I lay the notebook facedown in my lap, unable to read anymore. I knew about packing up stuff, about having to be ready to do that task. Two years later, and besides a few of his shirts, I still had all of Rob's belongings in boxes. If I hadn't moved upstairs, I probably wouldn't have touched any of it.

"Well?" Michael asked. "Anything interesting in there?"

I nodded, not trusting my voice. I turned the notebook over and resumed reading.

Joon said to not look for her. Divorce papers will be coming in the mail soon. For me to look out for them, sign and mail them to the name on the envelope. She doesn't want anything, nothing left for her here. Maybe she would've stayed

Dec. 3, 1962

Packed up all of the boy's stuff, hauled them down to the center.

Dec. 4, 1962

Quiet in the house. Decided to keep writing this down, maybe a letter to Joon would help. No divorce papers yet.

Dec. 8, 1962

Papers came today.

Dec. 12, 1962

Signed the papers, sent them back.

Dec. 13, 1962

The boy would've been 4 tomorrow.

Dec. 14, 1962

   Lost my job. Fight at work.

Man, this was depressing. Let's see—in 1962, Jack would've been in his mid- to late twenties. To've lost his son and then his wife ... that was a lot to happen to a young man. I closed the notebook, put it under my legal pad and paperback.

"Well?" Michael asked again.

I filled him in on what I'd read so far.

"Wow," he said, "that's rough. Nothing about the war in there?"

"No. At least not yet. Jack was like a lot of the guys—didn't talk about his time. They'd joked around, stuff about the Army being better then the Marines, or whatever, but nothing real serious."

"What did they talk about? I mean from what you've said, it was the same people day after day, right?"

"Yeah. It's funny because of the changes since I've worked there. When I started we opened at ten in the morning and closed at midnight. A couple of years ago, they started opening at five. Made the old farts unhappy, but the powers that be said they were losing money, so the hours were changed."

"What do you mean by old farts?"

"The World War II and Korean vets. They'd plan their whole days around coming in. These guys are retired now, and for the most part their wives were happy to get them out of the house for awhile." I chuckled at the memory. "I had a sign that said 'VFW: Adult Daycare Center.' The guys loved it, but Dick took it down. Asshole."

"Dick's a real stickler for rules, isn't he?"

I nodded. "I'll say. Well, for most things. He'll make exceptions if it benefits the club. He'll break or bend the rules if it's important enough to him. Like, Pete for example. He wasn't in the military, but he'll step up and fill in when needed. They've needed him to be a part of the

Honor Guard for funerals and parades. Like with Jack's funeral a couple of days ago."

"Doesn't he stand out? Since he's not in uniform?"

"No, not really. He— Whoa. I wonder if that's what's been bugging me about Sam. Brenda met him on Thursday. Could he be lying about having been in the military? Remember that website I told you about? Could Sam be the one with the fake medals?"

Twenty-Six

"Have you ever seen Sam's medals?" Michael asked. He'd just pulled onto I-10, the route we'd be on for most of the trip.

"Yeah, but I've never paid attention to them. Kevin, Dick, JC, all those guys have medals and ribbons. I don't know what they all stand for. Brenda was interested because her brother's pretty high up in the Army. A lieutenant colonel or something."

"What about the guys from the club? Have they ever said what rank they were?"

"Oh, hell, I'm sure they have at one time or another, but I don't remember. Really, other than the same couple stories, they didn't talk that much about their time in the military. They talked about their wives, hunting, and sports. Oh, and recipes. And how much better life was years ago. These are the old farts

I'm talking about. Kevin's closer to my age and still works, so he doesn't have that in common with Dick and Sam. Of course, JC still works, but he and Dick are really tight even though Dick's like fifteen years older."

"Are their wives friends? "

"Pam and Diane?" I snorted. "They spend time together because they have to. Between their being officers of the Ladies Auxiliary and their husband's friendship, they're pretty much forced together. I don't think they have much in common beyond the VFW. And of course their kids. Darlene Reid married Scott Nelson." Mentioning Scott made me think of Jack, and how Scott was close to the same age as Jack was in 1962. Compared to Jack then, Scott had it good now.

"How are Pam and Diane different?" he asked.

"Pam has money, Diane wants money, for starters. Pam's assertive, Diane isn't. Pam has a great sense of fashion, Diane's totally clueless." I thought about it some more. The way Pam stands up to JC, and how Diane was mousey with Dick. JC and Dick weren't much alike, either, come to think of it. Maybe opposites do attract. I couldn't imagine Pam and Dick together—both are too forceful.

Except for JC's display earlier, he doesn't lose his temper often. He's more annoying in a nasally, whiny way. Dick's aggressive, but quiet. I remembered how I'd suddenly run into him the other day.

"I just thought of something," I told Michael. "When I was in the club talking to Sam, Dick all of a sudden showed up. Never heard him come in the back door. It was Monday. The beer delivery guy was there. Dick must've come in while the door was still open."

"So?"

"I'm wondering how long Dick had been standing there. Damn. He was obviously eavesdropping on our conversation. I wish I could remember what Sam and I were talking about at the time."

"Don't push it. Maybe you'll remember later if you don't think about it too much."

"Kind of like what's been bugging me about Sam. Sheesh. So frustrating that I can't think what it could be." Unless it was the medals, but that didn't make sense because Sam didn't share his war experiences. What type of person would buy and wear fake medals? But Brenda had sent me that e-mail, so she must be on to something.

My head was starting to ache. I rubbed my temples and then stretched out my arms.

Michael looked at me. "You okay?"

"Yeah. I'm glad I ate that big breakfast, but now I'm sleepy." I yawned. "Sorry."

"Plus you were up earlier than usual this morning. Go ahead and take a nap. I don't mind."

"No, I'm okay. I want to make good use of our time."

"Okay. What else can you tell me about the Reids or the Nelsons? I'm curious about what you said about Pam having money. Does she come from a wealthy family? I can't imagine their hardware store making them rich."

"No, not at all. JC was constantly whining when Lowe's came to town. From the way he talks, they're just getting by. And Pam grew up poor, lower-middle class. She talks about her past, her history of drug abuse on her lecture tours."

"Lecture tours? Pam actually goes on tours? Where? Who invites her?"

"That's what she calls them." I shrugged. "And I think she invites herself. She goes to different schools in Clay and Duval Counties. Junior high and high schools. Pam even had a support group kind of thing going on for high school kids with known drug problems. But it got to be too much for her, so she stopped. Typical of the gossip mongers at the club, a rumor went around that she'd been kicked out because she was really dealing drugs."

"Does she get paid for these lectures?"

"She might. It would explain where she gets the money for her clothes. She sure doesn't shop at Wal-Mart like I do. And manicures—she goes to Jacksonville twice a month to get her nails done. Can you imagine?" I looked down at my short fingers and unpolished nails. "While I wouldn't mind an occasional manicure, I sure wouldn't throw away hard-earned money on one."

I laughed and continued, "Oh, that reminds me of Diane. I remember how she'd buy gambling tickets on the sly. Dick would be sitting at a table a few feet away, and Diane would come up to the bar, slide a twenty toward me, and I'd pass the tickets to her without him seeing. Diane never won much, and anything she did win, she put back in and lost."

"And he never caught on?"

"Diane's very sneaky when it comes to Dick, but there was one time she got caught. I clean her house once a week and she doesn't want Dick to know. He says it's her job as the wife." I shuddered. *The wife*. I hated that expression. It was almost as bad as *the old lady*. "Anyway, one time her check bounced and the bank contacted Dick. He was royally pissed. Gave her hell for 'throwing his hard-earned money away on something she should do herself.' From then on Diane paid me in cash."

"She has guts. What if he found out?"

"I think she cares more about keeping up with Pam than pissing off Dick. Although there was talk when Diane was gone for a few days after that happened. All sorts of speculation and rumors."

Michael asked, "Such as?"

"Somehow word got out about the bounced check. They all thought it too much of a coincidence when Diane suddenly went to visit her mother in Gainesville. People were saying Dick had roughed her up and she was laying low at home until the bruises cleared up."

"Is there a history of abuse between them?"

My mind flashed to Tuesday night at the club when Dick grabbed Diane's arm and yanked her away from talking to me. And how she'd been wearing long sleeves lately. I told Michael what I was thinking.

"So you think she's covering up bruises?"

"Could be." I shook my head. "No, wait a minute. That's not right. Diane wore long sleeves the day *before* Dick pulled her arm. Oh, hell, I don't know. Unless she did something else to piss him off. I know he left her to empty their car trunk, the rotten bastard, so maybe they'd had a fight that day. Would've been Monday."

"The same day you think Dick was eavesdropping on you and Sam?"

"Yeah." I closed my eyes and replayed the conversation that day with Sam. He'd given me a cup of coffee, asked if Jack's notebook was in the truck, if the police thought it could be a robbery. I told him that Bobby Lee said only my scrunchie was found. I shared what I remembered with Michael.

"Doesn't sound like much to me. And Dick said nothing to you?"

"Nope. Not even a greeting. But that's not unusual for him." I picked up my legal pad and flipped through my notes. "I keep going back to what Gussie said about two people and two cars. And how she didn't see Sam leave."

"I wouldn't think she stands there all day and night looking out her window. Did she say if Sam's truck was there?"

"I didn't ask, but Sam has a reserved spot on the other side of the parking lot. I'm pretty sure Gussie wouldn't be able to see it from her window." I didn't feel like looking through more of my notes, so I pulled Jack's notebook from my stack. I flipped open to the page I'd been reading.

Dec. 18, 1962

Spent last three days drunk. Joined a vets club near here. Good guys. Talked to one guy who has the same problem as me. Said I should take notes of everything. It's helping him remember. Doctors don't know what's wrong with him. He said his dreams are bad, real bad. Hard to get through most days. Forgets shit all the time. I still haven't told him about Daryl. Don't know if I will. But I am going to start keeping track, writing shit down, giving myself reminders.

Dec. 19, 1962

Back to work. Told the boss my story, said he'd give me another shot but to watch myself. VFW is a good place, good guys. They know. They just do.

Dec. 20, 1962

Writing in here is helping. I got notes all over the place. Haven't been forgetting as much, but I still keep all the damn lights on. Joon used to hate that. Dreams still bad.

Dec. 21, 1962

Not sleeping. Got to be at work in 2 hours.

"Michael, do you know anything about post-traumatic stress disorder? I think Jack may've had it back in 1962." I read the last page aloud to him. "See what I mean?"

"I know a little. Of course, they didn't have a name for it back then. PTSD began to become known in the 1980s, if I'm remembering right from what I read. It was called shell shock or battle fatigue for the World War I vets. From the little bit you just read to me, sure sounds like he suffered from it."

"Poor guy. I'm glad he at least had the VFW back then." I went back to reading.

The next thing I knew I felt the car slowing down. Michael was pulling off of the interstate.

"Oh, I'm sorry. I didn't mean to fall asleep."

"You needed a nap, don't worry about it. We should be at the hotel in a half hour."

"Good." The dashboard clock read 5:40. I retrieved Jack's notebook from where it had slid to the floor at my feet.

Dec. 22, 1962

> *Guy at the VFW told me about a place he goes to. Invited me to tag along. Said it might help. Told him I'd think about it. Not ready, if I ever am ready to tell him or anyone about what happened to Daryl. He thinks I'm just not talking about the bad war stuff. He told me it helps him to keep a diary, just write down whatever shit he doesn't want to talk about. I told him I already do that. Some shit is nobody's business. And what I did to Daryl isn't anybody's business.*

Twenty-Seven

"Okay, here it is," Michael said and swung into the Holiday Inn parking lot. Just after six o'clock, it was dusk. I wished we had arrived earlier in time to see the sun set over the Gulf. "I made reservations under my name. Connecting rooms."

I remembered Diane's remark about connecting bedrooms. This time I blushed and I grabbed my bag and followed him into the hotel. Our rooms weren't ready for some damn reason, so we went into the lounge to wait.

The only customers in the place, we had no trouble getting seats at the bar and the bartender, a pretty young thing named Stephanie according to her name tag, waited on us immediately.

As soon as we got our sodas, Michael's cell phone rang. Stephanie smiled and pointed to a sign behind her. No Cell Phones At the Bar.

Good idea. I should put one of those up behind my bar.

Damn. Where had that thought come from? I had no bar, no job. Hell, I was teetering on having no life.

I sipped my soda while I waited for Michael to return. The lounge was really nice. A little too dark for my taste, but the stools were comfortable and good music from the '70s played in the background. The bar had a back mirror just like my bar. *Let it go, Maggie, let it go.* Because it was a real bar, there were dozens of different liquor bottles lined up on the shelves. Tequila, Absolut, Grey Goose. The officers at the club were always adamant about keeping it simple—just cheaper stuff and no fancy drinks. That made me think of Abby and the first time I'd met her.

"That was Chris," Michael said as he sat down. "Everything's fine, she called to say hi."

"Good." I looked at the rows of bottles again. I finally realized what had been bugging me in the back of my mind and told Michael. "I knew something about the bar looked wrong. Sam never would've lined the bottles up like that, so why were they set up that way?"

"Because he lied to us and to the police."

Sadly, I nodded.

"Mr. Bradley, your rooms are ready." The young man from the front desk stood behind us. "Sorry for the delay. My manager says to give these to you," he said handing Michael two business-sized cards. "Dinner for two, our compliments."

Cool. Now I could pig out without worrying about how much it cost. Sheesh. Here I was thinking about food when I just figured out Sam's lie. We grabbed our bags and headed up to our rooms. I dropped my bag on the bed, unlocked the deadbolt on my connecting door, and knocked on Michael's side.

When he opened the door, I said, "Let's talk some more. Your room or mine?"

"Come on in," he said and moved aside to let me in.

Our rooms were identical, decorated in the standard hotel chain motif. Light aqua walls, floral bedspreads, paintings of beach scenes hanging on the walls. I'd brought my legal pad with me and dropped it on the round table by the window, then sat down.

"Give me a minute, I'll be right there." He walked back over to his bed and started unpacking. He lifted a shirt out of his bag, walked over to the tiny closet, and hung it up. I watched as he did this two more times with a pair of slacks, then a pair of shoes. Back and forth from the bed to the closet. Couldn't he carry more than one thing at a time? Sheesh. Tapping my fingers on the table, I hoped when he went into the bathroom with his shaving kit, he'd be about done. The shower curtain rattled and I pictured him putting his shampoo and his own bar of soap away. He came back out to his bag, pulled out briefs, socks, and a T-shirt and carefully placed them in the top drawer of the dresser.

I knew enough to wait until he'd completely finished. Sure enough, after he zipped up the bag and put it on the floor of the closet, he came over to the table.

"All set?" he asked and he sat down across from me.

I nodded. "Ready if you are." Thank God, finally. I got my pencil and legal pad ready to take notes while we talked.

"Now, back to Sam. It'd been bugging me that something was different about the liquor bottles. When Sam trained me, he was very specific on how the bottles were lined up on the shelves, so whoever was working could just grab the bottle needed. He also wanted them wiped clean every night. When I talked to Sam on Monday, the same day as the beer delivery, he almost knocked over a bottle. That's when I noticed the bottles seemed dusty, like they hadn't been cleaned in a couple days. It was the same day the bar itself felt sticky."

"Monday. The same day you saw Dick and Diane at the club."

"That's right. And it was on Sunday, the day I was 'arrested' that I first noticed the bottles looked different. They weren't lined up properly. The bottle of Jack Daniels was in the wrong place on the shelf. So much was going on, and I wanted to focus on the guys in the back of the room, that it didn't click until now."

"So, Sam either didn't train Abby as well as he did you, or he didn't close that night. And if he didn't, who did?"

"And why lie about it? Sam told Bobby Lee that he had closed, but he had to have left early. That would explain Gussie not seeing him come out with Pete and Abby. It's not a big deal if he asked an officer to lock up because they have security codes, but if he let Pete do it … yeah, that's serious. But, according to JC and Dick, they both left at eleven thirty. And Kevin—another officer—had left around the same time. So, all the officers were gone before closing that night."

Michael asked, "If Sam gave Pete his code, that's a big deal?"

"Oh, yeah, it'd be a very big deal. Sam could get into a lot of trouble," I said. "He could lose his job and even be suspended from the club. Sam's been a member of the VFW for over forty years. I don't think he could handle being kicked out."

"If Sam lied, then it makes sense that Pete closed, using Sam's code. I assume each officer and bartender has their own code?"

"Yeah, we do. Sam keeps a list of them in his office. Anyone could get to that list. Which would explain why it looked like I had been there at three thirty that morning. Someone used my code to set me up for Jack's murder."

"That and the scrunchie in Jack's truck," he said.

"Pretty lame, don't you think?"

"Explains why Chief Lee never arrested you. Maybe he actually does know what he's doing." He blinked his big brown eyes at me. "But, getting back to Sam—since Jack always wrote down any infractions, wouldn't Sam be worried? I mean, Jack would've known Sam left Pete to lock up."

"That part doesn't make sense. Unless Sam bribed him? Maybe gave him a year's supply of beer chips? That'd keep Jack quiet." But I couldn't see Sam doing that. First of all, we don't have that many beer chips, and I would've been suspicious. Wonder what excuse Sam would've come up with to explain why Jack Hoffman suddenly had all those beer chips.

I didn't want to believe it. Not of Sam. No way was he the killer. "We're on the wrong track. We have to be, Michael."

He shrugged. "I know you hate to believe it—so do I—but it does make sense."

"Yeah, but, c'mon. Sam? He's the Pillsbury Dough Boy. Sam wouldn't harm a fly."

Michael stood up and stretched. "I'm hungry. Let's go eat downstairs and we'll talk more. Okay?" He checked his pocket to make sure he had the meal cards.

I wanted to stay put, but he was in charge—well, the one with the car keys anyway. Plus he had the free food cards, so I went.

After we'd ordered and I was sipping another soda, I said, "No way in hell do I believe Sam killed Jack. I do believe he lied about closing that night, but that's as far as I'm willing to go."

He pulled a pen and a small notebook out of his shirt pocket. "Okay. Let's make a list of questions we want to ask Abby tonight."

"Abby'll be able to tell us whether or not Sam closed with her Saturday night. She can let us know if it was Pete, or even someone else. Also, who all was there that night at closing time?" I sighed and made a face. "Unfortunately, she was only there the one night, so she may not know people—who's who."

Michael shook his head. "Don't think that'll be a problem. You can just describe people to her. Pam, Diane, all of them are easy to distinguish."

"True."

Michael moved his pen and notebook aside when the waitress delivered our meals.

I looked at his plate and immediately wished I'd ordered that instead of what was in front of me. Feeling bold, I took a forkful of his pasta, making sure I'd also stabbed a shrimp with it. Delicious. I dug into my own stuffed flounder.

"Chris told me a joke when she called earlier. Want to hear it?"

"Sure," I mumbled, my mouth full.

"It's a knock-knock joke." He waited for me to stop chewing. "You ready?"

"Yep, go ahead."

He leaned closer. "Okay. You start it."

"Knock-knock."

"Who's there?" he said.

I opened my mouth, then closed it.

Michael burst out laughing at my confusion.

"Smartass," I said and joined in the laughter. "I'd tell you one of my jokes, but they're all dirty." I thought back to some of the good, funny times while working at the club. I hoped my next job would be somewhere I could be myself and not get in trouble for it. Smartass and all. I'd think about that later.

"You okay, Maggie?"

"Yeah, why?"

"You were laughing, then smiling, then a sad little look came over you."

"Oh, I'm fine," I said, and I told him about what I'd been thinking. "Once this is all over, I can concentrate on finding a job. I'm not worried. Not too much anyway." Thankfully my bills for the month were caught up. I'd deal with April when it arrived. Only a week away, but I'd deal with it somehow. Too bad I was a lousy cook or I could take Sally up on her job offer.

"Good. Do you want dessert? I'm just having coffee."

"Coffee sounds good to me too. I'll need to stay awake when we go see Abby. I've gotten into the habit of going to bed earlier." Just one week ago, I'd spent my one night off with a bag of popcorn and a novel. Good times, oh yeah. Tonight was band night, and I wondered how well Sam would handle it. Then he'd turn around and have to be back in the morning to have the Sunday brunch.

"What should we expect tonight, Michael? Any ideas?" Since there weren't any other pictures on the website, I didn't have much to go on. I pictured a real dive, the kind of place I'd be afraid of sitting down in. Oh, God, I prayed I wouldn't have to use a restroom. I'd have one more cup of coffee, then make sure it was all gone before we left.

"I did some checking with the local department—police department—and was told there's never been any trouble."

"So, it's not a strip joint?"

Michael shook his head. "According to the authorities, it's a nice, upscale place. And they would know."

Terrific. I'd packed jeans and a simple blouse. Could be I'd be underdressed. Maybe not as much as some of the other women, but still.

Twenty-Eight

As it turned out, my attire fit in fine. And I was glad to see I wasn't the only woman customer in the place. Groups of men and many couples were seated at the bar and at tables on the main floor.

A large stage, complete with two cages on either side of a brass pole, jutted out into the audience section. Michael and I found a table and sat down. A cocktail waitress clad in a French maid outfit, very sexy and alluring, welcomed us and took our drink orders.

I relaxed immediately. No need to be all leery or afraid or apprehensive. I'd even be comfortable using the restroom if I had to.

The waitress returned with our drinks. Michael paid her—including a nice, hefty tip, I was glad to see—and asked, "We're looking for Abby Quon. Is she working tonight?"

"She sure is. She's on at nine, about an hour from now. Would you like me to tell her you're here?" The waitress looked from Michael to me, then back to him. "Are y'all friends of hers?"

"I worked with her for a while," I answered. "At the same club."

She eyed me up and down. "Oh?"

So I didn't clarify it wasn't at a men's club. Let her think what she wanted.

Michael said, "We're Michael and Maggie. Any chance you could ask her to stop by our table before or after her dance?"

"Sure, I can. Be happy to." And she sauntered off. I watched her move to another table.

"Hell, I could look like that if I wanted to."

Michael raised one eyebrow.

"I could. If I were twenty-five years younger. And eight inches taller and about forty pounds lighter. Actually, if I was that tall, I wouldn't have to lose weight."

He smiled and shook his head at me.

I grinned back. "Hey, can you teach me how to do that trick with the one eyebrow? I've always thought it was so cool that some people can do that."

"Takes years and years of practice."

"Can you do this?" I leaned closer and rolled my tongue.

"Impressive. I never could do that."

"We make quite a pair," I said, leaning back in my chair. "Your eyebrow and my tongue."

He turned red. Score! It was fun making him, a grown man, blush.

"Hi, do I know you two?"

I looked up at the voice. Abby, dressed in a long white silky robe, a pink belt tied at the waist, stood at the table. No sign of the shiner.

"Hi, Abby. We met last week when you were in North DeSoto. I'm Maggie Lewis, this is Michael Bradley."

Michael stood and extended his hand. She shook it and looked at me. "Oh, yeah, I remember you. How's it going?"

"Good. Can you sit for a bit and talk with us?"

Michael pulled out a chair for her and they both sat down. Abby's robe slipped open a little, and as she crossed her legs, I saw the black fishnet stockings and hot pink spiked heels. "What can I do for you?"

It didn't seem to occur to her that we'd had to track her down. It also didn't seem to bother her.

"I assume it has something to do with that poor man getting murdered. I talked to your police chief about it," Abby said. "He called here the day after it happened."

That surprised me, but I guess it shouldn't have. It impressed me that Bobby Lee had actually followed through on that part of the investigation. This was only his second murder case. I sent a silent prayer up to Rob.

I turned my attention back to Abby, and said, "Michael and I were wondering about the night you worked at the club. If the man who was murdered—"

"Jack," Abby said.

"Um, yeah, Jack. Do you remember if he said or did something that night that might've provoked another person into killing him?"

Abby bit her bottom lip while she obviously tried to think back. "I can't recall. Of course, I wasn't always down at that end of the bar. When I was, I don't believe he said anything."

"How did he behave?" Michael asked.

"He got pretty drunk and seemed more quiet as the night wore on," she said.

"Drunk?" That didn't sound right. Jack could easily handle his beer. Had he been drinking whiskey? He knew better than that. "Was he drinking just beer, or something else?"

"Beer. The other guys kept buying him beer."

"What other guys? Maybe if you describe them to me I'll be able to tell who they were."

"It was JC and Dick," she said. "They and their wives, Pam and Diane, respectively, were sitting near Jack. Along with Kevin, Scott, and Pete."

Michael flashed a grin at her and said, "I love witnesses like you. You have an excellent memory. Especially for working only one night."

Yeah, yeah, yeah. Big deal. So she remembered a few names. I continued with my questions. "So you're not sure exactly if Jack said anything?"

"He was very quiet, like I said. Jack seemed morose the more he drank. The other guys were laughing because Jack was all fidgety."

"Fidgety? Why's that?"

Abby shrugged. "Said he lost his notebook. Do you think it was important?"

"Yeah, I think I do," I said. I explained to her about Jack and his habit of writing stuff down in his notebook. Of course, now I had a better idea of why and what he wrote. "I wonder why he didn't have it?"

She shrugged again. "I don't know. Scott asked him and he mumbled that he'd lost it."

I knew all about Jack and his mumbling.

Abby said, "I know Sam was getting angry about it."

That got my attention. "Angry about what?"

"About him getting drunk and how they kept giving him beer chips. After Scott, his parents, and the Reids left, Sam told me to slow down service to Jack. He didn't want Jack to leave totally wasted, didn't want him on the road driving."

"What time did they all leave?" Michael asked.

"Let's see … The Reids and Nelsons, along with their son, left together about eleven thirty or so. Kevin left a few minutes after them, and Sam—" Abby stopped herself short.

"It's okay," Michael told her. "We know Sam left early."

"I don't want to get him into any trouble. He's a nice man. Okay, so Sam left about five minutes after Kevin. He told Pete how to do the security, turn off bathroom lights, and lock up, then he left."

"And Jack was still there?"

Abby nodded. "Yes. Pete sat with him the rest of the night. They were the only two left in the bar. Poor man. Any time Jack tried ordering a beer from me, Pete would get into a conversation with him to distract him. He was doing the best he could to keep Jack from drinking too much more."

"What time did Jack leave?"

"Same time as Pete and me, about twelve thirty. We wanted to make sure he was okay, so I didn't kick him out after last call. He went out the front door, and Pete locked it behind him. Pete did a building security check, then we left through the back door." She smiled. "Pete was cute. He jiggled the doorknob a few times to make sure it was locked. Didn't want me or Sam to get in any trouble."

Apparently Pete didn't realize that he also could've gotten into trouble. The officers on the board wouldn't like hearing that a member had closed up and locked the doors. Definitely grounds for suspension, or even having his membership taken from him.

"And was Jack still there when you two left?"

"Yes. Pete found Jack's notebook stuffed behind a toilet in the men's room when he checked all the rooms, so he went over to Jack's truck and gave it to him. Plus Pete wanted to make sure he was okay. They talked for a few minutes and Jack said he was fine, he'd be okay to drive himself home."

"Did you actually hear Jack?"

"No, Pete had let me in his car, then he went over to Jack's truck. Pete told me all that when he came back to the car."

"So Jack was still sitting in his truck when you and Pete left?" I asked.

"Yeah," Abby said. "Pete told me that Jack didn't live too far away, so I wasn't very worried. He said Jack did that all the time."

I nodded, knowing it was the truth. Except for the part about Jack misplacing his notebook behind a toilet and getting drunk because JC and Dick were buying his beer, everything Abby said sounded logical. Like any other night at the club.

"Did you see anyone else around?" Michael asked. "Anyone else still in the parking lot, or nearby?"

"No one in the parking lot, and I didn't notice anyone nearby. Of course, I wasn't looking."

Michael arched that eyebrow of his.

"I was on my cell," Abby said and turned her head toward the bar. "See that gorgeous man behind the bar?"

Michael and I both looked. The hunky guy from the website. Oh, my God, he looked even better in person. My mouth dropped open.

Abby giggled at my reaction. "Yeah, I know." She waved at the hunk and he waved back. Looking at us again, she said, "That's Tyler. I was on the phone with him, listening to him beg me to come back."

Holy crap. I never would've left him in the first place. He could be dumber than dirt and poorer than me, it didn't matter as long as I could just look at him. I had to stop drooling and focus.

The first question came to mind and I asked, "Why'd you leave?"

Abby placed her hand on her tummy, caressed it. "In a few months I won't be able to dance. Tyler and I had a huge fight last week, the night Pete was in here. I'd told Tyler about the baby and he wasn't very happy. Actually, he became very angry."

I immediately thought of her black eye and asked, "Was he abusive? Did he hurt you?" I glared over at Hunky Tyler, then back at Abby.

"No, no, nothing like that. It just surprised him and he initially reacted badly to the news. He slammed his hand down on the bar, hit a bowl of peanuts, and it bounced up and the edge hit me right in the face. Total accident, but I was very upset at the time. Pete rescued me took me away from all this." Abby gestured with her hands. "Tyler came to his senses, decided he's ready to be a daddy, and begged me to come back."

"And you came back the next day?"

"Yeah, Pete dropped me off at the bus station early Sunday morning. He's an absolute doll, isn't he? He wanted to drive me all the way back here, but I wouldn't let him. He'd already done so much."

"Done so much?"

"He put me up for a couple of nights, found the job at the VFW for me. So, yeah, I consider that doing a lot, especially for a complete stranger. He didn't have to help me at all."

"You stayed at Pete's while you were in North DeSoto?" That amazed me because I knew Pete lived in a tiny mobile home. I couldn't imagine two adults living there comfortably even temporarily.

Abby must've heard the surprise in my voice. She said, "Well, yeah. It's not like I would've had to've worried about keeping him off of me. Y'know?" Abby winked at me.

Okay. I guessed Pete was the one who's gay. Was I the only woman who didn't know it? I'd known the man for years and never had a clue.

I shook my head, and said, "No, I was thinking more about the size of Pete's place—it's pretty small."

"Pete gave me his bed and he slept on the couch. It is small, but it was only for a couple nights." Abby glanced at her watch and said, "I have to get going in a few minutes. Is there anything else?"

"Um, yeah. Why would Pete come to this club? I mean, since he's gay."

Abby laughed. "In between our shows—the girls, I mean—we have gay cabaret. See all these men sitting alone, or with another man?

That's really what they're here to see. The straight couples are here to watch the girls."

What do you know? Equal opportunity stripping.

Abby pushed her chair back and stood. "I need to get going. You're going to stay for my act, aren't you?"

Michael and I looked at each other. We hadn't gotten that far in our plans.

"Wouldn't miss it, Abby," Michael said. "And thanks again. You were very helpful." He stood up and shook her hand.

"Wait, Abby, I have one more question," I said. It was hard to ask, but I did anyway. "When Pete came back from Jack's truck, did he have any blood on him?"

Abby frowned. "Of course not." To Michael she said, "You're welcome. Glad I could be of some help. Good-night. Hope you enjoy the show." She headed toward a door near the stage.

"I had to ask," I said.

"I know. You did a good job asking questions. You asked all the right ones."

I smiled. "Think I might make a good detective some day?"

"Let's not get carried away."

Music started playing and an amber spotlight hit center stage. Abby no longer had on the long robe. Instead, she wore a little one-piece outfit, the black satiny short skirt fringed with hot pink fur that matched the color of her shoes perfectly. Oh, man. There were days I couldn't even match my socks. Michael and I spent the next couple hours watching beautiful young women and hot men get almost naked. I was grateful to be sitting in the dark.

Twenty-Nine

It was close to midnight when we got back to our rooms. I was keyed up, not ready for sleep, but climbed into bed anyway. Michael wanted to meet in the hotel restaurant for breakfast at seven and get on the road by eight, so it was best to get some sleep. Not an easy thing to do. The light from the hall shone in through the bottom of the door, and the damned air conditioner rattled between its cycles. I punched pillows, tossed the sheets off, then back on all night depending on how warm or cool the room got. When I did manage to sleep, I dreamt about sliding down a pole with Hunky Tyler dressed as a fireman. I was sorry when my wake-up call came at six sharp. It would've been interesting to finish that dream.

What an awful time to be awake and out of bed. I stumbled through the dark, unfamiliar room and felt my way to the coffeemaker on the dresser. I'd set it all up before going to bed, so just had to push the button. By the time I got out of the bathroom, the coffee was ready. I would've killed for one of my ceramic mugs, and more sugar. And real milk. Man, I'd make sure to bring all of those the next time Michael and I stayed at a hotel.

Whoa. That was a strange thought. As if he and I were going to make this a habit. I decided to blame my warped thinking on the early-morning hour. I hated mornings. I hated hotels that gave only two dinky-ass packets of sugar and powdered creamer. I hated Styrofoam cups. Grumpy and not nearly caffeinated enough, I showered, packed my bag, and headed down to the restaurant for a decent cup of coffee.

The hostess showed me to a table and we passed a huge buffet on the way. Even before I sat down, I asked for a pot of coffee and within minutes a bouncy little waitress showed up with it. I'd make sure she got a wonderful tip.

I gulped down the first delicious cup and was pouring a second one when Michael joined me. He set his duffle bag on an empty chair.

"Hello," he said. "You're down here early. How are you this fine morning?"

I growled, then glared at him when he reached for the coffeepot.

He ignored me and poured a cup for himself. "Not a morning person, I take it?"

Not only did he steal my coffee, but he drank it black. Nasty. The second cup was beginning to do its trick, and I forced a small smile on my face.

"Good morning," I said. "Did you sleep as poorly as I did?"

Michael shook his head. "It was okay. I'm sorry you had a bad night."

The waitress came and we both ordered the buffet. My appetite grew as the caffeine kicked in.

"Want to eat first, then talk, or what?" Michael asked.

I pointed at the coffeepot. "More of that, then eat. Then talk."

"You do that and I'll go to the buffet. I'm hungry."

By the time we had both eaten and were working on our second pot of coffee, I was ready to talk. "We learned a lot from Abby last night, didn't we?"

"Yeah, she was very helpful. We confirmed Sam's lie, and that Pete's gay."

I still felt weird about not picking up on that, but I let it go for the time being. "Sam's lie is much more serious, don't you think? He could've actually lost his job."

"Yeah, but Pete had a whole image thing going on, hiding the truth from the club members, didn't he?"

"Yeah. He used to come in just about every weekend with a new woman hanging on him. Was it that important to him?"

Michael shrugged. "It's a men's military club. Definitely a macho thing going on for Pete."

"Pete loves the club, is very active for just being a social member. He likes being a part of it even though he wasn't in the military. Pretending to be a smooth Casanova was maybe the only way for him to feel he really belonged."

Michael sipped his coffee. "I imagine North DeSoto doesn't have much of a gay community."

"If there is, it's pretty well hidden," I said. "I've never really thought about it."

"Okay, so what have we learned?"

I got out my legal pad and pen. I jotted down as I answered. "Sam lied about closing. Pete's gay. Jack was alive when he and Abby left Saturday night. Someone took Jack's notebook and hid it in the bathroom, probably as a joke." I tapped the pen on the table while thinking, then said, "My guess would be Scott Nelson. Sounds like something he'd do. Just for kicks. Oh, and JC and Dick used up their chips to get Jack drunk.

Sorry rotten bastards. Why the hell would they do that? They're always talking about shit being detrimental to the club."

"What else?"

I cocked my head and looked at him across the table. "Is Kevin the one who lied about his medals? He's the only one left of who Brenda met." Damn. Kevin?

"Sounds that way to me. Makes sense, doesn't it? The night I met him, Pete talked about what a war hero Kevin was. Kevin seemed to clam up."

"Yeah, and I remember wondering about that at the time. So, he was lying all along? I wonder if he even served in the military. That's one hell of a serious lie."

"Keeping their lies from being revealed was very important to all three of them," Michael said.

"Damn. I just thought of something else about Kevin." I explained to him how the gambling board prizes, quantity and quality, had dropped off. "Kevin said they didn't have the money to spend the way they used to. That never made sense to me."

"Remind me, what position does Kevin hold?"

"President of the corporation, of the canteen, which translates to mean the bar. He gets all of the gambling board prizes. Hunting, fishing, camping gear, and supplies. Meat market gift certificates, stuff like that. Usually top-quality items that entice the members to spend money buying a chance to win."

"Is that all he does?"

"Oh, no. He organizes the monthly suppers and the Sunday breakfast, and hires the bands for the monthly Saturday band night. Even that's changed. We used to have a band every Saturday night. They said it was too expensive, so now they only do it on the last Saturday and have Sunday brunch the next day, which happens to be today. And instead of steak night, they switched it to a cheaper spaghetti supper.

Damn, now that I think about it, there's been an awful lot of changes since I started working there five years ago."

"When did the changes start? How long ago?" he asked.

"I'm not sure. Gradually. The last two, three years. Maybe longer?"

"Who were the officers? Were Dick and JC on the board? Was Kevin? What about when you first started working there?"

"Let's see." I closed my eyes to get a clear picture of when I interviewed for the job. I opened them, looked at Michael and said, "Kevin wasn't there. It's only been a year or so since he joined and he became president right away. JC, Dick, and Sam hired me. Dick was commander, and JC was quartermaster then. The commander position can only be held for two years, and Dick was on his second year when I started.

"Nobody else ran in the election four years ago, so JC and Dick flip-flopped positions. Dick took over as quartermaster and JC was commander. Then two years ago, they switched again. Sam's always been the steward since I've been there."

"So those three—Sam, Dick, and JC—have been around and have been officers of the club since you've been there?"

"Oh, yeah, and for years way before that."

The waitress dropped off the check. Michael looked at his watch. "You ready? I've already checked out, and it's close to seven thirty. The club closes at four o'clock today, right?"

"Right. Because of the breakfast, or brunch as Pam likes to call it. Hours are ten to four today."

While he paid, I said, "All of this makes sense, but we're no closer to finding Jack's killer. How do we go about doing that?"

"Remember what I said about sifting through the bull, and everyone having a secret? We're learning what secrets these men had. *Keeping* those secrets is important to them."

"It's like that expression: 'Three can keep a secret if two of them are dead.'"

228

Thirty

Seven thirty in the morning and the inside of the car felt like a hot oven. We rolled down the windows and let what little breeze there was circulate. I would've much rather been upstairs with the unruly air conditioning. But leaving now meant we'd be in North DeSoto just before two o'clock, which would give us time to talk to the guys before the club closed.

"I'll turn on the air once we get going," Michael said as he started the car. "Ready to go home?"

"Let's go." I buckled my seatbelt and asked, "What's our plan once we get back to North DeSoto? How much time will we have before you go pick up Chris?"

"We have plenty of time. We'll stop at home first, then go to the club. I don't pick Chris up until seven. Terri said she'd feed Chris and make sure her homework was done. She said if I showed up earlier, I was welcome to join them for dinner."

Well, isn't that cozy? I'd make sure Michael dropped me off before then so I wouldn't have to deal with that scenario again. Let him and Terri do whatever they wanted.

Oh, for God's sake, I really had to get a grip. I was his landlady, nothing more. And did I really want something more? Sheesh. I was giving myself a headache, and anyway, now was not the time to be thinking about it. I grabbed Jack's notebook and started reading.

Dec. 23, 1962

Christmas party at the VFW.

Dec. 29, 1962

Was asked to join the board at the VFW. Might do it.

Jan. 2, 1963

Happy fucking New Year.

Jan. 3, 1963

Elected 2 year trustee. Whatever the hell that is.

I had to smile at the last entry. It reminded me of how Kevin once told me he felt coerced into becoming the president. No one else would step up to do it. His name was placed on the ballot and that's all she wrote. Later, he said it was an honor.

Jan. 4, 1963

Going with my VFW buddy to the place he goes to.

Jan. 5, 1963

Sat around with a bunch of guys talking about war. We sat by the Navy flag. Most from WWII, a couple from Korea. Talked a lot about President Kennedy, Castro, Russia. My buddy was the youngest there. He broke down.

Amazing. It was almost like reading a history book. Instead of learning about the Bay of Pigs and the Cuban Missile Crisis, I was privy to the thoughts and reactions of someone who had been there. I wondered what happened to Jack's buddy. Another thought struck and I flipped through the pages looking for late November.

Nov. 22, 1963

~~Dear God~~ The President is dead. LBJ

The line through the first sentence had slashed the paper. I could almost feel the anguish. I turned the pages back to January of that year and continued reading. Most of the entries consisted of one or two lines. I spent hours reading, occasionally stopping to read something of historical interest to Michael. I found it curious that I never found out who Jack's buddy was. He never once wrote any names down.

Finally, in an entry in December, I found out what happened to Jack's son. I read it twice before I read it aloud to Michael.

Dec. 14, 1963

Happy birthday, Daryl. You would've been 5 today. I'm sorry, son. I'm sorry, Joon. Told the guys I wouldn't be coming in to the VFW today. Too much to do I told them. They don't need to know. Hard to believe its been over a year. Another Thanksgiving gone, another Christmas to get through. Joon, I'll never get that day back. I swear it was an accident. A mistake. My mind was, still is mostly, messed up. I forgot that one time. I write everything down now to keep me on track. It helps me now, but I know that it doesn't do any good for what I did that day. I didn't remember giving him the first shot. I swear, Joon. Daryl, I'm so sorry, son. I thought it was time for your medicine. I didn't remember giving you that first dose. You were such a good little boy, you never cried, never let on if you were scared of the needle, just always took your medicine like a man, a good soldier.

Thirty-One

"Home, sweet home," Michael said when he turned down our street. All I saw was a police cruiser sitting across from my house. The next thing I noticed was the empty driveway. My poor little car.

I tossed my bag on the bedroom floor, used the bathroom, then checked my answering machine. Brenda had left five messages and they all said the same thing: *"Where are you? I wish you had a cell phone. Did you get my e-mail? Call me, dammit!"*

I booted up the computer, cursing at its slowness. I clicked on my e-mail and up popped Brenda's. Another link and JPEG attached. The photo was a blurry shot of a man in uniform. The caption read, *Kevin Beamer before being ousted from Memorial Day parade.*

Oh, man. It sure did look like my Kevin Beamer. I clicked on the other link. A list of names of men who had been caught lying about their time served in the military. Kevin's name was on the list. The webpage had photographs and links to other pages demanding action be taken against these frauds. I printed out the list of names as well as Kevin's photo and turned off the computer. Michael was waiting for me when I went down to his car. I showed him the printout. He simply nodded.

———

The VFW parking lot was fairly empty when we got there. My stomach was in absolute knots. Even though I didn't have to go, I rushed to the bathroom while Michael went up to the bar. I splashed water on my face and looking in the mirror, I didn't look quite as washed out or drained as I had a week ago. A few deep breaths and I forced myself to go back out there.

Pete and a couple of other guys at the bar nodded or said hello as I walked by. Michael had left an empty stool between him and Pete, so I sat down. Sam came right over and took my order.

"How you doing, Pete?" I asked. Now that I had this knowledge about him, I felt really uncomfortable, not sure what to say. I wanted to blurt out that it didn't matter to me.

Sam served my drink and waved away my attempt to pay him. He looked much better than we'd left him yesterday morning, and I was glad to see him working behind the bar. I had hoped it wouldn't be that guy Cody. I needed to give the book pages directly back to Sam, no one else.

I was also relieved there were so few people around. They must have all cleared out after breakfast. I reached into my purse and pulled out the envelope that had the pages from the daily book. I slid it across the bar and said, "Sam, this is for you."

He frowned and took the envelope.

"Open it later when you're alone in your office," I said.

"Okay."

"Is Kevin working in the kitchen? I saw his bike out front."

Sam answered, "Yeah, he's in there helping Scott and JC. We were a little shorthanded for breakfast. Dick and Diane didn't show up and Pam was the only waitress. She's not real happy." Sam winked at me. Code for *Pam's never happy, so what's new?* I winked back.

Ah. That explained the weird tension I felt. Just wait until the truths about Sam, Pete, and Kevin came out. The members would hate them, but they'd blame me for disclosing what I knew. They'd all think it was better to leave well enough alone. It was a lose-lose situation—except for the fact that it might lead me and Michael to the killer. So what if I caused problems? It sure as hell wouldn't be the first time. And knowing me, it wouldn't be the last. I just hated the idea that learning these secrets could mean one of them killed Jack Hoffman.

"So, Pete, how are you?" I realized he'd never answered when I first asked him, that he had simply nodded. And, worse, no hug like usual.

"I'm fine, Maggie, and you?" He stared straight ahead.

"I'm good, thanks." But I wasn't. I sipped my beer, pretending everything was normal. I'd try again. "So, what's new?"

"Nothing."

"Oh." Okay. This wasn't going well at all. I needed to do something to make some progress. "Did Michael tell you he and I just came back from Ft. Walton Beach?"

Pete picked up his beer glass, swallowed what was left in it, and slammed the glass down on the bar. "See you later, Sam. Thanks."

I watched Pete's back as he walked away. Alrighty then. I wanted to chase after him, but somehow I knew that wouldn't be a good idea. Back to sipping my beer.

Sam took Pete's empty glass and pocketed the tip he'd left. I wanted to ask Sam if he was still my friend. I sure felt like I'd just lost one.

Without looking at him, I said to Michael, "Do something. Please."

"Hey, Sam do you guys need help cleaning up after breakfast? Maybe I could wash dishes or something?"

"That'd be great, Michael. Go on into the kitchen and tell JC and Kevin you're offering to help. We can never get enough volunteers. And it sure didn't help that the Reids never came in. Didn't even call or anything."

Michael slid off his stool. "Can I take this in with me?" He held up his glass of soda.

"Sure. Wait a second, will you?" Sam grabbed a plastic pitcher and filled it with beer. He handed it to Michael.

"They're not really supposed to drink while they're working, but they sure earned some cold beer."

Michael took the pitcher and walked away toward the kitchen. I didn't watch him. I now sat all alone at my end of the bar. Sam and the two other customers at the opposite end kept their attention on the TV.

Pathetic. Counting myself, only three customers in the place. I'd like to think my not working there was the reason, but my ego isn't quite that large. More than likely, the price increase in drinks had a lot to do with business dying. I turned toward the dining room and saw Pam still re-setting the tables. I could either sit here by myself drinking my beer, or I could be useful and help Pam. Neither sounded very appealing, but I knew the dangers of drinking too much. And if I sat here alone long enough, I knew I'd order another beer. I slid off the barstool.

"Hey, Pam, need any help?"

"Take the salt and pepper shakers off and put them away. You know where to put them, don't you?" She sniffed and walked away.

Oooh, a little passive-aggressive, are we? And the sniffing again. I was sure that came from snorting and nothing to do with her upper crustedness. I grabbed a tray from the waitress station to carry the shakers. The door to the kitchen was open and I peeked in. Kevin and Michael stood by the sinks, their backs to me, and I didn't see JC or Scott anywhere. I took the tray and got busy with my assigned task.

Only twenty tables in the dining room, so the job didn't take long. Pam had gone into the kitchen, and I wasn't about to go in there to ask what she wanted me to do next. I busied myself by looking at the framed photographs of all the past commanders and Ladies Auxiliary presidents hanging on the wall. Jack Hoffman's picture was draped with a black shroud. In another week or so, someone would take it down and put it away until the next time someone died.

Another example of loyalty, except this one made sense to me. A sign of respect. Just like the MIA/POW table, like all the framed photographs. These men and women had served their country, most of them during World War II and the Korean war, and then became active in the VFW upon returning home.

I thought about what Jack had said the last night I worked. Doing right by others, trusting each other. Again with the loyalty. Of course, he also had gone on about how the club was ruined when women joined. Knowing now about his history with his wife and son, Jack's resentment made a little more sense. I wondered how much of that resentment was directed at himself.

Terrific. Now I was starting to have a warped sense of understanding. I went back up to the bar. Sam left the other guys and came over to me.

"I swear I don't think working here is worth it. Things are really tense."

"How so, Sam?"

He shrugged his broad shoulders. "Just different. Really quiet. Everybody seems to be watching each other. Like we're all waiting for something to happen."

I almost blurted out what information we'd learned about Pete and Kevin. Then again, maybe that wouldn't be such a bad idea. Glancing furtively around, no one nearby, I saw my chance.

"Well," I said in a low voice, "Michael and I have found out a couple of things."

Sam leaned closer, his eyes wide, and guarded. "Oh, yeah, like what?"

"Did you know that Pete's gay?"

Sam snorted and stood upright. "Oh, please. Ain't no way in hell I'm going to believe that. No, not Pete. Phil maybe, but definitely not Pete. He likes girls. He's in here all the time with a different woman. Besides, what proof do you have?"

I told him about our visit with Abby in Ft. Walton Beach.

"I still don't buy it." Sam frowned, then said, "You said there were a couple of things. What's the other?" He leaned on the bar again closer to me.

"This nearly breaks my heart, and I hope to God it's not true because the person could get into a lot of trouble—"

"Is it about me?"

I wanted to hear about him not locking up the night Jack was killed from him, so I asked, "No, why? Have you done something?" I waited, hoping he'd tell me. Because if he didn't, I was afraid of what that meant.

He rubbed his hand across his mouth and said, "Of course not."

So much for giving him a chance to come clean. I said, "No, it's about Kevin." I reached into my purse, pulled out the printed photo, and showed it to Sam. "See? Right there is proof."

He squinted at the photo, then looked at me again.

I handed him the page from the website and waited while he read it.

"Holy shit. His name's right there and everything. Oh, man, I can't believe this. We're going to have to call an emergency meeting."

"Emergency meeting?" came a voice from behind me. Oh, shit. Kevin.

Sam shot up, glared past my head. "Try to explain this, Beamer." He shoved the piece of paper at Kevin. I turned and saw both he and Michael had come out of the kitchen. Michael frowned at me and I shrugged.

Kevin briefly glanced at the paper, then looked at each of us in turn.

"What have you got to say, Beamer?" Sam shouted. His face took on the same purple color as it had the previous morning.

Out of worry, I put my hand on Sam's arm hoping to calm him down. I was afraid his reaction would bring on a heart attack or stroke. Or violence? I stuffed down my nerves.

"What's going on?"

Terrific. Now Scott, JC, and Pam had come out of the kitchen.

"This is what's going on," Sam said and handed the paper to JC. "He's a liar, a traitor, bought his medals off of an online auction, never even served overseas."

JC finished reading and looked at Kevin. "Well, is it true?"

Kevin must've known there was no way out. He simply nodded. Without looking at any of us, and not saying a word, Kevin walked toward the front door.

"Damn liar," Sam yelled, one last parting shot.

Kevin came to a dead stop and turned. Looking directly at Sam, he said in a calm, quiet voice, "Yeah, Sam, let's talk about being a liar. You want to go next?"

Before Sam could answer, a shrill chirp of a cell phone pierced the quiet stillness. We all turned toward the sound. Scott, red-faced, quickly answered his phone. After a brief moment, his face paled and he shouted into the phone, "Okay, honey, okay. Calm down. Good. Okay, I'm on my way." He ended the call. "My wife needs me. She's called 911. Her father ... Dick's been stabbed. Diane's gone."

Thirty-Two

"I'm at a loss." Michael and I sat in his car outside the club. Pam, JC, and Scott had raced to the hospital to be with Dick and Scott's wife. And where the hell was Diane? What did Scott mean by *Diane's gone*?

"So, what do we do now?"

"Pete left earlier and doesn't know about Dick. Let's go talk to him. Where might Pete be? Any idea?"

I thought about it. "He doesn't belong to any other clubs in town, and I don't know of any bars he might go to. It's always been the VFW that he came to. He lives in a campground about twenty miles from here, but I don't know exactly which lot."

He glanced at his watch. "We have plenty of time before I have to pick up Chris. You want to see if we can find his place?"

"I was only there once when he had some of us over for a BBQ last summer. I rode with Sam, but I think I could find it again, so yeah, let's try." I gave him directions and said, "We'll pass a few farms and produce stands. You'll see signs from there for the forest hiking trails and campgrounds."

"Do you like camping?"

"Hell, no. My idea of roughing it is when the hotel doesn't have room service. Or only gives two lousy packets of sugar."

He just shook his head at me and laughed. I guess he thought I was joking.

After a while, I told him where to turn off. We made our way through the winding path and ended up at a visitor information shack. The nice lady inside gave me directions to Pete's site. She told me to beware of the alligators, and to not feed them. *No problem, lady. No problem at all.*

We drove another five minutes on a well-tended dirt road. Nestled among tall, scrawny pine trees sat Pete's home. A canopy attached to the roof extended out over a picnic table and chairs. Pete sat in one of the chairs and looked up as we approached.

"Let's get this over with," I said and got out of the car. I really didn't think Pete was a killer, but I couldn't deny that I would never have felt safe coming out here alone. There's no way anyone would hear a cry for help with how isolated these campsites were. Even so, I decided to keep a healthy distance between myself and Pete.

"Maggie. Michael," Pete said, nodding at us as we approached. "What can I do for you?"

"Hey, Pete, how's it going?" I waited for a smile, anything friendly. Nada. Zip. Zilch.

"Fine."

He was not going to make this easy for me. "We saw Abby last night. Nice club. She told us how you rescued her and all that. Didn't surprise me one bit since I know what a great guy you are."

"Yeah, okay."

I felt cold despite the heat. An unsmiling Pete was just unnatural. I looked at Michael and silently begged him to take over.

"Mind if we sit and talk for a bit, Pete? We came all this way to see you."

"I'll be leaving soon for work. Got a heavy week ahead of me." He seemed to mellow a bit when he looked at me again. Maybe the tears welling up in my eyes got to him. "All right, have a seat. I can give you a few minutes, I guess."

I brushed pine needles off the bench and sat down at the picnic table. Pete stayed in his chair across from me and Michael, his arms folded against his chest.

"Only have a few minutes. What's on your mind?"

I was starting to get a little ticked off at him. I mean, really. So what if people knew he was gay? That didn't make him a bad person. It wasn't my fault that information had to come out. Okay, maybe it was my fault, but still. He didn't have to act this way toward me.

"Pete, I'm really sorry, but—"

"I know Abby told you why I was at her club." He blew out a long breath. "She called me last night, realized you didn't know and maybe she shouldn't have said anything. Look, I'm not mad, really. You could've just asked me. I would have told you. Well, maybe I would've. Once word gets out, it's over. The friendships, the camaraderie, the whole idea of being a part of something important. The loss of all that hurts." He rubbed the heel of his palm across his eyes, then looked at me. He stood and I went over to him, fell into his warm embrace. I knew all about loss, and the pain that goes with it. I squeezed Pete's waist, then stepped back.

"We still have to tell you about Dick Reid."

"Dick? What happened to him?"

"We don't know anything definite yet," Michael said, telling Pete what little we knew.

"Oh, Jesus. First Jack, now Dick? What the hell is going on?"

———

Kevin's motorcycle was parked outside the Legion. I almost dreaded going in there, but I knew we had to. I was glad Kevin hadn't left town. After what happened to him, and knowing he didn't have family in North DeSoto, I figured he might. No reason to stay.

We found Kevin sitting at the bar, only one empty stool next to him. I moved onto it and put my hand on his arm. He smiled and looked surprised to see me.

"How you doing, Kevin?" I felt a weight lift off of me when I saw the smile.

"I've been better. But I'll be all right. How's Dick? Any word?"

I shook my head. Michael came up behind me and reached his hand out to shake Kevin's. "Can we go get a table and talk for a few minutes?"

"Sure," Kevin said. He picked up his beer bottle and followed us over to a round table with four chairs. I was glad it wouldn't be me and Michael sitting across from Kevin, interrogating him. This was more comfortable. As comfortable as it could be, I guess.

Before I could think of how to start, Kevin spoke up. "Why? Why'd you go looking on the Internet for information about me?"

I explained to him about Brenda and the photo, how it all got started. I told him how sorry I was that it ended the way it had.

"It was a stupid thing to do," he said. "I just wanted to belong. That's the only damn reason I did it. They don't look at social members the same, you know."

"Were you even in the military?" Michael asked.

"Hell, yeah. I didn't stoop that low." Kevin snorted. "Like that makes any difference. What I did was bad enough, and now I got caught so I have to live with it."

"What exactly did you do, Kevin?"

He looked around before speaking and then said, "Got kicked out, sent home, dishonorable discharge. I don't want to go into that. Let's just say I royally screwed up, and it bit me in the ass. Didn't mean too much to me until after 9/11, when the whole damned country had gone patriotic. I wanted to be part of that. I know it sounds crazy."

In a twisted sort of way it made sense to me. In a very sad, pathetic way.

"Getting ribbons off the Internet was a piece of cake. As easy as forging my DD214 to have it read I was honorably discharged. No one was any wiser." He looked at me and smiled again. "In a way I'm glad it's out in the open. I'll move on and won't look back."

Just like he moved on the last time he was caught? I wondered how many times there had been. Instead of voicing my thoughts, I said, "Thanks for being so open, Kevin. Michael and I appreciate it. Maybe you can help us with something else. Anything you can tell us about Jack Hoffman, why he was murdered, who might've done it?"

"I suppose it wouldn't hurt now to tell you. Jack called me Saturday morning, said he wanted me to fire you. That you were disrespectful, a real smartass. He wanted to call an emergency meeting to go over a couple things. Said he didn't want to wait until the next scheduled meeting. Jack was tired of the bullshit that was allowed to go on."

"Like what? Like JC and Dick meeting together on the sly? Making decisions on their own and getting the others to go along with them?"

244

Sheesh. I *was* a smartass. Not that there's anything wrong with that. I winced when I remembered Dick Reid and his current condition.

Kevin said, "No, none of that came up. Jack bitched about you for awhile, then started in about the book. He said he tried talking about it the night before with JC and Dick, but they didn't want to hear it."

Michael asked, "What about the book?"

"The daily book. Jack told me he was tired of it being rigged. Seemed the same people won over and over. He hadn't won in nearly eight years and it was time he did. He was really pissed."

"So, Jack tried talking to JC and Dick, what, on Friday night? My last night working there? I don't remember him talking to them." I also had been pretty busy that night, so there was a good chance I'd missed it.

Kevin nodded. "Jack said he went into the office while they were in there. He didn't want to talk to them while we were all sitting at the bar. He said it wasn't proper."

Jack must've gone to their office when I was in the bathroom. Now that I thought about it, I remembered Jack wasn't sitting at the bar after my break. Then I remembered something else.

"That day at Jack's funeral reception, you told Sam to not talk about what went on in the meetings. You stopped him from talking about Monday night's meeting, remember?"

"Yeah."

"That was the night y'all voted to suspend me, right? What—"

"Whoa, Maggie." Kevin raised his hands and said, "That wasn't unanimous, y'know. A lot of us voted in your favor. But JC and Dick had gathered enough voting members that would go along with them."

"Doesn't matter anymore." I shrugged. And I realized it really didn't matter. Somehow I knew things would work out. For the past two years I'd been running on automatic, doing what I had to do to just get through each day. I sat up straighter in my chair. "What else was talked about that night at the meeting?"

He hesitated for a second then said, "Raising the drink prices, shortening the hours, closing on Sundays and possibly Mondays. They—"

This time I interrupted him. "What are they thinking? I mean, I know the VFW is nonprofit and everything, but all of that is sure to cut business. They'll start losing money."

"The only two things decided on that night were suspending you and raising the prices. Oh, and putting Sam behind the bar full-time." Kevin took a swig from his beer bottle. "They said the club was turning into a bar, less of a military club."

"I get it," I said. "They were trying to make it less appealing to the social members, weren't they?"

He shrugged, said nothing. Was he still being loyal? And to whom, and why? Especially after the stunt that he'd pulled. I tried another tactic.

"The prizes you're supposed to get. Did they tell you to stop buying expensive items?"

Kevin nodded. "JC said I was spending too much money on them. Dick suggested I hold off until further notice."

It kept coming back to money. And to JC and Dick.

Michael asked, "What exactly did Jack say to you, do you remember?"

"Let's see … It was kind of hard to understand him—you know how he mumbled. He was mad about Maggie, about women belonging, about being blown off by Dick and JC. He said things were done right when he was commander."

"Yeah, I do remember him saying most of that. But what about the book and being blown off?"

"He said that he told JC and Dick he didn't like the way the book was being handled. That he wanted to bring it up in the next meeting. Jack said they more or less told him to mind his own damn business."

Poor Jack. Except for the part about firing me and women belonging, he just wanted things to be run the right way. Right according to whom? He was of the old school, but still. If the book was rigged, it should've been brought up. Wrong is wrong, no matter who was involved.

"And when they blew him off, he contacted me and wanted to call a special meeting for Sunday night. Of course, all hell broke loose Sunday morning, so it never happened." Kevin finished off his beer and scooted back his chair. Holding up his empty bottle, he asked, "Can I get you guys anything?"

Michael stood and I followed his lead. "No, thanks. I do have one more question, if that's okay. About how you implied Sam had lied about something."

"Shoot."

"How did you know Sam left early, letting Pete close up Saturday night?"

"My bike wouldn't start. I was fiddling with it when Sam came out. Poor guy had waited for the Nelsons and Reids, then me to leave. He didn't see me still out there."

"Why didn't you say anything?"

"Oh, yeah, like I was in any position to chew him out."

Thirty-Three

F or the third time in four days, I approached the doors of the North DeSoto General Hospital. Michael and I entered the brightly lit lobby and went straight to the information booth.

After confirming Dick had been admitted, we rode the elevator to the ICU unit and followed the signs to a locked door. Beyond a wall of glass windows, a nurse sat at a desk, her back to us. A row of cubicles stretched out in front of her where she could keep an eye on all the ICU patients. I could just barely hear beeping sounds from the machines hooked up to these patients.

"I'll handle this," Michael said. He pushed the buzzer. The nurse turned, looked up, and moved her hand to answer the buzzer, and he said, "We're here to see Dick Reid."

"Are you family?" her voice crackled through the speaker.

"No, ma'am, we're not. Just close friends."

"I'm sorry, but the family has issued a 'No Visitors' for the patient." She didn't sound at all sorry. Michael thanked her.

"Damn," I said. "Well, at least we know he's alive. That's good news anyway." We turned to head back to the elevator when the door behind us opened. Pam Nelson came through the door and stopped when she saw us, then rushed over.

"Maggie, oh God, poor Dick." Pam's eyes were red, and this time her sniffling was due to crying. I immediately felt sympathetic. The Nelsons and Reids had known each other for years. Even if Pam and Diane weren't genuine close friends, their husbands were. JC and Dick were practically joined at the hip. Sure, Pam was a bitch who thought she was better than most people, but seeing her all shaken up made me forget all that.

"How is he, Pam? Where's JC?"

She cocked her thumb over her shoulder. "He's in there with the family. It doesn't look good. Dick's in a coma. JC says he's going to stay until Dick either wakes up or ..." Pam couldn't finish the sentence.

"What about Diane? Has anyone heard from her? Seen her?"

She shook her head. "No. I don't know what's going on. Oh my God. Why did Diane try to kill her husband?"

Whoa. "Is that what you think happened, Pam?"

"Of course. What else could it be? She must've finally got tired of his abuse." She wiped her nose with her hanky and looked at me. "You do know about the abuse, don't you? I haven't said anything out of line?"

"I always suspected. I've seen the way Dick grabs her sometimes, and the long sleeves she wears even on the hottest days."

Pam nodded, her eyes filling up with tears. "I've tried so many times to get her to leave him, but ... JC told me to mind my business, that Dick was a good man. If you'll excuse me, I have an appointment." She rushed toward the elevator.

———

Sam's truck sat in front of his house when we pulled up.

"Good. I thought he'd be at home. Poor guy, he really has nowhere else to go. The club means everything to him." Man, after talking to Pete and Kevin, and reading Jack's notebook, I realized how important, how *significant* the VFW was to a lot of people. Me included. Hell, that job grounded me, gave me a reason to get out of bed every day since Rob's death.

Before Rob's murder, it was just a job. A paycheck. With all that had been happening, everything Michael and I were finding out, my heart was heavy when I got out of the car and walked with him toward Sam's front door.

Sam opened the door right away in response to my knock. He didn't seem at all surprised to see us. He led us into his living room, turned off the TV, and gestured for me and Michael to sit on the couch.

"Can I get y'all anything? A beer, iced tea?" After we declined, he plopped down into his recliner. A half dozen crushed beer cans lay on the floor at his feet, one sat on the table beside him. "So, what brings y'all here?"

Now that we were actually right there in front of Sam, I clammed up. I didn't want to know if he had anything to do with Jack's death. And he didn't ask about Dick.

Michael took the lead after he probably realized I wasn't going to. "We wanted to make sure you were doing okay, Sam."

Sam took a swig from his beer. "Yeah, I'm all right. Can't let the bastards bring you down. Didn't I always tell you that, Maggie?" He finished off his beer and crushed the can. "Can't let the bastards get to you."

I'd never seen Sam drunk and it made me strangely wary. I wanted to get out of there. Leave him alone with his misery. And his beer.

He leaned forward in his chair. "Almost made me have a heart attack. Wife's glad I quit. She was tired of seeing me so stressed out all the time. Ain't worth it. Screw 'em. Tired of doing their dirty work."

"What dirty work, Sam? What did JC and Dick have you do?" Michael asked.

He pointed at me. "Suspend her, first of all. Soon as she was arrested. Assholes. They didn't care. They didn't have to work behind the bar, especially for free." He poked his thumb into his chest. "I'm the one who had to do it. Sonofabitches. I'm not going to give 'em a chance to fire me, though. I left a message on JC's machine telling him I quit. I showed them."

"Is that why I was suspended? Because of Jack's murder?" I had to hear him say it.

"You ticked off too many board members in the past. Too damn mouthy for your own good."

I let it ride. Whatever they needed to tell themselves to get through the day. Like Sam said, screw 'em.

"One last question, Sam, then Maggie and I'll get out of your hair. Did you let Pete close up Saturday night?"

He waved his arms. "Hell, that's old news. Everybody's talking about Kevin now. Damn shame." He burst out laughing, a drunken ugly sound. "Correction: Guess it's Dick they're all talking about now."

"Sam, who stabbed Dick?" If he did it, maybe we'd catch him off guard as drunk as he was. "Who killed Jack?"

"Damned if I know." He lowered his head, kicked the beer cans scattering them across the room, then looked back up at me. "But it's my fault. Jack and his notebooks." Sam slapped his hand hard against his chest, his eyes welling up. "All my fault."

———

Michael and I sat in the car for a few minutes outside Sam's house. We couldn't get any more out of him, and before leaving I suggested that maybe a nap was in order. I heard the sound of the TV as we closed the front door behind us. Thank goodness he didn't smoke. One less thing to worry about.

"Wow, I've never seen him like that before. It's weird. And sad." I felt like crying, but didn't. "Jack's notebooks. What did he mean by that?"

"How old is Sam, do you know?"

"Actually, I do. His wife throws a birthday party every year. He'll be seventy-four this year."

"Army? Navy? Marines?"

"Navy. He signed up when he graduated high school, wanted to go to college on the GI Bill. He joined the Navy … oh my God, Sam joined in 1961. Cuban Missile crisis in October 1962. He was only seventeen years old." I pictured the dozen or more colored Post-it notes plastered on Sam's bulletin board above his desk. "Sam's the guy Jack wrote about becoming buddies with when he joined the VFW in 1962. The guy who suggested he write stuff down. That's why Sam's blaming himself."

"Sam'll be all right," Michael said. "He'll sleep it off, most likely. But he'll be okay. Now, we'd better get going or we'll be late to pick up Chris." He pulled out of Sam's driveway and we headed over to Terri's. "You look exhausted."

I turned my head and saw him looking at me. I smiled. "It's been a hell of a day. After everything that's happened, I'm not sure what to make of it all. Y'know, thinking of what to say to people is easy. Coming up with questions to ask is easy. What's hard is actually talking to them, asking those questions, then listening to them."

"Yeah. You know these people. In a way, you don't want to know the truth. You're afraid of the answers, what you're going to find out."

I couldn't disagree with him. "Maybe tomorrow will be a better day."

Thirty-Four

On Monday morning I woke to the sound of roaring and at first I thought it was the Gulf, and we were still in Ft. Walton Beach. I lay there thinking about last night when Michael and I went to pick up Chris. We ended up being a few minutes late, and Terri was not happy. Man, oh, man. The girls—Chris and her BFF Heather—had gotten into a huge argument and Terri was pulling her hair out trying to keep the peace. She demanded Michael remove his spoiled, bratty daughter from her home and to never set foot on their property again. I got to watch the whole scene from inside Michael's car.

Outside my bedroom window, I heard a horn and jumped out of bed. My car was home. Whoa. That stopped me dead. My car was *home*. Whatever. I threw on jeans and a clean T-shirt and rushed downstairs. Michael stood next to the tow-truck guy, signing papers on a clipboard.

"Good morning, Maggie," Michael said. "Or is it too early to wish you that yet? Should I wait until you've had your coffee?"

I slugged him right before hugging him. My beautiful car. New tires. New windshield wipers. Oh. No more ugly scratch.

"Thanks again, call us anytime," the guy said and climbed into his truck. As he drove by me, he shouted, "Glad to have a happy customer, Mrs. Bradley. Have a good day!"

Almost afraid to look at him, I turned toward Michael. We both blushed, then burst out laughing at the same time.

"How much do I owe you, Michael?"

"Breakfast at Sally's."

"Oh, c'mon, really."

"Okay." He cupped his chin, acted like he was considering it. "What about breakfast and you don't raise my rent?"

"You can't keep bailing me out like this."

"How about you don't use the word *bail*?" The laugh lines around his eyes crinkled.

I slugged him again. Yes, today was turning out to be a much better day.

A half hour later we pulled up and parked in front of Sally's. The early-morning crowd had apparently dispersed by the time we got there, so there were a few empty tables and booths. I headed for the counter.

"Your booth's open," Michael said and started walking toward it.

"No," I said. "Let's sit at the counter. I like it up there."

He shrugged and followed me.

"G'morning, Yankee, Maggie. What'll y'all have?" Sally rattled off the specials. We ordered. Sally came back with our coffee, and Michael's juice. In front of me she put a full sugar shaker and large glass of milk. "I seen what you do to your coffee. Reckon that'll hold you for a while."

I didn't argue with her. Michael cringed as I poured the sugar and milk in. I made a big show of taking a big gulp. "Ahhhh. Perfect." Inside I was doing my best to not spit it out. There *was* such a thing as too much sugar.

Sally set our plates in front of us, plopped more coffee in our cups, and left us alone to eat. I scraped the grits away from the scrambled eggs and home fries. "I will never acquire a taste for these. There's not enough butter and sugar in the world to make them appealing. I know I'm southern, but yuck."

"What I miss is scrapple. Haven't had that since we left Pennsylvania. Talk about huge differences between here and there. I can't even get a Genesee beer anywhere. Or pierogies. Or stromboli." After coating his food with pepper, he dug in.

I grabbed the ketchup bottle and poured some onto my scrambled eggs. I scooped up a mouthful and looked at Michael after he grunted. "What?" I asked.

"Ketchup on eggs? That's disgusting."

"It is not. I think putting pepper on everything is gross. Just because I don't like it doesn't mean I'm going to knock you for using it." I poured more ketchup on my eggs. "So there."

He laughed. "I learn something new about you every day."

"Well, hey, I didn't know you were from Pennsylvania. You told me you were from Orlando."

"True. I guess there's a lot we don't know about each other."

"You know, this is weird. We're just finding out things about each other now, after spending the last week digging up secrets about people I've known for five years. Lies they told for whatever reason."

"Yeah, we have." Michael nodded. "We've learned a lot."

"What I'm wondering now is, what's the difference between a lie or a secret, and simply not knowing everything about the person? I mean, I could call you a liar because you told me you were from Orlando."

He pushed his empty plate away and picked up his coffee mug. "Okay, I see what you're saying. I withheld information from you, but that doesn't make me a liar. It just means I didn't reveal everything about myself to you. I wasn't keeping anything a secret."

"If I had asked where you were from originally, you would've said Pennsylvania. So, it all depends on asking the right questions." I finished my breakfast and stacked my plate on his.

"I think you've done a very good job at asking the right questions." He clinked his coffee cup with mine.

Our cups were still in the air when Sally refilled them. "Hey, Maggie, you sure you don't want the job? You're out of work, I need a cook. I can teach you if you're willing to learn. Not like I'd let you poison any of my customers." She leaned forward, resting her chubby elbows on the counter. "Help me talk her into it, Yankee."

"Well, ma'am, it's up to her. I can't—"

"Shoot," she said. Sally straightened up, scowled at both me and Michael. "I'm an old woman. I can't be doing this like I been. All the ordering, the books, the cooking, the cleaning on top of taking care of this counter every day. I need help, and I think Maggie here will do just fine." And she walked off in a huff, muttering to herself.

I sat rooted to my stool, afraid to speak, move, or even breathe. Michael leaned over and said, "I think you ought to consider it."

"Really?" I tried to picture myself standing in front of a grill flipping pancakes and hamburgers. All I could see was fire and smoke. Something to think about though.

He wiped his mouth and tossed the napkin on our plates. "You ready to go home?"

There was that word again. "Yeah, let's go back to the house. I need to catch up on laundry, and a few other things. Do detectives get days off?"

"Yes, we do. Life continues to happen while we're working, and we have to make sure to take time for other stuff."

When we got back to the house, and after waving at Bobby Lee sitting in his cruiser across from my house *again*, I thought about what Michael had said about taking care of other stuff. After loading the washer, I headed toward one of the bedrooms. I had put this off long enough.

The day I moved to the upstairs level of the house, I had put the boxes of Rob's belongings in this room because it was the closest to the stairs. Smallest of the bedrooms, Rob and I had considered turning it into a huge walk-in closet.

I wasn't sure where to get started. Dozens of cardboard boxes were stacked against three of the walls. I grabbed the closest one and sat down in the middle of the room. Rob's yearbooks, trophies, awards, certificates from sports he'd received during high school. I set the box aside to decide on later. Hard to know just what to do with stuff like that. Clothing. I'd go through his clothes and pick out anything that I could donate or toss. I'd keep the few T-shirts I had in my dresser.

Several hours later, I had sorted through all of the boxes. Rob's clothes had been separated into boxes or garbage bags. I'd haul them all downstairs later. I'd have to find out if there was a Salvation Army or Goodwill nearby. Standing and stretching my tired muscles, I looked at what I'd accomplished. The one box of his high school stuff sat by itself, separated from the boxes I was tossing or donating. I took that box and put it in the closet, then left the room, closing the door behind me. A job well done.

While I loaded my damp clothes into the dryer, I realized two things. I hadn't cried once during the ordeal of going through Rob's things, and I hadn't gone to the cemetery to visit him since Friday. And that had been only to rant after getting pissed off at Phil. Before I could chastise myself, I realized I'd been talking to Rob the entire time I was in that bedroom. I didn't need to go to his grave to talk to him.

Thirty-Five

The grandfather clock chimed nine times. Wow. Six o'clock already. Time to decide what I'd have for dinner. I had a few frozen dinners, a new box of wine, and I'd treat myself to something fabulously fattening. Maybe even three glasses of wine. I had certainly earned a reward for the job I'd accomplished today. Maybe a fourth glass of wine with a frozen Snickers candy bar for dessert. I popped a fried chicken and mashed potatoes dinner in the microwave just as the phone rang. I answered it.

"Maggie?"

Pam Nelson? Oh, no. I figured the next words out of her mouth would be *Dick's dead*. I braced myself for the news.

"Hi, Maggie, it's Pam," she said. "How are you?"

Okay, this was different, but I went along. Pam was going through a rough time. I told her I was fine. *Now, just give me the news about Dick, lady.*

"Good. Me too. I'm calling to let you know I found another article about your house. Has some great photographs. You should come over now and check it out."

"Um, Pam, I'd love to, but I'm just sitting down to dinner. Maybe tomorrow?"

"I'm afraid I have appointments all day tomorrow *Diane's here* and tonight would be better."

Did she just whisper *Diane's here* in the middle of that? Not sure, I asked her.

"Yes, yes, tonight works better for me. And I know you'll love these photos I found. They're fabulous. Can you come now?"

"Okay, Pam, I'm on my way. Give me ten minutes."

I knew if I tore out of the driveway, Bobby Lee would be on my tail in a heartbeat. I wanted him to follow me to Pam's to see or hear anything that was about to go down. Sure enough, I looked in my rearview mirror and there he was, right behind me. I could've kissed his bald little head. I flew through the first yellow traffic light, hoping he would stay with me. Not the time to drive like Michael. God love Bobby Lee, he stayed on my ass.

The next light screwed me up. I got through it, but Bobby Lee got stuck. Watching for him in my mirror, I expected to hear his siren or see his flashing lights. Instead I saw a funeral procession. Damn. Who in the world has a funeral on a Monday evening? I was several hundred yards away and the line of cars was still going through the intersection. Only a few blocks from Pam's house, maybe he'd figure out where I was headed. I sent up a silent prayer.

Pam's front porch light came on when I pulled up in her driveway. I walked slowly up to the front door, giving Bobby Lee time to get there. I didn't want to go inside until he showed up. I rang the door-bell. Pam answered right away.

"C'mon in, Maggie. Thanks for coming. I really appreciate it."

I looked over my shoulder, and thank God, saw headlights cut through the darkening street. Pam closed the door behind me.

"The article is in the family room," Pam said. She shifted her eyes toward the opposite end of the house, toward the bedrooms and her office. "You'll love these photos, Maggie. Let's go in the family room."

I mouthed, *"Diane's back there?"* She gave me a brief nod. I wanted to let Pam know the police were on their way, but there was no safe way to get the message across. I followed her through the kitchen into the family room. She led me over to the low square coffee table sitting between the couch and the fireplace. On top of it sat a high tower of Pam's library books.

Books. Sally's books. Diane's books. JC's books. Jack's notebooks. That's when it clicked.

"Here it is, Maggie."

And that's when the lights went out.

I moved, as far away from Pam as possible. *C'mon, Bobby Lee, this would be a great time to show up and save my ass.* I edged up against the fireplace right into the damn brass tools, clanging them together. *Quiet,* I told myself. I couldn't see Pam, so I knew she couldn't see me. I had to be quiet as a mouse. I thought of mousey little Diane. Where was she? Was she really here? Was she in on this or was it all Pam's doing?

I remembered Gussie saying she'd seen two people visit the club around three thirty that morning. One went in the building and the other went to Jack's truck. Diane and Pam? Pam and JC?

Where the hell was Bobby Lee? Too much time had passed and I figured those headlights hadn't belonged to his cruiser after all.

"What's wrong, Maggie? Where are you? It's just a little power outage. I'm sure the lights will come back on soon."

I so wanted to believe her, I really did. But the glowing red lights on Pam's microwave and coffeemaker visible thanks to the open layout told me otherwise. Someone had turned off the lights deliberately. I had to be prepared for either Diane or JC. Given Dick's current condition, even weak little Diane could be dangerous with a knife, and JC had at least forty pounds on me. Or Scott; he was big too. Oh God, I hoped it wasn't all of them.

I reached behind me and as quietly as possible lifted one of the fireplace tools out of the holder. Good. The fireplace poker. With a weapon in my hand, I felt more confident, stronger. I had to find out who else was in the house.

"So, Pam, who all is in on this with you? Should I expect to have JC jump out at me? Or Diane? Or have you done something to her? To him?"

"Nice try, Maggie. Now, this is the way we're going to do this. Listen carefully."

At least I knew where she was. Unfortunately, she also knew I was standing next to the fireplace. I had to move. I slowly brought the poker up and laid it against my shoulder like a baseball bat.

"And what's that, Pam?" When she answered, I'd move in the opposite direction.

"We're going to go out to your car. You'll get in the passenger side, put the keys in the ignition, Diane will get in the driver's seat." Pam snorted. "What a joke. Diane in the driver's seat. But, as long as she follows my instructions *this* time, we won't have any problems."

Pam's voice was coming from my left, and it sounded like she was moving in my direction while she spoke. I inched slowly to my right, toward the kitchen. Closer to the front door. Damn, the room was dark, and I had to keep her talking so I'd know how close she was. I was behind the couch, just feet from the kitchen, when the microwave clock blinked out.

Someone was blocking it.

Where the hell was Bobby Lee? He had to know where I was. The poker weighed heavy on my shoulder. I stood between Pam and someone else in the middle of the family room. If I could get the someone else to move toward me on my right, and Pam to stay where she was, I had a chance. I'd make a run for the front door.

"Behind the couch, Pam. She's holding something in her hand."

Diane. Somehow she'd seen my weapon. Damn. I had moved right under the friggin' skylight, and the moon must've flashed on the brass poker. I lurched forward away from the light, and immediately felt rather than saw someone go by me. I swung the poker with all of my might. Made contact that reverberated up my arms. Something grabbed my ankle. I kicked out and brought down the poker at the same time. Made contact again. Then my feet were free and I ran like hell.

And slammed smack dab into somebody else. Somebody short and round and fat. *Please don't be JC.* Lights flashed on, and I was face to face with Chief of Police Bobby Lee. Diane Reid was stretched out on the floor, not moving. Pam must be behind me. The poker clanged and bounced when it hit the tile floor.

"Drop it, Pam." Bobby Lee shoved me aside and stepped forward, his raised gun never wavering. I crouched behind the gathering island. He'd told her to drop it. Drop what? A gun? God, I hoped not. With any luck, she'd brought a knife to a gunfight.

"Pam, drop the knife now." Okay, so now I knew. I cowered behind the island waiting for Bobby Lee to pull his trigger and shoot her, but nothing happened. My heart was slamming in my chest. I listened hard, but my ears only caught the sound of my own heavy breathing. My knees felt like they were going to buckle under me.

I slowly rose from the floor, peeking out when I got eye level to the top of the island. Pam stood with her back to the fireplace, facing me and Bobby Lee. I could just barely see Diane's legs. It looked like she hadn't moved.

Oh, please God, no. I never meant to kill her.

"Pam. Now. Last warning. Drop the knife." Bobby Lee took a step forward, his gun still raised before him. "Pam, I will shoot if you don't drop it."

I sure believed him. I'd never been more impressed with Bobby Lee than I was at that moment. Oh, hell, who was I kidding? I'd never been impressed with Bobby Lee *until* that moment.

Maybe if I stood up real fast, I'd scare Pam into either throwing or dropping the knife. Or I'd make Bobby Lee suddenly turn toward me and fire his gun. Okay. I'd take the chance of standing, but do it slowly to give the chief time to adapt. No sudden moves.

And as soon as my legs stopped shaking, I was going to stand and face the woman who'd made my life a living hell the last week. I thought I had it pretty much figured out, and I did not want Bobby Lee to shoot her before I could get answers out of her.

"Now, Maggie, that's far enough," Bobby Lee said as I slowly stood.

I ignored him and said to Pam, "You thought Jack knew you were stealing money from the club and he was going to turn you in. That was Friday night, the same night you came back behind the bar. You took one of my scrunchies. You tried to frame me."

Pam smirked. "I said all along that a woman could've done it." She raised her arm, and I got a good look at the knife she was holding.

Rob's knife? It had the same type of mother-of-pearl handle. But, how—? Yeah, now that made sense too. "You swiped that from my purse." I wanted to slap the smirk off her face. Instead, I waited for her to talk.

"Oh, all right. I admit it, Chief, I took the knife. But I'm not the one who stabbed Jack. I'm also not the one who stabbed Dick." She looked over at Diane, who was still sprawled out on the floor.

Was she implying Diane killed Jack and attempted to kill Dick? No ...

"You and JC were in on it together. You stole the knife and JC stabbed Jack. And now JC's just waiting for another chance at Dick. Pretending to be his friend, when he's the one who stabbed him in the first place!"

"Don't be silly, Maggie. My husband's too stupid to come up with this plan, and he's not brave enough to kill. JC's sitting by Dick's side waiting to see if he comes out of his coma and starts talking." She sniffed. "No, I'm afraid I'm going to have to implicate my good friend Diane Reid. She's the murderer. And the way she looks from here, you're also a murderer now, Maggie."

No way was I ready to believe I'd killed Diane with a few hits in the dark. I wanted to keep Pam talking, and Bobby Lee seemed okay with my goading her. "Diane? Your good friend? You two can't stand each other."

Her ferrety eyes bulged. "Precisely. I can't stand any of them, any of you. But with Diane dead and Dick almost there, there's almost nothing to stop me. Actually, it was quite clever. After Diane and I left Jack, we drove to the store. Used a lot of bleach, but we finally got all of the blood and any traces of it off of ourselves." She smiled maliciously. "We *are* capable of cleaning, you know. We'd just rather have you do it for us.

"But Dick was waiting up for Diane when she got home, wanted to know where she'd been, why she'd snuck out. After he shoved her around a bit, Diane told him what she'd done. Dick, being smarter than Diane, immediately figured out that I'd told her to leave your knife in the truck so our fine police department would find it. What Diane had failed to realize was that her fingerprints were all over the knife! Even if you didn't get arrested, Diane would. Dick is a jackass, but he's smarter than his wife. He must have driven Diane back to the club and made her get the knife out of that nasty little man's truck."

So that explained someone being in the club at three thirty in the morning. Dick had used my code to try to set me up. Hell, he probably had a beer while he was inside. He really was a jackass.

"Of course, I learned all this thanks to you letting JC know no weapon had been found. Took me longer than expected, but I finally convinced Diane to get the knife back from Dick. Poor dear stabbed him with it, and now here we are."

Her words chilled me. I knew she was a bitch, a snob, a drug addict, but never so cold and callous. But she had left out one detail. "What did you do, Pam? Steal Dick's heart medicine and poison Jack?"

Her arm wavered, and the gasp out of her sounded like a deflating tire.

Whoa. The shocked look on her face was priceless. She didn't know about the autopsy results. While I was at it, I asked another question.

"How did you get Diane involved? What motive did she have other than wanting to be like you?"

Pam's smirk returned. "Oh that. When it was Dick's turn to be quartermaster, he found out what JC had been doing, how he'd been handling two sets of books. Can you imagine? Dick Reid had the nerve to blackmail my husband. He wanted in on it. I used the money to maintain my lifestyle, my reputation. They used it to go traveling with us and to visit their god-awful grandchildren."

Pam dropped the knife and stepped forward. She held up her hands and spoke directly to Bobby Lee. "None of this has to do with me, Chief. I did the planning, but none of the killing. And it was no great loss. I mean, it was only Jack Hoffman."

I went flying around that island so fast the bitch never saw me coming.

Thirty-Six

"So, tell me the part about how you tackled her." Michael poured wine into our glasses. We were sitting on the patio the next day. Late afternoon, still an hour or so before dusk. Brenda and Chris were upstairs, busy in my kitchen. Michael had cleaned the grate and preheated the gas grill while I set the table, and now we were enjoying some wine. "Tell me again. It's my favorite part." He leaned forward, both elbows on the table and resting his chin in his hands.

I laughed at him and said, "Yeah, it's my favorite part too." I raised my glass to him and we clinked glasses. "Hey, last time we toasted each other, Sally came along and refilled our cups."

"Speaking of Sally, what did you decide? Are you going to go to work at the diner?"

"Yep. Can you imagine? But Sally is positive she can teach me to cook. She spent a lot of time today showing me around her kitchen and introducing me to customers. We're the talk of the town at the diner, did you know that?"

"Us? More like you. You saw the newspaper's front-page story today. Nice shot of you and Bobby Lee shaking hands." He grinned. "Unbelievable."

"I know, right?" After yesterday, and then this morning's newspaper interview, I saw the police chief in a different light. Much like how my opinion of Jack Hoffman changed the more I learned about him, how I felt I knew him better. Now, if only Bobby Lee would solve Rob's murder…

Michael jumped up from the table, breaking me out of my reverie. I turned to see where he was going.

"Howdy, folks," said Bobby Lee himself as he came around the corner and approached the table carrying a huge platter. Brenda and Chris followed him, their hands full. Michael took a bowl from Chris and set it down on the table, then led Bobby Lee over to the grill. I jumped up to grab one of Brenda's bowls.

"The police chief was kind enough to help me and Chris," Brenda said and grinned at me. She reached for the bottle of wine. "So I invited him to join us for dinner."

I looked over and watched as Michael took hamburger patties from the platter Bobby Lee was holding and placed them on the grate. Their backs were to us. I stuck my tongue out at Brenda, and Chris giggled. Crap. Not the best adult role model. Whatever.

"He just happened to be passing and saw Chris and me carrying stuff out your front door. He came to our rescue," she explained.

"Well, that was nice of you. The more the merrier," I said while looking at Chris. We moved the place settings to make room for one more. I hadn't told Brenda about my new job yet, but I wanted to wait until Michael was at the table. While he and Bobby Lee were at the grill, Brenda filled me in on her new shop in West Palm Beach and Chris let us know that she and Heather were best friends again. Before I could find out more from Chris, Michael and Bobby Lee came back to the table.

"I flipped the burgers, so we might as well fill our plates while they finish cooking," Michael said. "Should be five minutes or so."

"Everything looks so good," I said. I plopped serving spoons into the bowls of potato salad, macaroni salad, and baked beans. "Can't believe all this came out of my kitchen."

Brenda laughed and shook her head at me. "Yeah, that square contraption that heats up when you turn the knobs is amazing. Does so much more than reheat pizza." She sat down next to me, leaned over, and kissed my cheek. "You know I'm joking. Sort of."

I smiled at her and said, "I know you are, and I can't wait to tell you my good news." Because he knew what I was about to tell her, I winked at Michael. I really liked the way his dark brown eyes sparkled. I quickly turned back to Brenda. "I have a new job."

"That's wonderful news!" She hugged me. "Oh, I'm happy to hear that, hon. That deserves a toast." She raised her wineglass. "Here's to Maggie. Congratulations on the new job, and for helping the police chief solve his case."

"Hear, hear!" Bobby Lee clinked my glass.

"Daddy has some good news too," Chris piped up. "Can I tell them?"

"Hold on a minute, kiddo. Let's all grab our burgers first. They should be ready."

We grabbed our plates and followed Michael to the grill. I suddenly wasn't hungry. What was his good news? He hadn't said a word to me about anything. Were they moving? Did this have anything to do with Chris and Heather being friends again? Were he and Terri getting married?

Were they going back to Pennsylvania or Orlando? Time seemed to move slowly and I dreaded what was coming.

Once we were all settled back at the table, Chris asked, "Now, Daddy? Can I tell them now?" He nodded. "Daddy got his license. He's a full-pledged private eye," she proclaimed proudly.

I burst out laughing, then clamped a hand over my mouth. Oh, God. "I'm sorry for laughing, Chris. I'm not laughing at you, I swear, it's just that it was kind of funny how you announced the news. It's very good news and—"

Brenda kicked me under the table, and said, "Maggie's just happy to hear your wonderful announcement. She tends to ramble when she's this happy. Right, Maggie?"

"Um, yes, right. Brenda's absolutely right." I raised my glass and said, "Cheers to you, Michael, congratulations." I gulped some wine.

"I'm not finished. Daddy has more news."

Michael leaned over, whispered in her ear. "Oh," she said, giggling. "Full-*fledged*. Got it."

Here it comes. The part where he announces his engagement. I took a big bite out of my hamburger and waited.

"I do have more news. I did get my PI license, and I've found the perfect location downtown to set up an office."

That's it? Nothing about Terri and him. I felt silly for jumping to that conclusion, then wondered why I'd even had the thought. Why I was bothered by the possibility. Whatever. I took another bite.

"Oh! Is that your new job, Maggie?" Brenda asked. "You're going to work for Michael at his new office? Help solve more crimes? Cool, very cool."

Michael burst out laughing this time while I nearly choked on my food. Bobby Lee just stared at each of us in turn, sweat running down his bald little head.

I swallowed and said, "Don't worry, Chief, that's not happening. No, Brenda, my new job is at Sally's Diner. You know the place you liked so well? I start there Friday night."

"Great," Brenda said. "I bet the waitresses make good tips there."

Michael wiped his mouth with his napkin and arched that eyebrow of his. "Oh, it's not waitressing."

Brenda frowned. "What then? You won't make much money bussing tables or cleaning—oh, no. Are you serious? *You're* going to be a cook?"

Priceless. Her expression was priceless and everything I expected. "Yep. Sally is convinced she can teach me everything she knows."

Michael said, "Believe me, Maggie and I tried warning Sally, but like Maggie said, Sally's sure she can do it."

"And so am I," Brenda said, slapping the table. "Congratulations, hon. You too, Michael. Here's to new beginnings."

We raised our glasses again to each other. Good news all around. Bobby Lee solving Jack's murder, my new job, Brenda's new shop, Michael's new career and office, and Chris and Heather's restored friendship. We enjoyed the rest of our meal, and after tossing paper plates, plastic forks, and napkins in the trash can, we finished off the bottle of wine.

"Heather's mom helped Daddy get his new office," said Chris.

And here we go again. "Terri helped you?"

"Yeah, she's a realtor downtown. She's been showing me different places. While you and Bobby Lee were kicking butt last night, she called and we talked. We met today to take a look at the old bookstore. Terri's boyfriend used to own it until he opened a bigger store in the mall."

Brenda kicked me again. "Ow. I mean, oh, the old bookstore. Her boyfriend, cool. Hey, that means you, me, and Bobby Lee will all be working downtown now." I looked over at Bobby Lee. He wiped sweat from his forehead and I saw white gauze on his left hand.

I pointed to the bandage. "What happened?"

He squirmed in his chair and rubbed his other hand over his bald head. "Pam Nelson. She bit me."

Michael cleared his throat. "Um, kiddo, how about going inside to finish your homework? Grown-up talk."

Chris rolled her eyes but did as her father said.

I waited until Chris was in the house, then said, "Bit you? Oh, sheesh, Bobby Lee. Did you get a tetanus shot?"

"Yes," he said, chuckling. "Yes, I did."

"When? How? Why? Well, maybe not why because we know what a bitch she is, but when did she bite you?"

"It happened when I was putting her in the holding cell last night. Pam didn't want to go in there. Kept saying how Diane—oh, she's fine, by the way—was the one who killed Jack and stabbed Dick. She went on and on talking about Diane. Some garbled story about Diane being concerned about a cat and how she stopped to feed it, and clean out a litter box. Oh, and something about watering a dead plant."

So that's why there was a puddle for me to step into that day on Jack's porch with Brenda.

"Apparently Pam and Diane broke into Jack's house, stole boxes of notebooks. Does any of that make sense to you, Maggie?" Bobby Lee asked. He looked over at Michael. I didn't miss the winks exchanged between them.

"It sure does, Bobby Lee." I blushed. I kicked Brenda this time.

"Yes sir, it does," she said and batted her eyes.

I slugged down the last of my wine and said, "Well, everyone, this was very enjoyable, but I have an important errand." I scooted my chair back and stood.

Brenda took my hand and asked, "The cemetery, hon?"

I shook my head, kissed her hand, and said, "No, I don't have to do that every day anymore." We smiled at each other, and I told them I'd be back within the hour.

———

I went to Wal-Mart first and got what I needed there. Then on to my next stop.

The key was still under the potted dead plant. I carried my new purchase into Jack Hoffman's house.

"Kitty, here kitty," I called out. Nothing. "Come on, cat, just come on out." I pulled the cat carrier out of the plastic bag. The noise must've made it curious, and it came out. I unlatched the door on the carrier and gently pushed the cat inside. I'd have to find out its sex soon and come up with a decent name.

But for now, I just said, "Okay, cat, let's go home."

The End

Acknowledgments

Writing this acknowledgement page may have been some of the most difficult writing I've done because I was afraid of leaving anyone out. Each person was instrumental in helping get this book out into the world. It's been a long journey, so I'll start at the very beginning and go from there. There are so many of you. There are not enough ways to thank each and every one of you.

My son, Adam Matter, who in the third grade used his vocabulary word *author* in this sentence: "My Mom is an author. For real." Mumblety years later, it became true.

My husband, Dave, whom most people know I call The Saint. This page would be much longer if I listed all the reasons why.

My early readers, to whom I must apologize for putting them through those awful first drafts:

My sister Patti Peres, sister-in-law Pamela Gault Matter, Cassie Gamble, Robyn Fisler, Steve Ohnmeiss, Mary Olive Britt, Teresa Friedman, David Wilson, and Ron Williams.

My online critique group members Donnell Bell, Annette Dashofy, Chris Eberle, and Ron Voights. My Danville critique group members Dave Freas, Martha Johnson, Pamela Lee, and Andi Hummel. My Seascape mentors Hallie Ephron, Roberta Isleib, and S.W. Hubbard. My fellow Seascape mentees Michele Dorsey and Christine Falcone.

Jane Atkinson for helping me set goals and keeping me accountable this time.

Fabulous freelance editors Kristen Weber Dworkin, Alison Dasho, and Ramona DeFelice Long.

Daniel O'Shea, Jon Jordan, and Dan Malmon. They know why. Or maybe they don't, but I do.

Ben LeRoy, who introduced me to MI Acquisitions Editor Terri Bischoff, who gave me a chance. And then another chance. Thanks, Big Boss. MI editor Nicole Nugent, who really knows her way around commas. All 102,856 of them. My literary agent Jill Marsal for always being a phone call or e-mail away.

Last and certainly not least is the person I would've dedicated the book to if I weren't afraid of my mother haunting me: Susan Meier. Thank you for always believing in me and Maggie.

About the Author

Paula Matter (rhymes with *otter*) is the author of the Maggie Lewis mysteries, which take place in a small town in North Florida. Paula's short stories have been published in anthologies in the US and Germany. Originally from Miami, Florida, Paula kept moving north until she arrived in north central Pennsylvania, where she lives with her family.